D0344424

ALSO BY EDNA BUCHANAN

Shadows

Cold Case Squad

The Ice Maiden

You Only Die Twice

Garden of Evil

Pulse

Margin of Error

Act of Betrayal

Suitable for Framing

Miami, It's Murder

Contents Under Pressure

Never Let Them See You Cry

Nobody Lives Forever

The Corpse Had a Familiar Face

Carr: Five Years of Rape and Murder

LOVE KILLS

A Britt Montero Novel

EDNA BUCHANAN

SIMON & SCHUSTER
New York • London • Toronto • Sydney

SIMON & SCHUSTER
Rockefeller Center
1230 Avenue of the Americas
New York, NY 10020

This book is a work of fiction. Names, characters, places, and incidents either are products of the author's imagination or are used fictitiously. Any resemblance to actual events or locales or persons, living or dead, is entirely coincidental.

For information about special discounts for bulk purchases,
please contact Simon & Schuster Special Sales
at 1-800-456-6798 or business@simonandschuster.com.

Designed by Dana Sloan
Manufactured in the United States of America
10 9 8 7 6 5 4 3 2 1

Library of Congress Cataloging-in-Publication Data
Buchanan, Edna.
Love kills : a Britt Montero novel / by Edna Buchanan.
p. cm.
1. Montero, Britt (Fictitious character)—Fiction. 2. Women journalists—Fiction.
3. Miami (Fla.)—Fiction. I. Title.
PS3552.U324 L68 2007
813'.54—dc22
2006039050

ISBN-13: 978-0-7432-9476-8
ISBN-10: 0-7432-9476-9

For the tough and savvy redhead with a gun:
Lieutenant Joy Gellatly, the best
and the brightest of the Savannah Chatham
Metropolitan Police Department

The person most likely to murder you sits across the breakfast table.
Your nearest and dearest, the one who sleeps on the pillow next to yours
and shares your checking account, can be far more lethal
than any sinister stranger lurking in the shadows.
Love kills.

—Edna Buchanan, *Never Let Them See You Cry* (1992)

And so, all the night-tide, I lie down by the side
Of my darling, my darling, my life and my bride,
In her sepulchre there by the sea—
In her tomb by the side of the sea.

—Edgar Allan Poe, "Annabel Lee"

LOVE KILLS

PROLOGUE

Operating the huge machine that groaned and howled like a prehistoric monster as it savaged everything in its path was what he enjoyed most about the job.

But not today.

The driver wiped the sweat from his face and yearned for a cold beer, just one, to settle his stomach. A shame his rig wasn't air-conditioned. He'd lost his sunglasses and his Florida Marlins cap somewhere between last night's happy hour and this morning's painful dawn. His head throbbed, his stomach churned, and he truly regretted how much he'd had to drink.

A flock of snowy white birds with curved pink beaks swooped gracefully overhead, flying low, like a scene in an animated Disney movie. He wondered what sort of birds they were and then sighed. No way to take a quick break and pick up an Alka-Seltzer out here. Not yet. This desolate stretch of real estate had been considered the wilderness fringe of the Everglades until recently. But soon it would be transformed into shopping centers, paved parking lots, and fast-food joints. Miami's relentless creep inched west, despite protests from granola-eating tree huggers hoping to cling to paradise a little bit longer.

Progress. He grinned and gunned the engine, guiding the machine as it snarled and ripped at the saw grass, a patch of Florida holly, and a small willow grove. He moved ancient shells, broken limestone, and tangled roots mixed with black muck that smelled of age and rot. Engine straining, the big machine's blade rang against stone outcroppings as he labored to clear the site.

Was it his imagination, or did his sweat smell like the beer he drank the night before? He hoped the crew chief wouldn't get too close. He had never worked in humidity so oppressive. Never again on a work night, he swore. What was that girl's name? He could barely remember her face.

Sweat snaked down the small of his back, tickling his spine. He comforted himself with thoughts of his paycheck, the richest he had ever earned.

Bombarded by one killer hurricane after another, in the midst of a huge building-and-rebuilding boom, Miami suffered a critical shortage of construction workers. Even unskilled day laborers were now paid more than they'd ever dreamed of in their wildest fantasies. His own brother-in-law, whom he'd followed down from North Carolina, was making a fortune, rescreening storm-damaged pool and patio enclosures, many for the second or third time. Any man who could swing a hammer or pick up a shovel had more work than he could handle.

Disaster, he thought, is damn good for the economy.

He wiped his face on his dusty work shirt. His eyes stung and his nose ran like an open faucet from a rising cloud of grit, loose soil, and pollen. As he bulldozed the debris, exotic plants, and rocks into what had become the only hill on this vast flat landscape, an object broke loose from the top. It bounced crazily down the side of his man-made mountain, glancing off tree limbs and stones. For an instant, it hurtled straight at him and then deflected off a jagged chunk of oolite.

The driver squinted into the glare until his eyeballs ached. *A rock?* No. *A coconut?* No coconut palms grew out here. *What is that?* He shielded both eyes and stood up, momentarily dizzy. *Can it be . . . ? Nah, no way.*

"Hey! You all see that?" He waved down to a surveyor wearing an orange hard hat. "What the hell?" Without waiting for an answer he cut off the power. The engine shuddered and died. He jumped down from the cab, his steel-tipped construction boots making sucking sounds as he approached the fallen object.

Huge empty eye sockets stared back at him. Nauseated, he recoiled with a cry. That was no coconut.

Investigators approached the site as if it were an archaeological dig. Old Indian burial mounds are common in and around the great swamp. Too often the occupants are disturbed, their skeletons disinterred by heavy equipment as the city pushes west. Homicide detectives and the medical examiner hoped the remains would be those of a long-dead Indian.

They were disappointed.

This empty skull had never hosted the hopes, dreams, and gray matter of some ancient native Floridian. That much was obvious to the naked eye. The maxilla, the still-intact upper jawbone, bore clear evidence of modern dentistry: porcelain crowns and gold inlays.

To the detectives' further dismay, something else was also obvious: a bullet hole in the right occipital bone at the back of the skull. The small-caliber slug had exited through the hard palate of the mouth.

The job was shut down as they launched a search for more bones.

"Where's the bulldozer operator who unearthed it?" asked Cold Case Squad Sergeant Craig Burch. He had been called out to the scene with his team, Detectives Pete Nazario, Sam Stone, and Joe Corso.

"Over there." A middle-aged patrolman gestured toward the shade of a papery-barked melaleuca, the lone tree still standing. "Talking to his wife back in North Carolina. Had to borrow a cell phone. Says he lost his somewhere last night."

The detectives pulled on rubber gloves and, joined by Miami-Dade County's chief medical examiner and Dr. Everett Wyatt, a forensic odontologist, they measured from where the skull was found to a point a hundred feet behind the bulldozer. They photographed the site, set up a perimeter, drew a map, and with small flags blocked out a huge rectangular grid to mine for the mother lode.

Using trowels and hand tools, they painstakingly sifted every bit of soil, sand, or muck. By dusk, they had recovered a femur, a long leg bone, and a human rib cage entangled in the rotted tatters of a work shirt. They also unearthed torn strips from a heavy tarpaulin, the shreds of a leather belt in the loops of a pair of nearly disintegrated men's trousers, and—the prize package of the day—a partially intact billfold.

"Somebody took great pains to encase the body in a strong tarpaulin that was nonbiodegradable and made to last, like a roof tarp," the chief medical examiner said, his shiny round face alight with interest. "The joke's on them. Had the body simply been dumped as it was, there would have been nothing left to find."

"And we wouldn't be here," Corso said glumly.

"Correct," the chief said. "Animals would have scattered the bones. Whatever splinters and fragments they left would have deteriorated in the sun and the climate. That billfold and its contents would have shriveled down to a small mass of indecipherable pulp. The remains would never have been found, much less identified. But, instead, whoever left him here wrapped him in a way that preserved enough for us to recover."

"If it was a roof tarp," Burch said thoughtfully, "that might be a hint of how long he's been out here. Andrew hit in August of 'ninety-two."

He removed his sunglasses and studied the billfold, which lay on the hood of an unmarked car. A faint monogram was still visible, the initials S.N.Y. etched into the worn leather. Frowning, he repeated the initials aloud, twice, as though he had heard them before. The third time his expression changed.

"Jeez, Doc! Know who this might be?"

"Yes. That occurred to me too." The chief medical examiner wiped the misted lenses of his gold-rimmed glasses with his handkerchief.

"I'm with you," Nazario said quickly, "on the same page, but I always expected that hombre to surface alive somewhere, not like this." He scanned the barren site around them, now eerily quiet. Even the birds had fled. "I would never have expected him to turn up here. I thought he was far from Miami."

"Let's not jump to conclusions," Corso said. "This doesn't have to be a homicide, it doesn't have to be our case. He mighta come out here to commit suicide. It's a head shot. We bring a metal detector out here, maybe we find his gun."

"Pretty difficult to shoot yourself in the back of the head from that angle," the chief said mildly.

"Maybe in the lab it'll turn out to be an exit wound," Corso said hopefully. "Or something else. This place is a suicide magnet. Every wacko with a death wish comes here to disappear; they don't want their families to know."

"Let's see," Burch said. "He shoots himself in the head, tosses the gun, rolls up in a tarp, falls into a shallow grave, and covers himself. Good thinking."

"Stranger things have happened," Corso said defensively. "All I'm saying is—"

"If he is who we think," Nazario said quietly, "he wasn't the type to put a gun to his head. But a whole lot of other people would've liked to."

The chief took a closer look at the skull. "It appears that the bullet entered the back of his head, went through the brain, and exited the mouth. Here"—he pointed with a pencil—"you can see the beveling."

Dr. Wyatt peered over his shoulder. "See the burr marks on that upper right molar? That dental work was done shortly before his death. That may help."

"We'll know more when we piece things together back at the morgue," the chief said. "His dental records should give us a positive ID."

"Who we talking about, Sarge?" Sam Stone, the squad's youngest detective, looked puzzled. He took pride in being well informed. He loved modern forensics and high-tech detecting, was a quick study, and had familiarized himself with most of the department's old cold cases before even joining the squad, but he couldn't place who they were talking about. "You think he's an old homicide suspect?"

"Nope. This all went down before your time, kid. I was still in patrol. There was no homicide involved. Then."

"So, why . . . ?"

"The case was an A.P.E." Nazario grinned. "The fallout was *grande.*"

"A.P.E.?" Stone looked more puzzled.

The medical examiner chuckled. "Acute Political Emergency." His gloved fingers gingerly opened the billfold. "Good memory, Sergeant. I suspect you're right. Look at this."

Burch bent closer to read an old business card tucked behind a clouded plastic window. The telephone number handwritten across it was faded.

"Hah! I knew it! Has to be him."

"Who?" Stone demanded impatiently. They filled him in.

The man had vanished. But no fearful loved ones ever reported him missing. Their biggest fear was probably that he would come back. He must have been one of the most disliked men of his time.

"When he disappeared," Burch explained, "you couldn't count the people who hoped it was permanent."

"Looks like one of them made sure of it," Nazario said.

The skull blindly returned their stares until the chief placed it in a brown paper bag and sealed it with an evidence sticker. Though it had not yet been scientifically confirmed, they all knew his identity.

And they all knew who had seen him last.

Burch mopped his brow and scowled at the old business card.

Corso examined the Everglades muck on his Guccis and muttered curses under his breath.

"At least we know who we have to talk to first," Nazario said.

"Yeah," Burch said. "Where the hell is Britt Montero?"

BRITT

CHAPTER ONE

You can leave Miami, but Miami never leaves you.

In my dream I am there again. The lusty pulse beat of the city stirs forgotten longings. Like an absentminded lover, I wonder why I stayed away so long. Then something sinister worms its way into my consciousness. My heart races, pounding faster and faster, until my dream ends like all the others.

I see the flames, feel the heat, hear the screams. Some are mine.

I wake up gasping, drenched in perspiration, my adrenaline-charged body alert to danger. From where? What unfamiliar room is this? Where am I? The smell of smoke lingers as it all rushes back in a vivid explosion of memory.

No matter where I go, I feel Miami's magnetic pull and mystical intrigue, even in my dreams.

That explains my father's obsession with Veradero. The same siren song that haunts me inexorably drew him back to the place of his birth, to Cuba and his execution on San Juan Hill at the hands of Fidel Castro. Others called my father a hero, a martyr, a patriot. My mother never forgave him, but in this room, in this bed, tonight, I do. He is always with me. *Estamos juntos.*

A restless sigh in the night reminds me that someone else is here as well.

Throwing back the thin sheet, I swing my feet onto the cool tiles, pad barefoot across the well-worn floor, and peer into the shadows. The outline of a familiar figure deep in slumber is somehow comforting. I escape my fiery dreams by slipping out the door onto fine white sand still warm from the sun.

The mantle of night sky drapes endlessly around me. It is the same sky. The same sea, wild and swollen, hisses in fierce, whispering rivulets along an ever-changing shoreline, but the smells, sounds, and rhythms here are different from Miami. Thousands more stars crowd the moon and stud the sky, their light reflecting hope upon the shimmering face of dark and soulless water.

I inhale the salt air, walk wet hard-packed sand, and block my recurring dreams by searching out my favorite heavenly beacon, my signal fire in the sky.

The Southern Cross comforts me. It always has, it always will. My mother refuses to believe me because I was only three at the time, but I remember being held high in my father's arms on a brilliant night like this, as he pointed out the five stars of the Southern Cross and told me stories.

Early sailors used the North Star to guide their ships at night. But the North Star cannot be seen from the equator. When Portuguese navigator Ferdinand Magellan explored the new world after Columbus and sailed down the coast of South America, his crew became disoriented. The familiar stars and constellations they used as landmarks had disappeared or moved into strange positions. The farther south they sailed, the stranger the skies appeared. The terrified mariners feared that they had ventured into a new universe and that the stars they had always relied upon to lead them home were gone forever.

With mutiny imminent, Magellan put into port for the winter so his crew could study the new skies and make sense of the strange star patterns.

One of the most prominent was the Southern Cross. Playing upon their superstition, the intrepid explorer convinced his men they had nothing to fear because the Christian cross was with them, a heavenly omen to guide them through uncharted waters in uncertain times.

On that long-ago starry night in an uncertain time between Memorial Day and the rainy season, my father held me and pointed due south, to the Southern Cross and Cuba.

Like the explorer's frightened and superstitious crew, I now look to the Southern Cross as my guide through dark uncharted waters. In this uncertain time, more than ever.

Sensing something different, I look to the horizon, where a strange vessel bobs gently at anchor offshore. Who are you, riding the tide in shadow beneath this same spectacular sky? Voyagers I will never meet, sharing this brilliant night off this small remote island, a tiny speck on a troubled planet sailing at breakneck speed through the universe. Where are you bound? I wonder. Godspeed. I wish I could go with you.

It is nearly dawn as I creep softly into the cottage, careful not to disturb my weary guest. I sigh as I close the door behind me. I have cherished the silence of this sanctuary, communing only with the wind, the birds, and the sea. Traffic, telephones, police radios, emergency signals, and deadlines do not exist here. No television, no fax machines, only me and my thoughts. But I know in my heart that this quiet time in my life is over. My solitude has ended.

Forever.

Sorrowfully, by dawn's first light, I study my visitor, who still slumbers in the small living room, her hair spread across the pillow, hair as red as fire.

CHAPTER TWO

"Hey!"

The woman can sleep anywhere, at any time: in small planes, speeding boats, during deadly riots, revolutions, political coups, killer storms, and behind enemy lines. Yet she always captures the big one, the heart-stopping moment, the football at the fingertips, the front-page picture. Nobody is better at being in the right place at the right time.

"Hey!" I said again. A toenail painted with hot pink polish protruded from beneath the sheet. I nudged it and Lottie Dane, the best photographer I ever worked with, the best friend I ever had, stirred, stretched, and yawned awake, alert, comfortable, and at home, as always, wherever she happened to be.

An hour later, we were trudging across white sand carrying surfboards. Her unannounced arrival the night before hadn't totally surprised me.

Good reporters—and photographers—can track down just about anybody. What did surprise me about Lottie's arrival was how happy I was to see her. Fearless and dedicated, funny and full of life, she is more outgoing than I, with a Texas twang in her molasses-smooth voice and a readier laugh.

Unlike me, she had slept soundly and radiated energy. Born in Gun Barrel, Texas, she had learned to surf in the rough waters off Galveston.

Where I grew up, surfing off Miami Beach was sporadic and dependent on rare inclement weather. This out island's towering surf and splendid isolation were its chief attractions.

Lottie, a sturdy and statuesque five-eight, looked like a tomboy in her blue two-piece L. L. Bean bathing suit, her freckled nose smeared with sunblock, her frizzy red hair as wild and unmanageable as ever.

"Not bad." She surveyed the pristine, almost empty beach. "Surf's up."

Fishing boats dotted a blue-green sea. The vessel I had seen anchored offshore in the dark must have sailed at daybreak. It was no longer even a speck on the horizon.

"I could stay here forever," I said fervently.

"Paradise," she agreed.

"Well, there *is* one weird local," I said. "He roams the sand dunes at night stark naked, posing like a statue on the highest one. I guess he's playing king of the mountain."

"Is he hot?"

"More hairy Sasquatch than hot. Maybe that's why he thinks he doesn't need clothes. Seems harmless enough. The locals act like he's part of the scenery. Nobody complains."

"Let me know if you see 'im," she said. "Shouldn't have left my camera at the cottage."

We had reached the special place where the waves barreled in out of deep water. Mostly I watched her, as she paddled furiously to catch them as they hit the reef. Hitting that shallow shelf was like a free fall into a trough, the energy converting tons of water into a powerful bottom turn. I watched a wave sweep over her and then collapse, pasting her to the bottom turbulence. She fell, opened her eyes, and swam down beneath the power. Free and exhilarated, she rode one steep makeable wave after another. That was the part I'd always loved, with no time to think of anything but the waves and the primitive high brought by riding them.

"How'd you find this spot?" Lottie panted, as she paused for breath knee deep in the surf.

"Met a surfer rat from Daytona. Came here to surf four or five years ago and forgot to go home. He stays at the other end of the beach. This is one of his secret spots."

She rolled her eyes. "A guy, huh?"

"For Pete's sake, Lottie. He showed me some surfing tips and shared this spot with me. That's all."

"Too bad," she murmured sympathetically, then asked again, "Is *he* hot?"

I sighed. "Why are you always thinking about sex and romance? There's a time and a place for everything. This isn't it. Not for me."

Lottie has been divorced for years, with no children. But she yearns for family, and hope springs eternal in her heart.

"I just hoped maybe that was why *you* forgot to come home."

Later, we sat on the white sand in the shade of coconut palms to unwrap the fruit and sandwiches we'd brought. "What bums me," I said, "is that I still don't get it. I've always been intuitive, like my Aunt Odalys, the one who practices Santería. She can sense bad things before they happen. You and I know more than anybody how life can spin out of control in a heartbeat. We go to work every day hoping for the best but expecting the worst, and we're usually right. But, damn, McDonald's death totally blindsided me. Sucker-punched when I least expected it. Not a clue, no warning, not even a whisper from that little voice we all have in our heads."

"Only natural," she said flatly. "You were on a high, in love, returning from a romantic vacation, sporting a new engagement ring. Who'da thought?"

"I wrote about sudden death and tragedy every day," I said. "I'd work weekends and holidays because there was more action then:

Christmas Day tragedies, Fourth of July shootings. Remember the dad shot to death at his surprise birthday party? I would comfort the survivors. I believed I knew how they felt. I didn't. But I do now.

"I didn't expect to live in a world without M in it. I keep feeling nostalgic for times that never happened: the honeymoon we didn't have, our first Christmas tree, becoming parents. All the days and nights, weekends, and holidays as we grew old together. The wedding that never was. You were going to catch the bouquet, you know."

"Damn straight," she said. "No matter who I had to wrestle to the ground." She shoved her wet hair out of her eyes and turned to me, her expression serious. "The newsroom sure isn't the same without you, Britt. You can run, but you can't hide forever. Speakin' of forever"—she leaned back against the trunk of a coconut palm, relaxing with a contented sigh—"you can almost see it from here. Wish I hadn't left my camera back at your place. Would've liked to make a picture of that little wipeout of yours. It'd look good on the bulletin board in the newsroom."

The photo ops here were endless.

"I could make some pictures for a travel piece," she mused lazily. "But you know what would happen."

"Right. The world would beat a path and ruin all this. Same thing that happens when a food critic writes a rave about your favorite restaurant. The paper hits the street, readers mob the place, and regulars can't get a table. The quality of the food and service drop because the staff is overworked. Prices soar because the owner has to hire more help. And it's never the same."

She nodded, nibbling on her sandwich and basking in the warm sun. "A travel piece would turn this stretch of sand into wall-to-wall beach blanket Bingo."

"Littered with beer cans, broken glass, and used condoms."

"Damn right. Paris Hilton would show up. That's a sure sign. Cruise ships would make it a stop on their itinerary. They'd dump their garbage offshore, screw up the reef, and kill all the sea life. Developers would be right behind them, building luxury high-rises and resort hotels you and I couldn't afford, right down to the waterline."

She stood, stretched, and brushed the sand off her long legs.

"God bless the power of the press."

We surveyed our surroundings, more aware than ever of their fragile beauty and grateful for our good luck at being there.

"Damn, still wish I had my camera."

"Me too."

At low tide, the reef was too exposed to surf, so we strolled the sand watching for sea life as we collected gleaming lettered olive shells, swirling Scotch bonnets, and angel wings. Then I spotted something awash in the shallows, propelled by the tide into a coral pocket on the reef.

A gift from the sea, but it wasn't aquatic.

My glad cry startled gulls into flight as I splashed through ankle-deep water to snatch up my find.

"Can you believe this?" I waved it in the air. "What did we just wish for?"

"The good Lord always provides," she said, eyes piously raised to the cerulean sky.

The camera was waterproof, preloaded, and disposable. We scanned the beach. Not a soul in sight.

"They say to be careful what you wish for, you might get it," I said. "I wonder who lost it."

An unexpected breeze suddenly whipped across the water, and I felt a chill.

"No telling. Lemme see that." She checked the camera and grinned gleefully. "Don't look much the worse for wear," she said. "No damage. Twenty-seven shots, twenty-four exposed. We've got us three pictures to play with."

"Maybe we'll know who lost it when we see the film."

Thunderclouds began to tumble across the horizon, and the sea beyond the reef turned dark.

Traffic was deadlier, city officials sleazier, and the scandals hotter than ever.

Lottie filled me in on the hometown news that evening, without my asking, as we dined beneath the thatched roof of an open-air restaurant on fish caught that day.

Another Miami city commissioner had been arrested, this one for brawling with police at the airport. A thief dubbed the Human Fly was bedeviling the cops and the Chamber of Commerce, climbing tall buildings, scaling balconies, and stealing from the sky-high apartments of the rich and famous, who were now poorer and furious. Community leaders, for reasons known only to them and to the devil, had launched long-term construction projects that simultaneously blocked all of Miami and Miami Beach's traffic-clogged north-south arteries.

"We're damn close to permanent gridlock," she said. "Just wait till the next big hurricane boils up and they order everybody to evacuate."

"SOS," I said breezily. Same old shit.

She shook her head. "Britt. In Miami, it's always crazy new shit. We went from a major drought, with wildfires charring half the state, to flash-flood warnings without a breath between. Ain't no normal anymore, not even for a day. Alligators are slithering out of the swamps and attacking people; the drought fried their environment. Now it's mating season and they're on the prowl. Gators killed three women in a week. One woman was scuba diving, another was drugged outa her mind, sitting on the edge of a canal dangling her tootsies in the gator's habitat. They found the arms of the first girl in a big gator's belly, but not until they'd captured and cut open every poor swamp critter they could find. Somebody had shot that last one with a BB gun, blinded 'im in one eye. He musta had trouble hunting. Now it's open season and every shit kicker with a gun is hunting down gators and killing 'em, poor things."

The drought ended suddenly, she said, when a gigantic thunderstorm dropped more rain in three hours than there'd been in three months. Lightning and gale-force winds toppled trees onto cars. Screened-in patios got torn out again, and thousands of families in Miami-Dade and Broward counties lost power. There were flash floods and more destruction to houses and apartment buildings still protected only by blue tarps after last hurricane season's roof damage.

"They had to open Red Cross shelters for a thunderstorm, for God's sake, two months before hurricane season," she said.

Traffic fatalities had become nightmarish, outnumbering murders, which themselves had doubled since last year.

" 'Member, you grew up there. Never was like this before. Even when I first got to Miami, there'd be maybe one spectacular major wreck, like a giant exploding tanker truck, every two weeks or so. Now it's every rush hour. Just before I left, there were two major unrelated tanker-truck crashes in less than an hour, ten miles apart. Same ol' story: fishtail, jackknife, topple over. Nine thousand gallons of gasoline splashing across the Golden Glades interchange at the height of rush hour. At least neither of those killed a whole carload of tourists like the one the day before.

"That happened the day after workers drilling a fence posthole ruptured a natural-gas line on Collins Avenue. Buildings were evacuated. People panicked. Businesses closed. Total gridlock for four hours. Some drivers abandoned their cars and ran. Wasn't pretty, I can tell you. No wonder Florida has three times the national average of mental illness." She daintily sipped her drink while I gazed dreamily at the red-violet sunset, watched the palms sway, and wished the waves could carry my worries out to sea.

The long-planned $450 million Center for the Performing Arts had actually opened. "Downtown's still a mess," she said. "Sidewalks all tore up. Small businesses going bankrupt. Latest tally on the Center's cost overrun is another $102 mil, and of course they never did plan for parking."

The project had been on the drawing board for three decades or so. I was surprised it had actually opened. "I thought it would be like that church in Sweden," I said.

Lottie blinked and cocked her head curiously.

"They broke ground in 1260, in Uppsala, Sweden. None of their children or grandchildren lived to see it finished—a hundred and seventy-five years later in 1435."

Lottie wrinkled her nose and scratched her sunburned shoulder, bright red despite all the sunscreen. "Where do you find all those obscure stories that never fit into newspapers or cocktail party conversations?"

"I read a lot," I said testily.

"I'm not criticizing. It's part of your girlish charm." She ordered another rum drink and continued bringing me up to speed.

"More construction workers are getting killed on the job than all the cops, firemen, cabdrivers, and convenience-store clerks put together. Three men drowned in tons of hot quick-drying cement, buried alive at a luxury high-rise oceanfront site. They were pouring concrete on the roof when a frame broke. It buried the workers on the floor below and hardened before anybody could pull 'em out."

I hate when people go to work in the morning and never come home. It's always painful to write about a man or a woman who meets a violent sudden end only because he or she is at work—which, at that moment, is the wrong place at the wrong time. It's lousy to die trying to earn an honest living and care for your family.

"Who were they?"

"Two Haitians and a Mexican," she said. "Came to join the boom, find their piece of the dream, and feed their folks back home. The apartment prices on that condo project start at a million five. They died building a place they could never live in, or even be welcome at, except maybe as busboys in its rooftop restaurant."

"They'd have lived longer busing tables," I said.

"Except as busboys they'd have no place to live, 'cause all the affordable housing is being torn down or converted to pricey condos. . . . We're living in interesting times, Britt. I feel like a character in a horror flick. Floods, fires, monsters crawling out of the swamp and eating people alive, big machines crashing, burning, and exploding, men buried in quick-drying cement. But it's no movie. It's real life."

Our conversation seemed surreal in this serene setting beneath a crescent moon.

"And you suggest I go back there? Why?"

"'Cause it's a great news town, Britt, and you're a news junkie, just like me. Reporting is what you do best. You and Miami are made for each other."

I knew she was right. "How *are* things at the word factory?" I finally asked.

"Worse since the anthrax scare." She sighed. "Our incoming mail is all diverted to an off-site mail room, where it's opened by an eighty-year-old man hired by security."

"Why him?" I wondered aloud. "Is he considered expendable? Is he an old snoop who loves reading other people's mail, or is he a wild and crazy octogenarian who lives and breathes for danger?" I wistfully recalled the letters that arrived daily at my desk, penned by wackos, gadflies, indignant readers, eager tipsters, jailed felons, and the guy with the foot fetish.

"Maybe he works cheap." She shrugged. "All I know is that he wears gloves and a surgical mask and is shaky with the scissors. It's hell, Britt. The mail arrives in pieces with crucial parts missing or mixed up with bits of somebody's else letter. Reading it is like trying to put together a jigsaw puzzle. Everybody's complaining."

But she had good news too.

The Heat won the championship and thousands of crazed Miamians descended on downtown. Confetti cannons blasted. Fans partied hard. They did not attack one another or the cops. Nobody got hurt or went to jail. Hard to imagine.

And the news about our friend Ryan Battle, the feature writer who labors at the desk behind mine, was excellent. His leukemia was still in remission.

" 'Member Nell Hunter, that new reporter, the cute little one from Long Island?"

"The blonde?"

"That's her. Broke Ryan's heart."

"Not again," I lamented.

"No sweat, he bounced back," she said. "Now he's hot for an intern, purty little thing from Kansas City. Saw them canoodling at the Eighteen Hundred Club the other night.

"Nell may be cute as a button, but she's a certified bitch. Wrote a story that burned Sam Stone, the Cold Case Squad detective. Included all kinds of personal stuff about his dead parents and ambushed his elderly grandmother. I felt bad for 'im. He was real upset. No surprise there. The desk sent Nell out to cover a story on your beat a couple weeks ago."

"Oh?" I didn't think I'd care, so the hot surge of resentment surprised me. "How'd she do?"

Lottie shook her head. "Not too well. The first Miami cop she met asked, 'Where's Britt?' Nell didn't take that kindly. Then she meets the Cold Case sergeant, Craig Burch. As he's answering her questions, he calls 'er *Hon*.

" 'I am *not* your honey,' she says, and blasts him in front of his detectives."

"Is she crazy?"

"Appears to be," Lottie said. "Burch is good people. Most likely he said it 'cause he couldn't remember her name. She sure showed her ass. They showed her the door. So she beefed to their lieutenant." She paused for effect.

"She went to K. C. Riley?"

Lottie nodded slyly.

"Why on *earth* would she do that?"

Lottie rolled her eyes and looked innocent.

"Lottie! You didn't!" I put down my dessert fork and stared accusingly.

She shrugged and confessed. "Nell called me, mad as a red-assed dog, bitchin' about *sexist pigs.* Wanted my advice. How would Britt Montero have handled it? I just tried to help."

"Oh, sure, you and Mother Teresa."

"I told her you would've marched back into that cop shop straight into the office of their lieutenant—who, of course, just happens to be a sister," Lottie said sweetly. "You would've demanded that those detectives be reprimanded and ordered to apologize—and to cooperate fully and respectfully with her in the future." She blinked coquettishly. "Isn't that what you would've done?"

"She didn't!" I whispered.

"She did, bless her heart."

I pressed my napkin to my mouth but failed to suppress the laughter. "You know how obnoxious K.C. can be," I gasped, when finally able to speak. "You know how ferociously she backs up her detectives. Is Nell still alive?"

"Alive but not well. K.C. got all red in the face, cussed Nell out, and had two patrolmen escort her out of the building. The front desk sergeant was told to bar Nell from the station." Lottie gazed out at the soft palm-shaded twilight, shaking her head sadly. "Too bad it happened to be windy and raining real hard, what with her car parked such a distance away and all. Poor thing."

"You are the worst." I laughed aloud.

"Nell showed up back in the newsroom, hair all plastered down, teary-eyed and totally pissed. Looked like a drowned rat. You could see her nipples right through that little blouse she wears. Said she won't go back there, ever. Nobody covers the police beat now, Britt, at least not like you did."

"How is K. C. Riley?" I asked quietly.

"Seems to be coping. Better than you are, I guess. Feisty as ever. Fights the good fight every day. Heard she went to hostage negotiation school, passed at the top."

"I guess it's easier for someone like her. She's cold," I said.

"You shouldn't hate her 'cause you both wanted the same man. She had him first, as I recall. And you have a lot more than that in common."

I grimaced, shook my head in disbelief, and changed the subject. "Anyone else ever ask about me?"

"Nope," she said shortly. "You know what a short memory Miami has."

My misery must have shown.

"I'm kidding." Lottie leaned forward, her honest brown eyes sympathetic. "Every day. Especially lately. Your ears must have been burning all last week."

"Is that so?"

"Yup. Another reason to come home, Britt: The Cold Case Squad is looking for you. I said I didn't know where you were. They want to talk to you."

"What about?"

"Some homicide."

"Which one?" I asked, suddenly interested.

"Wouldn't say. But I get the impression they think you're somehow involved."

"What sort of case?" I scrolled my memory bank for possibilities and came up blank. "When did it happen? Did they mention the victim?"

She shook her head. "You know how we can usually finesse information out of Burch, Nazario, Stone—even Joe Corso if you play 'im right. But they're stonewalling till they talk to you."

I frowned.

She looked pleased when I agreed to go back to Miami with her. "I didn't aim to push you," she said. "Sure you're all right with it?"

I nodded. I'd known my exile was nearing its end before she arrived.

"I'm broke," I confessed. "Think I'll have any trouble getting my old job back?"

"No way."

It was the end of one chapter and the beginning of a whole new one.

CHAPTER THREE

We shot the mystery camera's last three frames on the beach at dawn.

A shell collector snapped the last one of us together, with our surfboards. She was an elderly woman, her skin turned to parchment beneath a big straw hat, and the pockets of her baggy shorts stuffed with long-spined stars, baby's ear moons, and other jewels from the deep. Then we hurried back to the cottage to gulp tea, eat some fruit, and pack.

Lottie was due to return to work, and if I didn't join her I'd soon be living under a bridge. So we wasted no time. By two o'clock that afternoon our dusty taxicab was bouncing along a rut-filled road to the far side of the island to catch the three o'clock seaplane, one of three flights a week.

The tiny plane skimmed blue-green waves for heart-stopping moments, startling dolphins and pelicans, then swooped us into a brilliant sky under clouds that pierced the cavernous lazuline blue like stalagmites.

The pilot, a grizzled Vietnam veteran, said he hadn't been back to the States in years. He had done mountain rescues in the Andes and then worked for a time as a seagoing repo man, stealing boats from deadbeat owners behind in their payments. The money was good but he wearied of being chased, shot at, and cursed. "Had enough of that in Nam and then after we came home."

We spent a few hours in Nassau, speed-shopped the straw market for souvenirs, and then went on to Miami aboard a plane packed with the same fellow travelers who seem to be on every flight: Howling Baby, Sneezing Senior, Coughing Man, and Overweight Woman Drenched in Noxious Perfume.

Coming home, drinking in Miami from the sky, never fails to take my breath away, even though the city I love is gone now, replaced by a swollen, overbuilt metropolis, where the only remaining small patches of green visible from the air are cemeteries and sports stadiums. Endless rivers of traffic crept along every clogged artery. The surf snaked along the shoreline like a green river, while sky and sea blended seamlessly at the horizon.

Homesick, heartsick, a little bit nauseous, I stepped back into messy reality, my heart pounding with anticipation.

As we cleared customs, Lottie and I wondered aloud if we would ever identify the owners of the lost camera. I had left my number with several locals on the island, offering to send the photos should the owner show up.

Lottie drove me home in the company car she'd left at the airport. Culture shock overwhelmed me: traffic noise, heat, and humidity exacerbated by the scorching pavement and miles of concrete barriers that block sea breezes. Construction cranes towered at every turn. Cranes have become the new state bird, I thought.

Home, my little garden apartment—one of twelve in two rows facing each other across a tree-shaded lawn guarded by pink hibiscus hedges—had not changed.

I'd left my dog Bitsy, my cat Billy Boots, and my house keys with Helen Goldstein, my landlady. Leaving my four-footed companions in familiar surroundings with someone they loved and I trusted left me feeling far less guilt. At eighty-two, married sixty-three years, Helen Goldstein is one of the youngest people I know.

Welcoming aromas wafted from her kitchen as she threw open the door. There was flour on her hands and cheeks, and she wore an apron emblazoned with the words HARDLY ANYBODY GOT SICK LAST TIME I COOKED.

She had been baking rugelach, kugel, and kichel, little cookies with a sprinkling of sugar. Our surprise arrival delighted her. The hugs, happy laughter, and Bitsy's barking brought her husband, Hy, rushing in from the living room where he had been watching the TV news.

Bitsy, the little dog I inherited from a policewoman killed in the riots, had not forgotten me. Billy Boots, my black-and-white tuxedo cat, perched high on the embroidered back of an armchair, sneering disdainfully at the dog's hysterical welcome. Tail twitching, the cat stared straight through me, as though I were an imperfect stranger intruding on his turf. He arched his neck, displaying a bright flowered collar and a silver bell that were new to me. Well fed and well groomed, both animals looked cleaner and shinier than on my watch, clear evidence that I couldn't even properly nurture a cat and a small mop of a dog. What would Francie, who'd smuggled Bitsy into her patrol car on the midnight shift, think, had she only survived that deadly moment in time?

Mrs. Goldstein held me at arm's length, gave me a complete once-over from head to toe, spun me around, did it again, and delightedly announced that I looked wonderful. "Are you eating enough?" she demanded, before severely scolding me. "You couldn't have called first?" She would have prepared a meal.

"That's why I didn't. You'd fuss. You've done enough."

I turned to hug Mrs. G again, with Bitsy, now trembling, panting, and drooling, in my arms. My clumsy move brought us too close to the chairback and Billy took two swift swipes, just missing the little dog's nose.

"Billy, you know better!"

The cat ignored me, leaped lightly to the floor, closed his eyes, and rubbed against Mrs. Goldstein's ankles, purring loudly.

Despite my pleas of exhaustion and a long list of chores to be done, my landlady insisted we sit, to nosh on her fresh-baked goods and drink a glass of tea. Afterward, we all trooped across the courtyard to my apartment. Bitsy bounded ahead, to lead the way, while Billy followed at a discreet distance, as though it were mere coincidence that we all happened to be strolling in the same direction.

The Goldsteins exchanged a conspiratorial glance as I inserted my key, and when I opened the door he hit the light switch with a flourish. Both beamed at my gasp. Hy Goldstein had painted my apartment in my absence: bed and bath the palest shade of pink, like dawn's faint blush, and the kitchen in sunshine yellow with cream trim and turquoise accents.

I'd come home to a lighter, brighter, freshly painted world. Even my furniture had been repaired and rearranged, and somehow they'd managed to keep my window herb garden alive and thriving.

They hoped it would lift my spirits, they said. It did, despite my tears.

Lottie and I made a quick run for essentials to the big new Publix supermarket on the bay before she left. After trying to start my T-Bird without success, I called AAA to recharge the battery. They took more than an hour to arrive. The driver jump-started the car but warned me to take it to a garage for a long, slow charge or a new battery.

I didn't call my mother. All I hungered for now was sleep, in my own bed, and this time I slept like the dead, blessedly dreamless, waking at dawn, disoriented for only a moment. How I love my apartment! What a comfort to wake with Bitsy curled up at my feet and Billy's big green eyes gazing into mine. Purring loudly, he had obviously forgiven me my absence. I was home.

For the first time in months, I applied lipstick, eyebrow pencil, and a little mascara, then donned a navy blue skirt and a white blouse that showed off my tan. I pored over the Goldsteins' morning newspaper, then called to restart my home delivery. I fortified myself with a cup of Cuban coffee before making the call I dreaded, to my friend Onnie in the *Miami News* library. Slowly I punched the familiar numbers.

It felt awkward, but I knew there were those in the newsroom who would stare and whisper when they first saw us together. I had to warn her that I was back.

We both wept.

"Welcome home, Britt," Onnie finally said, her voice solemn. "Thanks for the heads-up. I've missed you. Darryl will be so excited. He asks for you every day."

My next call was to Fred Douglas, city editor at the *News.* He didn't sound surprised when I asked to see him. Lottie must have spilled the news.

The T-Bird sprang to life at once, a good omen. The familiar drive west across the causeway and the sight of the *News* building on Biscayne Bay were a comfort. For most of my adult life, that behemoth has been my rock and my sole security. A strange car was parked in my space beneath the building, so I left the T-Bird in visitors' parking across the street. My *Miami News* ID still gained me entry; I bustled by a new security guard without a challenge. So far, so good.

Ryan rushed from his desk for a hug moments after I stepped off the elevator and into the newsroom. I felt the stares, heard the murmurs, and the voices calling my name from other desks. Fred was in his small glass-front office.

"Look at you, Montero!" he boomed. "Must have been quite a vacation."

I was tanner than I'd ever been, my hair longer and sun-streaked. "Yep," I said jauntily. "But now it's back to the salt mine. I hope."

My stomach did a free fall as he paused to survey me thoughtfully. I had left suddenly, uncertain about my plans, and Fred had warned he couldn't guarantee me a job if and when I returned.

"When do you want to start?"

I shrugged casually, weak with relief. "This afternoon?"

He smiled. Fred is a rarity in the business, smart and creative, a tough editor with a heart.

"Do we renegotiate salary?" I asked brightly.

"Don't push your luck, Montero. I'll probably catch heat for this as it is. The budget's tight and we're in a hiring freeze."

"So it's back to my old beat?"

He gazed past me, out his picture window toward the cranes punctuating Miami Beach's pastel skyline. "I'm thinking of moving Santiago off the City Hall beat and sending you in there."

My heart hit the floor. I had covered city politics briefly, early in my career. My whole head, including my teeth, would ache as day-long city commission meetings stretched into evening and the early morning hours, as our erratic and volatile city fathers insulted, threatened, and occasionally threw punches at lobbyists, cops, irate taxpayers, city employees, and one another.

"That a problem?" Fred's eyes took on an edgy, questioning glint.

I shrugged. "I liked the police beat. Sort of made it my own. I did a good job."

His lips tightened. "There's no lack of crime at City Hall," he said tersely. "A helluva lot of One-A stories come out of Dinner Key. Graft, greed, and corruption, malfeasance, misfeasance, and nonfeasance, politicians doing perp walks—everything from low comedy to Greek tragedy wrapped up on one beat. What more could a reporter want?"

He was right. A city commissioner, a former war hero driven to the brink by personal demons and political and legal problems, had fired a fatal bullet into his own head in the newspaper's lobby last year.

How inflexible was Fred, I wondered. I didn't want to argue myself out of a job, but pushed anyway. "I was really good on the police beat," I repeated stubbornly. "From what I hear, nobody's really covering the cops." I glanced meaningfully at the newspapers stacked on his desk. "Who knows what stories we've missed?"

"The competition did beat us badly on the last few big cop-shop stories." He leaned back in his chair, cracked his knuckles, and contemplated the ceiling.

"It's where I would do you the most good."

He remained reluctant. "City Hall is a gold mine for an enterprising reporter who knows how to dig," he said persuasively. "Change is healthy. Show 'em how it's done, Montero. I think it's best, under the circumstances."

"I've had enough change." Did he detect the quaver in my voice? I hated to sound pathetic. "I need to go back to something familiar for a while."

"Sure you can handle it?" The concern in his eyes looked fatherly.

"Absolutely. No sweat," I said, wondering in sudden panic if I could. Was he right?

Now that I had doubts, his seemed to lessen. "Have it your way, Montero, if you feel that strongly. But at the first sign it isn't working, come to me. Got that?"

"Got it." I stood to go, before he, or others, could change his mind.

"Sure you don't need more time to settle in?"

I shook my head, my hand on the doorknob.

"Your buddy Lieutenant Riley from the Cold Case Squad has called, looking for you."

"I heard."

"What's that about?"

I hitched my shoulders and shook my head again, eager to bolt while I was ahead. "No clue."

"Should Mark Seybold talk to her first?"

I didn't think the paper's ferocious and fearless in-house attorney should be involved so soon. "Let me check, see what's up. It may be nothing. I'll let you know. Anything else?"

"Yeah. Looks like you and Lottie were a blast on the beach." Fred's trademark bow tie bobbed as he chuckled. "Didn't know you were a surfer girl."

I blinked in surprise.

"The picture on the bulletin board."

Gretchen, the editor from hell, smirked as I left his office. Her pin-striped navy business suit with a pale blue Brooks Brothers shirt projected the bright and impeccable image of a rising young news executive, totally masking her ambitious mean-spirited incompetence.

I ignored her and beelined for the bulletin board. Lottie and I were the centerpiece, framed by our surfboards, heads tilted together, our hair, haloed by the rising sun, streaming like banners in the ocean breeze. Newsroom habitués had already posted several humorous and not too flattering captions, comments, and critiques.

I found Lottie sipping herbal tea, back in the photo bureau.

"Hey. You developed the pictures! Where are they?"

"Mornin' to you too," she drawled, and put down her mug. DON'T LET THE BASTARDS GET YOU DOWN was lettered on the side.

"You see Fred?"

"I'm back on the job."

"You go, girl."

"The pictures. Where are they?"

She dropped a few enlargements in front of me, a copy of the bulletin-board photo on top.

"My favorite," she said.

"Nice job. You do these this morning?"

"Nope. Walgreens one-hour service, last night."

The next picture was Lottie, one hand on her hip, the other holding a conch shell to her ear like a telephone.

The last was me, leaning against the trunk of a palm tree.

"What's on the others?"

She shrugged. "A couple of tourists."

"Let's see. Maybe I'll recognize them."

"Doubt it." She shook her head and turned away.

"Where are they?" I began to paw impatiently through the other photos on her desk.

Reluctantly, she handed me a folder. "Recognize anybody?"

I shuffled through them like a deck of oversized playing cards, glimpsing freeze-framed moments in the lives of happy strangers. I looked more closely at the handsome couple.

"Betcha they're newlyweds. Look, you can see their wedding rings. Crap! They lost their honeymoon pictures!"

The photos had been shot on a white-sand beach and aboard a trawler, probably a forty-footer. No one else in sight, just the two lovers, radiating the white-hot fire of passion and adventure at starting their life together cruising through paradise.

Tears stung my eyes.

Had events played out differently, that might have been Kendall McDonald and me embarked on our own tropical honeymoon.

"One of 'em musta dropped the camera overboard or lost it in the sand," she said. "It wasn't likely, but I checked all the wedding pictures that ran for the last five weeks, just in case. Didn't see their faces. No way to identify 'em. But ain't he a hunk?" She picked up a glossy print. "Would've been nice to return these. I blew 'em up trying to make out the boat's name or registration number. No luck. They could be from anywhere." She shook her head, slipped a wide shot under the magnifier, and flipped on the light.

I peered over her shoulder. A pretty girl with long, flowing sandy-colored hair waved at her husband from aboard their boat, her radiant smile frozen in time, her tan golden, her shorts white, with a red crop top.

"Nice shots, but not one at the right angle," Lottie grumbled.

"No big deal." I sounded morose. "At least they still have each other."

She heaved an I-told-you-so sigh and cut her eyes at me. "Damn. I didn't want you to see 'em."

"Life's not fair," I murmured.

"It ain't. Never was. But like they say, 'You can sum life up in three words: It goes on.' "

"I wish I hadn't come back," I whispered. "I don't know if I can do this, Lottie. Maybe I should move in with my mom for a while. Find a job someplace else, maybe another state."

"Think your life's a living hell now? Try moving in with that woman for a while. Not that I have anything against her, bless her heart, but you know your mother. And sure, it really makes sense to move to a town where you have no friends, no sources, and no clue how to find Main Street. That sound like a plan?"

I blew my nose.

She scowled. "Would you just quit that, Britt? Now?"

"What?" I brushed my leaky eyes with my fingers.

"Your poor-pitiful-me routine. It's getting old fast."

My jaw must have dropped. She looked serious.

"Get over it and get on with your life! Think about something, or somebody, else for a change. Everybody since Adam and Eve has had loss and heartache. If it ain't hit 'em yet, it's headed right at 'em, barreling straight down that highway from hell. As my Aunt Paula always said, 'Any day you wake up on the right side of the dirt is a good day.'

"Whenever life went straight to hell in a handbasket, you always knew where to find Aunt Paula: in her kitchen, fixin' the world's best biscuits and spoon bread. That's how you survive. Do what you do best. Don't run away."

She dropped her voice and leaned forward to make her point.

"Comfort the afflicted and afflict the comfortable, that's a journalist's job. You know it, Britt. It's what you do best. McDonald didn't fall in love with some whiny-ass little crybaby. He fell for a strong, self-reliant woman. So would you please do me a personal favor and start acting like one?" She waited for an answer, arms crossed, lips pursed, her freckled face grim.

"How could you?" I was shocked. "You're my best friend."

"Damn straight. Who else would tell you?"

"Thanks so much for your concern," I snapped, and marched off in a snit.

She called my name but I didn't look back.

I picked up my mail and messages, still stung by Lottie's mean-spirited lack of sympathy. My resentment spilled over and focused on whoever had been using my desk, my space, my direct phone line. The intruder had added insult to injury by dumping the contents of my desk drawers into storage boxes stacked on the floor in a nearby hall. I was lucky they hadn't been discarded with the trash. In no mood to tippy-toe, I grimly reclaimed my turf. I swept the squatter's notebooks, papers, and personal items off my desk into two cardboard boxes from the wire room. What new hell was this? Today, many reporters file their stories from out in the field while others work from home. There is no shortage of newsroom desks. Whoever had invaded my space had to know it was mine.

That person had answered my phone and talked to my sources. The mail and notebooks I examined identified the guilty party: Nell Hunter. With not-so-gay abandon, I tossed her belongings aside and replaced them with my own.

Later, as I read through my mail and messages, she appeared, clutching a notebook, in a big hurry.

"Excuse me," she said, in her chirpy little voice. "I'm on deadline." Her sweeping gesture suggested I vacate at once.

I gazed up at her placidly.

"This is my desk." Her chirps grew impatient.

"No," I said, smiling sweetly. "It isn't."

"Britt?"

"That's right."

Her brown eyes widened in shock. "I didn't recognize you," she blurted. "Nobody mentioned you coming back. I've been using your desk. It's just so . . . so convenient."

"I'm sure."

"Do you mind?" She gestured again, as though I were a pesky rodent.

"Yes," I said. "I do."

She focused on my desk and looked alarmed. "My notes?"

"In one of those boxes over there, I think," I said vaguely, and made a little gesture of my own before turning back to my reading.

She was still standing there, open mouth revealing shiny little white teeth, when I glanced up moments later.

"Nell? Would that be your car parked in my space under the building?"

Her face reddened. "I'll move it right after I turn in my copy."

When I looked up again she was crouched, her peasant skirt collecting dust from the floor, as she furiously ransacked one of the boxes, searching for her notes.

"Nell?"

She glanced up warily.

"Did you take any messages for me?"

She sighed bitterly. "Call the Cold Case Squad."

"Grrreat to have you back," Ryan murmured, from the desk behind me. "Welcome home, Britt."

Lottie had been right about one thing. My overstuffed mailbox yielded at least two calls apiece from each member of the Cold Case Squad: Sergeant Craig Burch, Detectives Stone, Nazario, and Corso, and—the most recent—their lieutenant, K. C. Riley. Hers was more a command than request: *Britt: Call me or Burch, ASAP.*

• • •

The barricades, detours, and torn-up streets made the short trip to Miami Police Headquarters torturous. But I practically sang as I turned and twisted through traffic. I was home, on my beat. I turned my dashboard scanner up full blast, immersing myself in the endless chatter of police calls, trying hard to think of nothing else.

Once there, I took a deep breath and walked into the lobby, plunked my purse onto the X-ray machine's conveyor belt, and stepped through the metal detector. The desk sergeant called homicide to announce my arrival, listened for a moment, eyeing me idly, and hung up.

"They're expecting you." He signaled another officer, who used his key card to activate the elevator for me.

As I approached the Cold Case Squad's cubicles, Lieutenant Riley emerged from her office. Fit and tanned, as usual, she looked even thinner than I remembered. Her dark blond hair hung almost straight, shoulder length, with a slight natural wave. She saw me and stopped abruptly.

"Hey, Lieutenant."

She stared for a long moment.

"You're full of surprises, aren't you, Montero?" Her face reddening, she wheeled, returned to her office, and firmly closed the door.

I stood there for a moment, and then Craig Burch glanced up from his desk. "Hey, guys, cancel the Amber Alert!" he boomed. "Look who's here!"

"Holy shit." Corso rolled his eyes.

Emma, the lieutenant's secretary, clasped her hand over her mouth.

"*Dios mío*," Nazario said.

"This is a surprise, Britt," Stone said. "But it's good to see you."

"You rang?" I said.

"Yeah, more than once," Burch said. "We need to talk to you."

"About?"

"The last time you saw Spencer York."

"He's turned up?" I grinned in spite of myself, elated at the prospect of a good story my first day back on the job. "Where's he been?"

Their expressions told me.

I sighed and lost the grin.

"Dead?" I couldn't imagine him dead. The man was bigger than life, though it wasn't a stretch to imagine killing him.

I'd even fantasized about it once myself.

CHAPTER FOUR

"Let's talk." Burch jerked his head toward the conference room.

I followed, despite reservations. The good news was that it wasn't a room where suspects are interviewed.

Nazario politely pulled out a chair for me.

"My editor wanted to know if the paper's lawyer should talk to you first. Do I need him?"

"Your choice," Burch said.

I studied their faces. Curious, noncommittal, even friendly. Typical detective faces.

"You may have been the last person to see him alive," he said.

"So he *is* dead."

"Oh, yeah," Burch said.

"Very." Corso plopped his thick torso into a chair directly across the table.

I thought for a moment. "The last time I ever saw or heard from him was the day he was released from jail. I interviewed him just before he jumped bond and took off."

"It looks less like he took off and more like he was taken out," Burch said. "How'd that interview of yours come about? Was he pissed off at you?"

That would make sense to most people, since Spencer York's arrest was the direct result of a story I wrote about him.

"No, oddly enough. The publicity thrilled him, he wanted more. The guy had a humongous ego. Loved to be the center of attention. He looked forward to his trial, couldn't wait. Said he planned to represent himself. He was so elated at the prospect I almost felt sorry for the prosecutors. That's why it surprised me when they said he jumped bond and skipped town. What really happened to him?"

They told me.

"So he was here all along." I imagined him in the ground just west of Miami, oozing body fluids, his flesh slowly decomposing into Everglades muck as a clamoring world searched everywhere else for him.

"Sure it's him?"

They nodded.

"Did the ME determine a cause?"

The detectives exchanged glances.

"GSW," Burch said.

"What kind of gun? Did you find the bullet?" I flipped open my notebook. "Casings? Caliber? Any suspects?"

"We're the ones asking questions here," Burch said. "We're not giving interviews."

"He was a bad man. Nobody liked him," I offered.

"An understatement if I ever heard one," Burch said.

Spencer Nathan York was America's most prolific kidnapper. A hired gun for divorced fathers, he called himself the Custody Crusader and was a combative foe of what he described as a growing tide of feminism that had swept over the family courts, depriving fathers of their rights.

He had tracked his clients' ex-wives to twenty-five states and abducted more than two hundred children, whom he returned—to their fathers.

He saw himself as a hero. Instead of a Superman cape he wore faded army fatigues, thick glasses, and a graying crew cut. His crusade, he said, was to change the judges, the courts, and the laws that were unfair to men.

He offered his services to fathers whose ex-wives had moved out of state with their children. He'd advise the dads to file for custody, alleging that the mother had absconded with the youngsters, denying the fathers their court-mandated visitation. When the mothers failed to appear for court, the local family court judges usually granted the fathers' custody petitions.

The Custody Crusader would then track down the mothers and snatch their children.

I was a cub reporter, shuffling through routine Miami police reports, when an unusual incident caught my eye. The complainant was one Brenda Cunningham, age twenty-five and divorced, a relatively new resident from Arkansas. As she removed grocery bags from her ten-year-old Chevy outside her rented Miami duplex, a beefy middle-aged stranger in camouflage attire burst through the hedge and snatched up her three-year-old son, Jason.

Groceries scattered as she screamed and rushed to save her child. As she and the stranger scuffled over Jason, her ex-husband, James, emerged from a parked car across the street. Seeing him only made the terrified young mother more frantic.

The Crusader sprayed her with Mace and announced that he was taking legal custody of Jason. Blinded and hysterical, she continued to fight. Her ex-husband dashed to join the fray, and the two men escaped with the shrieking child, leaving the mother bruised, battered, and temporarily blind.

She and neighbors called police.

Before a patrolman arrived, however, the police chief's legal office and the local FBI received faxed copies of the father's official custody order. The Crusader followed up with telephone calls on his way out of town to confirm that the faxes had been received, knowing that at that time local police departments would not become involved in interstate custody disputes.

The police officer who responded to Brenda's plea for help said there was nothing he could do. Her problem was a civil matter she had to resolve in family court. He noted in his report that the child was safe with his father, who had legal custody in their home state of Arkansas. Neither the police nor the FBI intervened. Nobody opened a kidnapping investigation.

Spencer Nathan York, the Custody Crusader, was not difficult to locate. He included his name, address, and Texas telephone number with the legal papers he had faxed to authorities. I suggested I interview him, and my editors sent me to Texas.

Notorious criminals can be downright charming, colorful, and charismatic. That explains how they get away with their bad behavior long enough to become notorious. That was not the case with the Custody Crusader. He was rude, crude, and obnoxious. He called the divorced mothers bad parents, greedy sluts, and loose women who frequented bars, drank alcohol, and cavorted with strange men instead of devoting themselves to raising their children. Women, he warned, had far too many rights. His crusade was for change.

I also managed to interview Jason's father and was permitted to watch—from a distance—as the little boy happily romped with his new puppy in his paternal grandparents' walled-in backyard.

Jason's mother, Brenda, a waitress, could not afford to wage a legal battle back in Arkansas. However, my story created a stir, arousing the ire of Miami women's groups and the state attorney, who charged York with felony assault and reckless child endangerment during his skirmish with Brenda.

The Custody Crusader did not fight extradition. His asking price for a child snatch was $5,000 a head plus expenses. But most working fathers are cash-strapped after contentious divorces, and York actually received little or nothing for most abductions. His motives were altruistic, he insisted, not financial. He did it, he said, for the cause. He operated on a shoestring and was broke.

That is why those familiar with the case were surprised when York's $20,000 bond was posted and he was released pending trial.

"We're interested in that last interview with him," Burch said. "Where was it? Was he alone or was someone with him? Did he mention any threats or express concern about his safety? Did he say where he was going when you two parted company?"

"He called *me*," I said. "I think it was just as he was being released. As I recall, it sounded like jail noises in the background. I was surprised he had bonded out. He wanted to fill me in on the latest developments in his case. My editor told me not to meet him alone somewhere, since my story had resulted in his arrest. I didn't anticipate any problem but suggested he come to the paper, and he did.

"He was alone. Couldn't have been happier, couldn't hide his excitement. He loved playing martyr for the cause. He'd demanded a speedy trial and was counting the hours. Wanted TV and the wire services to report his rants about discrimination against divorced fathers. The man loved to talk, loved it even more when somebody paid attention and took notes. I asked how he managed to post bond. He said he didn't. He bragged it was from a donor, a supporter who admired his work. We talked. Had coffee. I wrote the story."

"What was the last thing he said to you?" Stone asked.

I thought about it, then remembered. "He asked when the story would be in the paper. I said, 'Probably tomorrow.' Then he walked out of the newsroom and off the map. I never saw him again. I was surprised he didn't call after reading the story."

The prosecutor had pleaded for a higher bond, calling York an itinerant kidnapper and a flight risk, but the judge had set it at the minimum. Nobody expected him to post it.

The state attorney was apoplectic when York failed to appear for his next pretrial hearing. Women's groups and female politicians raised hell when York could not be found. So did male politicos eager to court women voters. The Miami Police Department endured media scrutiny and high-profile criticism for their insensitive response to Brenda Cunningham's call for help and their handling of the case. In the next election the judge was replaced by a woman who ran against him.

The story took on a life of its own as cops and prosecutors waged a nationwide manhunt for the elusive fugitive. Rewards were offered. But as the years slipped by, the furor simmered down, sliding from the front to the back page and then out of the newspaper and out of public consciousness altogether.

"So, he talks to you and you write a story that lands him in jail. So when he bonds out, the first thing he does is talk to you again?" Corso said. "Was this guy a glutton for punishment, or what?"

"No. He wanted to use me—and the newspaper—for publicity. You know the type. My story brought him the attention he wanted, but celebrity is a double-edged sword. It also resulted in his arrest. But he was convinced his trial would make him and his cause famous."

"Have to agree with the guy on some things," Corso said. "But he must've had delusions of grandeur, thinking if he changed the system he'd be the patron saint of divorced dads."

"It goes without saying that he probably had a bad experience in divorce court himself," Burch said.

"In that first interview, in Texas," I said, "he vaguely alluded to a long-ago divorce but didn't go into detail."

"Did he say where he was going when he left the paper?"

"All I know is that he intended to stay in Miami, study Florida law, and prepare for trial. He asked for directions to the University of Miami law library."

"Where was he staying?"

I shrugged. "Up till then, Dade County Jail. Said he had to find a cheap place, a rooming house or motel."

"Did he mention any names, people he knew here? Anything more about the good Samaritan who posted his bond?"

"No. I tried to call the guy for comment, but as you know, he used a false ID with a nonexistent address."

"You have any ideas about who killed York?"

I shook my head. "I assume you've spoken to Brenda."

"Stone's talked to her," Burch said.

"She wouldn't have been able to post his bond," I said. "She worked at a local IHOP. If she'd had any money, she would have hired a lawyer to get her son back. I tried to call her after York was declared a fugitive. Her phone was disconnected. A neighbor said she left town.

"I didn't like Spencer York," I said, realizing as I heard my own words that it was not the wisest comment under the circumstances. "I mean, I liked the fact he'd still talk to me and probably would continue to do so, no matter what I wrote about him or how much trouble it caused him. He didn't care what anybody wrote about him as long as they spelled his name right. We had no quarrel. He was happy. And so was I, for my own reasons. I was a rookie reporter. My interview with the Custody Crusader was one of my first stories picked up by the wire services. Larry King even talked about it on his show."

The detectives appeared unimpressed.

"How did you make positive ID?"

"Dental. Finally found a dentist he'd used in Waco," Burch said. "His sister still lives there. Agreed to give us a DNA sample if we needed it. He was her only sibling, but they apparently weren't close. Seemed relieved to hear he wasn't coming back."

The detectives asked me to include their phone number in the story with an appeal to anyone who might have information.

"Thanks, Britt," Stone said. "It took a lot of nerve for you to come back here like this."

I shrugged, my personal and professional thoughts all jumbled together. What could I say?

K. C. Riley was still in her office as I left. I wanted to stop and say hello, but she didn't look up. From where I stood, she looked red in the face. I knew why, but I knocked anyway, then tentatively edged her door open.

She looked up at me and sighed. "What is it?"

"Thought I'd say hello." Our eyes met.

"Well, just look at you," she said, leaning back in her chair. "Bigger than life and back in town."

I did a double take at the framed photograph in a prominent place on her bookshelf. I had seen it before but was surprised to see it still displayed in her office. Blue sky above, liquid sky below. Two people aboard a boat. She was one of them, sunshine in her hair, in cut-off shorts and a bathing suit top. Laughing as she held up a puny grouper. Major Kendall McDonald, my fiancé, stood grinning beside her, wearing a Florida Marlins baseball cap, his right hand on her shoulder.

My mouth felt dry and my eyes began to tear. "I just wanted to let you know that I got your message and did speak to your detectives about the York case."

"And I got your message. I'm busy, Britt." She picked up the papers she'd been working on.

"Sorry to interrupt you."

"You make it a habit. It's as though it's your life's work," she said, as I closed the door behind me.

I left the station biting my lip. I forced myself to focus on the story, on Spencer York and how he had so eagerly anticipated his big moment in court. It never came. By his trial date he was a wanted man, a fugitive at the center of a media frenzy, the target of a high-profile manhunt.

How he would have loved it. But he missed it all. He never got to star in his own courtroom drama. Instead, he knew nothing, saw nothing, wrapped in a tarp, doing the big dirt sleep, with only the heat and maggots for company. Ironic, almost sad. Life is sad, I thought, and full of broken dreams.

My pager began to chirp. Lottie. Wants to apologize, I thought righteously. It's about time.

I didn't answer.

As I drove back to the *News*, my cell phone rang. The caller ID displayed the photo bureau number.

I ignored it, still stung by her words. Let her regret them a little longer, I thought. Amid the cacophony of car horns, rumbles, and traffic noises, my beeper sounded again. Three cement mixers blocked the turn onto Biscayne Boulevard as I waited through three traffic light cycles. Drivers behind me cursed and leaned on their horns as their blood pressure climbed.

How many would stroke out? I wondered with a sigh. How would an ambulance, or a victim trying to reach an emergency room, survive this traffic gulag?

I examined my beeper. Lottie again. This time she had punched in 911. Emergency.

Wow, I thought, she's really sorry. I felt guilty. *She is my dearest friend.* I glared at a driver trying to inch his PT Cruiser in front of me and called her, but now all I could reach was a busy signal.

CHAPTER FIVE

"Lottie's looking for you," said the assistant city editor I briefed on the Spencer York story.

Moments later I scooped up the persistently ringing phone on my desk.

"Britt?" It was her voice.

"I'm sorry too," I blurted.

The silence was deafening. "Hell," she finally said, stretching the word into two syllables. "I ain't apologizing for nothing. You're the one didn't answer my messages."

"You're not sorry?"

"No way." Before she hung up, she said, "Check your mailbox."

I did. Nothing special. Mostly routine press releases from the police public information office, artfully composed to impart as little information as possible, and an alert from the Coast Guard on two missing boaters. . . .

I almost spit up my coffee.

A U.S. Coast Guard air and sea search was under way for newlyweds from Boston. The couple and their forty-foot trawler, *Calypso Dancer*, had vanished on their island-hopping honeymoon.

The faces beneath the MISSING banner made my heart skip. The golden couple who had lost their honeymoon photos to the sea were now lost themselves.

"Oh, my God!"

"What's wrong, Britt?" Ryan asked from behind me.

I waved the flyer. "I know these people!"

His eyes widened. "Who are they?"

"Newlyweds. From Boston. I mean, I don't actually know them, they're the people whose camera we found."

Now we had names to match the faces: Vanessa Holt, twenty-six, and her husband, Marsh Holt, thirty-two.

The narrative stated in stilted Coast Guard jargon that nothing had been found: no wreckage, oil slicks, or reported sightings. There had been no distress calls. The search was hampered by the fact that no one was certain how long the couple had been missing. They had filed no precise itinerary, and friends and family had not been immediately alarmed.

Maybe no news is good news, I thought, staring at their faces. My phone interrupted.

"Did you see it?" Lottie demanded impatiently.

"It's them," I said urgently. "It's them. I'm on it. Make copies of the best pictures for the city desk."

"Did that." She paused. "I hope they're not dead, Britt."

"Me too."

I called the Coast Guard, then Boston.

"Did they find anything?" Norman Hansen, the father of the missing bride, asked when I identified myself. The fear and anguish in his voice were palpable.

"Not yet. I just spoke to the Coast Guard. The search area is huge, but we have some photos that may help narrow it down."

"Something terrible happened." His voice trembled.

In the background his wife asked, "Is it the airline?"

"No, Molly, a reporter," he said. "In Miami."

She picked up an extension. I could hear her labored breathing.

"This is not necessarily terrible," I said. "They may have simply lost track of time; you know how honeymooners are."

"No," he said firmly. "Nessa's not like that. She's extremely reliable. When she didn't come back to start rehearsals, we knew it was something terrible."

"Rehearsals?"

Vanessa, it seemed, played first cello for the Boston Symphony, quite an accomplishment at age twenty-six. The radiant girl with the long hair was a talented musician. Their pride was evident despite their panic and anxiety. The newlyweds had been due back in Boston on Friday. Rehearsals began on Monday. The weekend had come and gone without a word, a call, or a message.

"She devoted her whole life to music, to the Symphony," her father said, "until she met Marsh. He's a wonderful young man. We were so happy. But when they didn't come back and didn't call, we knew."

His wife choked back a sob. "We feel so helpless. . . . We're trying to book a flight."

"We're coming down," he said, "to look for them."

"Don't be so quick to assume the worst." I tried to comfort them. "Island time is different. Things move more slowly. They may have engine trouble, could be marooned somewhere. Maybe adrift. Coast Guard Search and Rescue is good. They'll find them. Last week they rescued several boaters who'd been adrift for five days. Wait a day or two. It's a big ocean. There's not much you could do here now. When they do come home," I added cheerfully, "this will be a story you'll tell your grandchildren someday."

"Please God." His wife choked.

I asked how to reach Marsh's parents.

"He lost them at an early age," Molly Hansen said. "He has little family, but he fit right in with us. He's the son we never had. We love him and he loves us." An engineer from the Midwest, he had met Vanessa shortly after his transfer to Boston and he had swept her off her feet: love at first sight, or something close to it. He proposed only months after they met, after first asking her parents' permission.

The wedding was lavish and rich in music. Fellow musicians had performed; others were members of the wedding party. Marsh had rented the *Calypso Dancer* for their romantic two-week island-hopping honeymoon.

The parents sounded sweet and scared silly. Vanessa was their only child.

"Don't panic," I said again. "No news is good news at this point. No distress calls went out. There have been no reports of a boat in trouble. No wreckage has been spotted. I'll stay on it and call you the minute I hear anything." The Hansens, in turn, promised to lend the *News* one of the couple's wedding pictures. Lottie arranged for a Boston service to pick it up at their home and transmit it.

The frightened parents sounded temporarily reassured by the time I hung up. Now I regretted my initial envy of Vanessa and Marsh, husband and wife for less than four weeks. How random fate and Mother Nature can be, I thought. How quickly life can turn on a dime.

Had the newlyweds been swallowed by the shadowy seas of the Bermuda Triangle? Were they targeted by pirates or drug smugglers? Or are they simply still out there, I wondered wistfully, sipping daiquiris and making love on a palm-lined stretch of sugar-white beach, having lost all track of time?

The last option had my vote.

Between calls to the Coast Guard, I contacted local feminists and politicians for reactions to the fate of the Custody Crusader. The once-outraged prosecutor was now a prominent criminal defense attorney. The deposed judge, caught up in a career-crashing whirlwind of criticism and controversy for releasing Spencer York on low bond, was beyond mortal reach, dead for more than a year. Too bad, I thought. He would have felt vindicated. When Spencer York failed to appear for trial, it was not the fault of a too-lenient judge. An unknown killer was the culprit.

Whoever murdered York and hid his corpse had effectively killed the judge's career and reputation as well.

The voices now were not as strident as at the height of the controversy. Laws had changed. Miami was a different city. The most vocal critics had moved on to other issues, other outrages. Some had left South Florida, others were gone from the planet. Miami is known for its short memory, which may be why we keep making the same mistakes.

He was no longer politically controversial, but the legend of Spencer York's disappearance had now morphed into a murder mystery, a good read. It was time to introduce the Custody Crusader posthumously to a whole new generation of *Miami News* readers.

I called York's sister, Sheila, near Waco. She hung up. Unlike her brother, she obviously didn't like talking to reporters and didn't want her name in the newspaper. I sighed. How could siblings be so different? Did they share the same father? I wondered. Had Spencer York been granted a onetime opportunity to speak out from beyond the grave, it would have been to a reporter.

As usual when people hang up on me, I counted to ten and redialed.

"Britt Montero again," I said sweetly. "We were cut off. Sorry. It must be the thunderstorm we're having. I know this is a bad time, how upset you must be at the loss of your brother, but we need some information about Spencer. I hate talking to strangers when I know you're the most accurate source."

As usual, it worked.

"What kind of information?" she said warily.

"Just a little background," I said.

"Like what?"

"Was he your only brother?"

"There was another, but he died when he was two, fell down the well."

"How awful. So there were just the two of you growing up together?"

"Yes. We were three years apart. He was the oldest."

"What is it that you remember most about your brother?" I asked.

"Difficult. He was always difficult. We weren't close."

"I know how that can be." I did sympathize. "But it's never easy. It's always hard to lose a family member, especially a sibling."

She must have some positive childhood memory of the man, however fleeting, I thought. Hopefully, he said or did something decent, had been kind to his sister at least once in his life. "Even if you weren't close, he was still family."

"You're right," she said. The little catch in her throat seemed to surprise even her. "I guess you sort of think what it might've been like, had Spencer not been the way he was. I always thought the wrong brother had died as a child, or that maybe they mixed Spencer up with somebody else's baby in the maternity ward, and he wasn't really related to us. That sort of thing does happen."

It piqued her interest to hear I had met Spencer myself. The last time she spoke to him, he had called collect, she said, from Miami. She accepted the charges because she hadn't heard from him for nearly two years and thought it might be an emergency. He told her to read the papers and watch the TV news, boasting that she'd soon see and hear his name.

She'd been embarrassed when she did see his name—on wanted posters. Deputies visited her home several times that first year or so, to determine whether she was harboring the fugitive sought for jumping bond in Miami. They asked if Spencer had been in contact with her. He hadn't. She feared he might. That possibility unnerved her every time a car door slammed, the doorbell rang, or the dogs barked. But after five years or so, she confided, she had come to believe that Spencer was dead.

I asked why.

"Because, you know," she said matter-of-factly, "bad pennies have a way of turning up."

Made sense.

I wrote the story, my impressions of York's dysfunctional family mingling with the plight of the warm, close-knit Hansens, who now faced the painful possibility of loved ones lost.

There are families, I thought, and then there are families.

That reminded me to call my mother.

I had intended to wait but decided I had better make contact before she saw my byline in the newspaper.

Should I invite her to my apartment? Go to hers? Or meet her on neutral turf, in a public place?

I turned in my stories, went over the copy with Bobby, the assistant city editor in the slot, to be sure he had no questions or drastic changes in mind, and then called her.

"I'm at work but I'll be off soon," I said. "Want to grab a bite somewhere, or stop by my apartment for a snack or a drink?"

"Oh, sweetheart." She sounded crestfallen. "How I wish you'd called sooner. I'm meeting Russell for drinks at the Van Dyke at ten. But I can stop on the way for a cup of tea, a hug, and a word about the divine new things we're showing in the fall. I've already seen a darling little form-fitting white sheath that has your name written all over it."

I laughed out loud.

"It's so good to hear your voice," she said warmly. "I've missed you."

"Me too," I said. "Love you, Mom."

I raced home. No time for elaborate preparations, she'd arrive in less than an hour. I cleaned out Billy's sandbox, found some green tea and crackers in the cupboard, and took Bitsy for a quick walk around the block.

Who is Russell? I wondered. After belatedly learning the truth about my father's death in Cuba thirty years ago, that he had not abandoned us, my mother had finally grieved, and then begun to heal and build a social life. These days, it was far busier than mine.

Moments after I brought Bitsy back inside, there was a knock at the door. She's here! I thought in a moment of panic. I'd hoped to freshen my lipstick and comb my hair. I will never be the fashion plate she would like, but it makes her happy if I appear to be trying.

"You're early," I cried, throwing open the door.

"For what?" asked Mrs. Goldstein, my landlady.

"I thought you were my mother," I said, relieved. "She's on the way. I'm making tea."

"Oh." Her eyebrows lifted. She looked serious. "So, I won't stay. But there is something you should know, Britt. I need only a minute. Then I'll bring some rugelach to go with the tea."

I smiled expectantly.

"It's not easy, Britt. When Hy and I settled here we thought this is where we would stay for the rest of our lives. Where else?" She shrugged.

I felt my smile fade. "What are you saying?" My knees suddenly felt weak.

"What can I say? We're not renewing any more leases. Fair, it's not. But every day, they knock at our door, they call, they stuff letters in the mailbox."

"You're not . . . ?" I couldn't bring myself to say the words.

"The real estate agents, the developers. They've got us fuh-shimmeled; they don't stop. One wants to convert this place into condos. His fuh-cocktuh vision is apartments 'for the young, hip, and edgy.' This is what he tells us. Another is buying up everything around us. He wants this piece to complete a parcel for his project."

"What project?" I whispered.

"A Home Depot."

"Oh, no," I pleaded. "You can't."

"Who would believe the money? More than we ever dreamed this place could be worth. Leave, we would never. But to live here now is so expensive. Oy! Our taxes are up; so is the insurance—the windstorm, the homeowner's, the flood, the liability—and the utilities. Every storm season, double and triple. Soon we'll have to raise the rent so much most tenants can't afford to stay. Then, maybe, we would break even. To live our lives out in this place we love is what we wanted. So, who can afford it?"

"You can raise my rent," I babbled. "I'm back to work now."

"I'm sorry," she said. "Tomorrow it's not, or next week. But it's a matter of time. Not a long time. We didn't want to tell you, especially now. We looked forward to you coming back. But fair we have to be. Don't say anything. We didn't tell the other tenants yet, but they see the handwriting on the wall."

"What will you do?"

She shrugged. "What can you do? We don't feel old. But some days . . . With the storms, the repairs, the new city codes, it's harder to take care of everything here. To go to a place for people our age we'd hate. They're all so old. Century Village is not for us." She looked miserable. Her faded blue eyes were bright with tears. "But there is a place upstate, near Ocala, that sounds nice."

I wanted to protest, to say, But you've lived in Miami Beach since you met and married. More than sixty years. You're part of this city's history; it's part of yours. Your roots, the story of your life is here.

I didn't.

Instead, I took her hand. "The most important thing is to do what's best for you both. The happiest home I've ever had is this one, and that's because of you. I love you two. I wish we could live this way forever, but we both know nothing is forever."

I smiled and hugged her, when what I really wanted to do was scream, stamp, and weep hysterically. I blew my nose as she hurried back across the courtyard for the rugelach.

* * *

The hand-painted table looked nice. My grandmother's china teapot, the fragile cups, the dainty spoons and tiny sugar cubes, with Mrs. Goldstein's baked treats the pièce de résistance.

My stomach rumbled. I hadn't eaten since morning and felt ravenous. I decided to treat myself and order a pizza later. The promise of an entire mushroom pizza all to myself was a comfort.

My mother was actually late. In a hurry. Hair sleek, heels high, skirt short. We fell into each other's arms at the door. Then she took an uncertain step back, stared at me for a long moment, and screamed.

CHAPTER SIX

"Good God, Britt! Why didn't you tell me you were pregnant!"

I shrugged. "I didn't want you to be upset."

"Upset?" Her eyes looked wild. "How could you? What were you thinking?" She raised her voice. "Did you think at all? This is not the life I wanted for you, ever! How could you be so reckless?"

"I'm sorry."

"What are you going to do?" She paced my apartment, shoulders rigid, lips pressed tightly together, trying not to lose control.

"I think that's obvious." Truthfully, nothing was obvious to me at the moment. I was still trying to wrap my brain around the news that soon I wouldn't even have a place to live.

"I wouldn't wish your situation on my worst enemy," she said bitterly. "I've lived it. Do you realize how difficult a life it is? I did it myself."

"No, you didn't," I protested. "Not really. My grandmother mostly raised me. But don't worry, I'll make sure that doesn't happen this time."

She frowned, scrabbling in her handbag for a cigarette. "What on earth are you talking about? Your grandmother is dead."

"You're the grandmother."

Her eyes opened wider, as she unleashed another hysterical tirade. "How could he? How could you? *Why*?"

"This wasn't deliberate, Mom. We were in the islands. McDonald proposed. I said yes. Remember, we called you? We were so happy, so relaxed. This wasn't intentional."

"It's utterly insane. It's not how I raised you!"

"I love him, Mom." I tried to speak rationally, softly, calmly. The last thing I wanted was to argue with her. "Please listen. When McDonald was killed, I almost asked if they could remove semen from his body so I could be inseminated. Believe it or not, the thought actually crossed my mind."

She stared at me as though I were an insane stranger.

"Maybe I was crazy with grief, but I'd read about the procedure. It's been done. But as much as I wanted a part of him to live on, I knew it was selfish. No child should be deprived of the stability of a two-parent home or the chance to know his father. I remembered how hard it was to grow up without my dad. But then, a few weeks after the funeral, I discovered it had happened anyway. There must be a reason. That's why I left for a while, to try to sort it out."

"What will you do?" she demanded. "How will you live?"

"I don't know, exactly."

"You've ruined your life! Your youth, your education, your future! It's ruined. You've flushed it all down the drain!"

She began to weep. Then she grimaced and gently touched my face. "You didn't use sun protection either!" she cried accusingly. "First you ruin your skin, then your entire life."

She teetered dramatically across my small living room on her stilettos, flung herself onto my couch, and pounded the pillows hysterically.

Billy Boots watched in horror, poised for flight, back arched, hair standing on end.

Bitsy rolled over and exposed her belly, totally vulnerable, as if to say, *Kill me now.* I shared both their reactions.

"How can you embarrass me this way?" she shrieked.

"That's it, isn't it? It's all about you."

She turned off the tears, sat up abruptly, and snatched her cell phone. Was she dialing 911? Turning me over to the police?

"Who are you calling?"

"Russell, he's waiting," she whimpered. She hiccuped and blew her nose. "I have to let him know I'm not coming. That I have a family emergency and can't leave."

The horror was all mine. *She plans to stay?*

"No, no, no! Don't let me spoil your evening or his. It's not fair. Don't do that! And I don't want to argue, Mom. I'm not up to it." I collapsed into my favorite armchair, suddenly exhausted. "I've had some other bad news. And I need some sleep. I have to work in the morning."

She cut off her cell call before it connected. "Are you all right?" For the first time, she showed concern rather than anger. "You can't keep that job, Britt," she added. "It's too dangerous for a woman in your condition."

"Believe it or not, Mom, cops, firefighters, soldiers, and astronauts all have babies. I even know some reporters who are mothers."

"How can you do this to me?" she whimpered.

I gave her a quick hug, stopped arguing, and began to get ready for bed, hoping it would convince her to go meet her date. She soon wiped her eyes, repaired her makeup, and recombed her little-Dutch-girl haircut.

"We need to talk more about this, Britt," she said, before leaving.

"Mom?" I said, as she reached the door.

She turned and gazed at me in my baggy pajamas—actually an old large Miami Dolphins T-shirt over a loose drawstring bottom—then closed her eyes for a moment, as though the sight was too much to bear.

"You can forget the form-fitting sheath with my name on it."

Even she had to smile, if only for a moment.

* * *

Restless after she left, I remembered the box of McDonald's things in the bottom of my hall closet. I suddenly wanted to hold something that had belonged to him. They were mostly books, a few novels, an autobiography of Chuck Yeager. At the bottom was his Miami High School yearbook.

I thumbed through the pages, eager to see how McDonald looked as a teenager. Here was something to show our child someday.

His youthful clear-eyed look and familiar smile took my breath away. Friends, fellow students, and teachers had signed the book, but there was only one notation on the page with his high school picture. The writing was graceful, legible, in blue ink. *Always in my heart, Love, Kathy.*

The signature was followed by the outline of a tiny heart pierced by an arrow.

I swallowed and stared at it for a long time.

Her photo was on another page. Blonder and sweet-faced, with eyes full of fun, she was somebody I probably would have liked had I known her back then. No hint in that tender young face of the strong woman she would become, wearing a badge and a gun.

Wait for me. Love, Ken, he had written.

Turning the pages, I picked out their faces in group shots. Found one of her at bat in a softball game. He played football.

Kendall McDonald and Kathleen Constance Riley, voted most glamorous couple, said the caption under a photo of them together.

They wore the flirtatious electric glow of teenage sweethearts. I recognized the look. I'd seen it just hours ago in her office, in that fishing photo shot nearly two decades later.

Under his picture it said *Most likely to be found with Kathy.* Beneath hers, *Most likely to be found in Kendall's convertible.* I closed the book.

My eyes flooded. How I envied all those years, all the history they had shared.

I forgot the pizza, stuffed my miserable face with rugelach, brushed my teeth, and fell into bed. I stared at the ceiling and then tossed and turned, as dark shapes crept in between the sheets with me. Jumbled horrors I couldn't quite recall ended in a flaming encore performance of my recurring dream. I woke up dazed and disoriented, a displaced person who didn't belong here or anywhere.

Without turning on the lights, I wandered outside with Bitsy and Billy and sat on a cold stone bench in the courtyard. The seductive scents of night-blooming jasmine, gardenias, and home filled the inky darkness before dawn. Home. My home. For how long? I wondered. Imagining this garden, this abode I loved, a denuded and barren construction site stung like a knife wound to my heart. Where will I go? I wondered. What can I do?

I searched the sky for comfort, cat purring in my lap, little dog at my feet. Like people, earthbound landmarks age and disappear, despite our struggles to save them, I thought. Only the heavens remain constant.

Venus, the morning star, rose in the northeast as I watched Aries the Ram pursue Pegasus, the winged horse, across the eastern sky. Eventually, familiar sounds returned me to earthly matters, the plop of morning papers hitting the ground.

COLD CASE
SQUAD

MIAMI, FLORIDA

"Could've knocked me over with a feather when she walked in here." Corso grinned. "Who knew?"

"Not Riley, that's obvious," Burch said. "See the look on her face? One look at that belly bump and she locked herself in her office. She was so hot to move on the York case, to find out what Montero knew, but she just turned around and closed her door."

"Have to hand it to Britt for coming back here. Took a lot of nerve," Stone said quietly.

"Nobody ever said she didn't have chutzpah," Corso said. "Wonder what she and Riley talked about in there."

"Didn't take long, whatever it was," Burch said.

"McDonald sure had a way with the ladies," Nazario said.

"The whole damn thing is awkward," Burch said. "I've only seen that look on Riley's face twice. The last time was when McDonald got killed. The other was way back when that dentist shotgunned his seven-year-old kid in the face to spite his ex-wife.

"I drank for four straight days after that one myself. Couldn't stop seeing it. When his father racked one into the chamber and aimed the gun at him, the kid was scared and covered his eyes with his hands. His little fingers wound up embedded in what was left of his face."

"Uh-oh," Nazario said.

Riley had emerged from her office. "Did the reporter know anything?" she asked briskly.

"Nothing we didn't already know," Burch said. "She talked to York at the paper. He was alone, mentioned no names. His immediate plans were to find himself a cheap room and hit the law books. She didn't think he'd run. He was high on publicity, couldn't wait to play Perry Mason at his own trial. We'll do a supplement."

The quiet Cuban-born detective is blessed with an uncanny talent invaluable to an investigator, even though it does not provide probable cause for arrest, or testimony admissible in court. His colleagues swear that he always knows without fail when somebody is lying.

She turned to Nazario. "What did your built-in shit detector say?"

"What Britt said was true," Nazario said. "In all the time we've dealt with her, she never lied. This was no different."

Riley folded her arms and perched casually on the corner of Burch's desk. "So who would've guessed? Any of you know she was pregnant?"

They all denied it.

"A surprise to us," Corso said. "We had nothing to do with it."

She nodded, eyes hollow. "So where do we stand on Spencer York?"

"Talked to Brenda Cunningham," Stone said. "Brenda Cunningham Grokowski. Resides in Oregon with her second husband, Mike, a long-distance trucker. Has two more kids, little girls. Hasn't been able to afford to go back to court to fight her ex for the boy's custody. Hasn't seen Jason since he was four. He's a teenager now."

"How'd she react when she heard York was dead?"

"With relief. Said she would've killed him herself back then if she'd had the chance. She's still angry that he never went to trial for the assault on her and Jason."

"Just when did she meet Mike the trucker?" Riley asked thoughtfully. "Was he Brenda's man of the moment when she was roughed up by our victim?"

"Nope," Stone said. "Claims she had no boyfriend at the time. Had casually dated a co-worker at IHOP. With her son gone and no trial on the horizon once York disappeared, she got depressed, lost her job, and was about to be evicted. Did a stint as a topless dancer at the Pink Pussycat. Not her finest hour. When a friend, another dancer, moved to Oregon, she went along, sort of spur-of-the-moment, she said. They shared the cross-country drive. She landed a job in Portland, found Jesus, and met the trucker in church. Said he's never been to Florida."

"Check him out anyway," Riley said. "See if that's true, if he has a rap sheet, or ever owned a gun. What about her ex, Jason's father?"

"Called the guy," Nazario said. "Says he's not sorry he had his kid snatched. Has no clue who wasted York or why. Suggested we check Brenda's boyfriends."

"Anything else?"

He nodded. "I'm looking into York's last confirmed sighting. When he left the *News* building, he went over to WAVE radio to be interviewed by a talk-show host. Listeners called in, including somebody from a support group for divorced dads. He invited the Custody Crusader to speak at their meeting the following night.

"His bondsman says he established back then that York did address that dinner meeting of Fathers First. They met once a month. The *News* story on York appeared in that morning's paper. They had a full house. I can't find anybody who saw him after that. Two weeks later, he failed to appear at a pretrial hearing."

"So his killer nailed him between the meeting that night and his missed court appearance," Riley said. "Leaves us with a two-week window."

"I'm thinking," said Burch, "that he had to be killed closer to the night he met with the fathers. York wasn't shy. He was a big-mouthed son of a bitch who craved attention and was on a roll. Yet nobody heard anything from him after that night."

"The group's defunct," Nazario said, "but I'm looking for a membership list from back in the day."

Burch stopped by Riley's office before going home. Still at her desk, she was poring over old reports.

He noted the framed photograph, still in a prominent place on her bookshelf: Riley and Kendall McDonald at a department fishing tournament.

"You okay?" he asked.

"Sure. Have to admit that one took me aback. Would've been nice to have a heads-up. Thanks for asking. First thing in the morning," she said without a pause, "have Stone check other Florida jurisdictions for custody snatches during that two-week window."

It was a smooth transition, switching gears from a deeply personal matter back to business without a blink. He had to hand it to her. Probably too good for Kendall McDonald. What had the guy been thinking?

"Spencer York's fifteen minutes of fame in the press might have attracted new clients," she said. "More loving fathers eager to have their kids snatched by a lunatic who would Mace and knock down their mothers in front of them. He needed money to survive and to finance his legal defense. Despite his arrest, he probably wouldn't have turned down a job. Maybe he tried a snatch that went bad."

"Jeez," Burch said. "As a parent, I can't imagine what those guys were thinking."

"You don't have to be a parent," she said sharply, "to imagine the trauma to those kids." She chewed her upper lip and stared at him accusingly as she toyed with a metal paperweight in the shape of a hand grenade. "And the mothers. Imagine what they thought, seeing that nutcase escape with their children."

"It'd make anybody crazy," Burch said quickly. "York claimed he snatched more than two hundred kids over the years."

"Which means that any twelve-year-old he took five years earlier would have been old enough to fire a gun by the time he was killed," she said.

"Hell, we see fourteen-year-olds shooting people every day. Some are better marksmen than cops you and I both know."

"It certainly widens the suspect pool," she said.

"Funny," he said. "Usually, the richer the murder victim, the more suspects there are. Money always makes people want you dead. But this guy was dirt poor and everybody still wanted to kill him."

"We have our work cut out for us."

"Montero's writing a story. When news that York's dead hits the street, it may shake something loose."

"Don't count on it," she said. "Input from the reading public might help once in a blue moon, but nothing beats solid detective work. Say hello to Connie for me. How are the kids?"

"Good. Great. This case makes me want to go home and hug 'em all. You know that me and Connie have had our ups and downs through the years, even separated for a while, came thisclose to a split," he said, demonstrating with his thumb and index finger. "Now we're good, but even if things had gone south, I still can't fathom how anybody could hire York. Can you believe that Corso thinks the Custody Crusader wasn't all that bad, even had some good ideas?" Burch shook his head as he turned to leave.

"What do you expect?" Riley said. "He's stuck on stupid, a longtime nominee for jerkhood."

Burch glanced back after punching the elevator button. Riley had picked up the framed photo of herself with Major McDonald. He paused, hoping to see her fling it into her wastepaper basket. She didn't. He sighed as the doors yawned open.

Pete Nazario didn't go right home. Instead, he swung by the home of Colin Dyson, the founder and former president of Fathers First.

Dyson operated an insurance agency and lived in a well-landscaped Mediterranean-style corner home in upscale Miami Shores. Expensive cars—a midnight-blue Jaguar sedan and a pearl-gray BMW convertible—sat in the driveway.

The man who answered the door was husky, dark-haired, and middle-aged, with ferociously shaggy eyebrows. He wore shirtsleeves, dress slacks, and a gold Rolex. He held a half-empty glass.

Nazario smelled liquor on his breath, but the man wasn't drunk. The detective introduced himself, flashed his badge, and asked for Colin Dyson.

"What now?" the man barked impatiently.

"Colin Dyson?"

"Who wants to know?"

Nazario handed the man his card. "Are you Colin Dyson, former president of Fathers First?"

A wary flame flickered in the coal-black eyes beneath the shaggy unibrow. The man slipped quickly out onto the shadowy porch, just as a woman's voice inside sang out, "Who is it, honey?"

"Nobody. A salesman," he called back sharply, and closed the door firmly behind him.

"The group disbanded six–seven years ago," Dyson said. He shrugged, but his voice was tight, eyes intense.

Nazario blinked. The man's demeanor had escalated from guarded to hostile in a heartbeat. He clearly had no intention of inviting the detective inside for a chat.

"We need some information," Nazario said.

"About what?" The tone was arrogant.

"The night Spencer York, the Custody Crusader, spoke to your organization."

Dyson stared at the detective for a long moment, full lips parted, his expression odd. "That was a long time ago."

Nazario nodded in agreement. "Nine years. I'm with the Cold Case Squad."

The woman called out again, from just inside the door. "Dy? Who's out there?"

Her voice galvanized him into action. "I'm not talking to you without a lawyer. Get the hell off my property." Dyson spat out the words and ducked back into the house. The heavy door slammed so hard that Nazario's ears rang. He heard the deadbolt's quick metallic snap and then the woman's querulous voice.

Nazario picked up his card, which Dyson had dropped, slid it under the door, and returned to his car, parked out front. He saw the drapes inside move as someone watched him settle into the driver's seat.

He turned the key in the ignition and drove away. Slowly, he circled the block, then parked down the street. Twelve minutes later, Dyson left home in a hurry, slamming the front door behind him.

The big man stood for a moment as though sniffing the air. He scanned his surroundings and, satisfied that he wasn't being watched, tore out of the driveway in the Jaguar. He didn't slow down at all for the stop sign at the end of the block.

Nazario followed, staying several car lengths back as Dyson cut off other motorists, swerved from lane to lane without signaling, and accelerated through intersections as traffic signals changed.

"*Dios mío*," the detective murmured. Even he, known for driving as though he were being chased by the devil, found it difficult to keep Dyson in sight.

He was game. He would have followed right through the last red light that Dyson ran, but had to hit the brakes to avoid T-boning a huge elongated intercity bus that had lumbered into the intersection.

Nazario stood on the brakes. They came so close to colliding that he could see the horrified expressions on passengers' faces as they saw his oncoming car skidding toward them, brakes screeching.

He feared he'd lost Dyson, but then he spotted the Jaguar parked in a space outside a small commercial building just west of Biscayne Boulevard: GOLD AND GRAY, ATTORNEYS AT LAW.

Nazario smiled.

He smiled all the way home to Casa de Luna. The annual property taxes on this multimillion-dollar chunk of Miami Beach real estate exceeded his yearly income, but he was a lucky man. Wealthy residents, fond of traveling but concerned about home security, sometimes offer a policeman free lodging in the servants' quarters, guest cottage, or garage apartment. The owner enjoys peace of mind and the policeman a rent-free place to stay.

As the historic old mansions disappear, falling to high-rises, hotels, and loft apartments, such offers are increasingly rare and coveted by cops who are divorced, or separated—as Burch was, when he first occupied this sanctuary—or single, like Nazario. When Burch and Connie reconciled, Nazario inherited the digs at Casa de Luna.

He rode herd on the landscaper, the twice-a-week maid, the car washer, and the pool man. Should a hurricane threaten, his job was to secure the premises. Each night he checked the house, the alarm system, and the doors and windows. Not long ago he also wound up riding herd on the owner's sad, bad, errant daughter, Fleur. A small price to pay for this retreat.

Casa de Luna, old Spanish-style architecture, elegant and graceful, with bubbling fountains, lavish gardens, and a pristine infinity-edge pool, was built in the 1920s but had since been renovated, updated, restored, and refurbished, inside and out, no expense spared.

The owner, W. P. Adair, Wall Street–rich, robust, and full of life for a man in his sixties, was currently traveling in Europe with a young trophy wife, his third or fourth, a knockout named Shelley.

Nazario parked his car in the fragrant shadows of the long driveway, drank in the salty breeze off the sea, just across the Intracoastal Waterway and Collins Avenue, and climbed the stairs to the apartment above the four-car garage.

Some might think it small—it had originally been built for a live-in housekeeper—but it was actually larger and more comfortable than many places the detective had lived.

Not bad for a Pedro Pan kid who arrived alone on a flight from Cuba. He never saw his parents again and spent the rest of his childhood shuttled between orphanages and foster homes all over the country before finding his way back to Miami as a young man. He never had, or required, many possessions. He was accustomed to living simply. And this was by far the best place he'd ever lived.

Not bad.

He thought about Colin Dyson, racing to his lawyer's office in his big Jaguar, and smiled again.

Tonight he felt richer than W. P. Adair.

"Sounds like we got lucky." Lieutenant K. C. Riley wore a wide grin at the morning briefing.

"The guy's guilty of something," Corso said.

"Dyson has a record," Stone reported from his computer terminal. "Domestic battery, traffic, and a DUI. No major felonies."

"Not yet," Corso said, cheerfully rubbing his hands.

"His lawyer just called." Nazario hung up the phone. "He's bringing Dyson in."

"You were right, Pete," K. C. Riley murmured, when Dyson and his lawyer, Franklin Gray, stepped off the elevator. "He does have a unibrow—you know, like Frida Kahlo."

"Frida who?" Corso said. "You talking about that new female recruit in—"

"Shhh," she said.

Dyson looked subdued in an expensive suit and tie.

"I read the newspaper this morning about the York case, the homicide you're investigating," said Gray, well known as a high-priced and aggressive criminal defense attorney. "I advised my client, who is guilty of absolutely nothing, that under the circumstances it would be in his best interests to cooperate."

They gathered in the conference room with a tape recorder on the table.

"I was stupid," Dyson sheepishly admitted.

"We're interested in the night York spoke at the Fathers First meeting," Nazario said.

"Look." Dyson turned both palms up, the open gesture of a man with nothing to hide. "To our group of screwed-over fathers, York was like a visiting celebrity. He'd gone to jail for the cause. He might be going back. They gave the guy a standing ovation. There was a lot of anger and passion in the room that night."

"So they treated York like their patron saint," Corso said, glancing at Burch.

"Right. But if any crime was committed"—Dyson's forefinger jabbed the air—"I was the victim. That son of a bitch ran off with my money. He ripped me off to finance his getaway."

"How so?" Nazario asked

"I hired him to snatch my kid, Colin Junior. He never grabbed the kid. He never did a goddamn thing."

The detectives exchanged glances.

"My ex-wife moved to Georgia—Savannah—with my only kid. He was eleven. I had visitation, but I had a life, a fiancée, a business to run. How am I gonna fly to Savannah every other weekend? Or fly him down? Impossible."

Fathers First met in their usual place that night, a hotel banquet room near the airport. The menu never varied: steak, baked potatoes, and chocolate cake for dessert. They paid York a modest $200 speaker's fee. He delivered a rousing fire-and-brimstone, half-hour, give-'em-hell talk and then participated in another thirty minutes of Q and A with his audience. Afterward, they passed the hat for donations to help defray his expenses.

"Everybody kicked in, tens, twenties, hundred-dollar bills," Dyson said. "We had a packed house. York wound up with a paper bag full of cash."

Several members then gathered at the bar and bought York drinks.

"A few of us were interested in his services," Dyson said. "I offered to drive him back to his room."

"And where was that?" Burch said.

"Some motel over on Southwest Seventh Avenue."

"Remember the name?"

He squinted, brow furrowed. "Sea Spray, Sea Bird, Sea something . . . Had a little lounge off the main lobby. We had a few drinks and talked. He said he had to stay a little more low key, operate under the radar, because of his pending case, but he was up for it, more than willing. I agreed to pay him five thousand dollars, two thousand down and the rest, plus expenses, when I got my kid. I gave him pictures of my ex-wife and my son, and their Savannah address and handed him two thousand bucks that night. Cash. Never saw him again."

"You always carry that much money?" Riley asked.

"No, but after I read the news story that morning, I took it with me just in case. It was stupid to give it to him. I guess I got carried away by the excitement of the meeting, and the Jack Daniel's I was drinking probably didn't help my judgment. I couldn't wait to see the look on my ex-wife's face when she got knocked on her ass and we took the kid."

"When did you realize York was gone?" Burch said.

"He told me to petition for custody here in Miami-Dade first. I went to see my lawyer the next day, to start the ball rolling. York was supposed to call. He didn't. I had some questions, but he didn't answer the phone in his room for a couple of days. I finally drove over there. The clerk said he didn't check out; he skipped out, still owing them money. I kept expecting him to surface. But a couple weeks later they said he'd jumped bond. That's when I knew I'd been ripped."

"Sure you didn't hunt him down for payback?" Burch said.

"Hell, no. I never would've been able to get custody of my kid if I got arrested."

"*Did* you get custody of your boy?" Nazario asked.

Dyson's face screwed up in an expression of disgust. "Yeah. Biggest mistake of my life. That little bastard cost me a goddamn fortune. Lawyers up the wazoo. And what did it get me? A kid who didn't appreciate a goddamn thing I did for 'im. Started running away at twelve, smashed up my car when he was fourteen, stole money from me, always in and out of trouble, and when he was nineteen he slept with his stepmother, the bitch. I threw 'em both outa the house."

"How old was the stepmom?" Burch asked.

"Twenty-four. What the hell does that have to do with anything?" he demanded angrily.

"Just curious." Burch sighed. This was not what he had hoped to hear.

"You ever own a gun?" Nazario asked.

Dyson hesitated.

"Don't answer that," his lawyer said. "My client has been completely forthcoming. When he saw the newspaper and realized what you're investigating, he wanted to put everything on the table. Mr. Dyson should not be treated like a suspect."

"Did you physically harm Spencer York in any way?" Nazario asked thoughtfully.

"Nah. I would have loved to rip him limb from limb"—Dyson shrugged—"but I couldn't find him."

"Where's your son now?" Burch asked.

"Beats me. I see him in my neighborhood, I call the cops."

"How lovely," Riley said later. "What a delightful cast of characters. Is there anybody who *wouldn't* have loved to kill Spencer York?"

"Dyson said he'll supply us with the names of the others in the group," Nazario said. "He tossed the records but said he has an old mailing list. He also agreed to take a ride with us to see if he can point out the Sea-something motel if we have no luck finding it."

"The bad news," Riley said, "is that York went from flat broke that morning to having about three thousand cash in his pocket, according to Dyson. Which means we can add every low-life robber, sneak thief, con man, and mugger in Miami to our list of suspects. If York was flashing that roll around, it could have been anybody."

"How ironic would that be," Burch said, "if the shooter was some stranger who didn't even know who York was? That would really leave our case FUBAR."

"Fucked up beyond all recognition," Corso said, nodding.

"Unlikely," Riley said thoughtfully. "Most robbers who shoot strangers just leave the bodies where they fall, they don't bother to hide them. But just in case," she told Stone, "access records and print out a list of all the armed robberies, known suspects, and missing persons reported in that sector, along Southwest Seventh, during the three months before York disappeared and the three after. Especially in the area of his motel, if and when we find it." She turned to Nazario. "How truthful was Dyson?"

He thought for a moment, then shook his head. "He wasn't lying when he said he wanted to rip York limb from limb or to see his ex-wife's face when they snatched his son. And he was truthful about giving York the money. He's so hostile, the rest is hard to read. Last night I really thought he might be the one," Nazario said, his spaniel eyes sad.

Riley frowned. "Let's not rule him out yet. His son was old enough then to remember if he met York. Why don't you find Colin Junior and see what he knows."

BRITT

CHAPTER SEVEN

I slid my morning paper out of its condomlike sheath: two bylines. Not bad for my first day back. I couldn't be accused of not doing my job—yet. The missing newlyweds had hit the front page, probably because of our exclusive photos. The wedding shot had caught the couple surrounded by well-wishers in a joyously exuberant moment as they left the church in their first public appearance as husband and wife.

The fate of the Custody Crusader was keyed to out front and led the local page.

I listlessly forced down Rice Krispies with milk, along with a banana for potassium, and drove to the paper early.

Where else did I have to go?

Nagging images from my dark dreams overnight nudged persistently at my consciousness. Spencer York's angry accusing eyes, their righteous indignation magnified by the thick lenses of his spectacles, his slightly stooped, bulky, middle-aged frame in incongruous combat fatigues. That tough-talking, harmless-looking fellow was no lovable curmudgeon, nobody's favorite uncle. He considered himself a warrior, at war with women.

I had rented a car in Texas, and as we drove somewhere, chatting during our day-long interview, his harangue about women became so offensive and vitriolic I had to restrain myself from pulling over and physically kicking him out of the passenger seat and into a roadside ditch.

I have spent time talking to serial murderers, Satan worshipers, crooked cops, wife beaters, and baby killers and never lost my cool. But Spencer York was something else.

He spewed outrageous theories: for example, that most women are totally unaware of basic feminine hygiene, accounting for what he described as America's huge epidemic of yeast infections and the resulting profits to pharmaceutical companies.

He chortled when he described how he stalked Brenda Cunningham, how he wrenched little Jason away from her as she screamed, begged, and struggled. He had spied on her in the dark and it paid off, he gloated. He had personally seen her leave in a car with a man and return home close to midnight. Proof positive, he said, that she was an unclean disease-spreading slut and a totally unfit mother. He wished he could have used a baseball bat, he said regretfully, instead of mere Mace when she dared fight to keep her son.

He had clearly tried to provoke me. Would the last person he provoked ever be prosecuted?

And, if so, would a jury convict? Some people would probably want to shower the killer with fresh-baked pies and medals for marksmanship, good fellowship, and public service.

Where were my notes from that outrageous interview? Did they still exist? I file notebooks by date, but over the years they had multiplied like kittens, far too many for my desk drawer.

So, I had packed away the oldest. I remembered marking my name and DO NOT THROW AWAY on the cardboard boxes and storing them atop a row of newsroom filing cabinets.

I scanned the vast, nearly empty newsroom. That row of filing cabinets had vanished, probably when the newsroom was remodeled two years ago. Sleek, more modern cabinets were posted like sentinels outside the editors' glass-enclosed offices. They were locked and bore signs warning that nothing was to be stored on top of them.

I checked the wire room and the hallways all the way to photo, then walked back to the library, known as the morgue in the good old days when reporting was more fun.

Onnie, always an early riser, was busy at her desk, marking with red grease pencil the stories in the morning paper that would be entered into the computer database.

She greeted me cheerfully. Tall and angular, she was an abused wife and mother, bruised in both body and spirit, when we first met. She'd been skinny as a rail, all sharp elbows and cheekbones, her collarbones like birds' wings. I aided and abetted her escape. We packed her meager possessions in a U-Haul trailer attached to the back of my T-Bird to make her getaway before her violent husband and his brothers were released from jail.

Now pert and clear-eyed, she has added some weight and makeup. Her hair is still in cornrows, her dark skin the color of burnt toast. She is good-natured, smart, and hard working, with high energy and an unwavering determination.

"You're just being polite," I said plaintively, when she asked how I was. "You don't really want to know."

"Of course I do." She put down the pencil, her intelligent black eyes concerned as I plopped heavily into the chair beside her desk.

"I'm pregnant, unmarried, and broke. My mother is totally freaked out and has probably disowned me. My best friend has abandoned me. I'm about to become homeless. I can't find my old notebooks. And, oh, yeah, my car is about to conk out," I added, remembering the AAA driver's admonition to charge the battery. "Otherwise, my life is just peachy."

"Whatchu talking about?" She looked more puzzled than sympathetic. "I haven't abandoned you."

I had to smile. "I meant Lottie."

"Right. You have so many friends. But you were my best friend when I needed it most, and I'll never forget it. I wouldn't have this job or my life without you. Now, I don't know about all the trials and tribulations you mentioned, but I can help with a few right now. First, I know Lottie hasn't abandoned you. You two are like sisters. She thinks the world of you. You have more friends in high places than you think, Britt. God loves you too. *I can do all things through Christ who strengthens me.* Make that your mantra. Repeat it whenever you feel lost or scared. It works.

"Now, about those notebooks. Did they happen to be in cardboard boxes with your name on them?"

"Right!" A slim shaft of hope pierced my gloom.

"I saw them when they remodeled the newsroom. They asked if we wanted those ratty old filing cabinets. We took them and I brought the boxes along. They should be here somewhere."

I followed as she trotted briskly into the bowels of the library, past shelves of books written by former *News* staffers, past rows of old high school yearbooks, reference material, and stacks of city directories.

"There they are!" I marveled. "That's them, I think!"

I was right. We carried them out to the front.

"Now, where were we? What was next?" she said. "Your car?"

I elaborated.

She nodded. "If it has tires or testicles it will give you trouble. No problem. You work later than I do. When I get off I'll drive your car to Sears for a slow charge. My Honda is out in the parking lot; I'll leave you the keys so you can use it."

"But how will you get home from Sears?"

"I won't. I can do a little shopping, grab a bite to eat, and then bring your car here or back to your place if you've already gone home."

"You'd do that for me, Onnie?"

"Sure. That shortens the list."

"Sounds like a plan. But wait, what about Darryl? Who will pick him up from school?"

"It's his night out. No problem."

"His night out? For Pete's sake, he's seven years old."

She laughed. "His night out with Kathy."

"Kathy who?"

"Riley."

I did a double take. "You don't mean K. C. Riley, the Cold Case Squad lieutenant?"

She nodded. "He really looks forward to it. She's been wonderful."

"I didn't know you even knew her," I said, stunned.

They had met briefly at Kendall McDonald's funeral, she said.

For a time McDonald had been seeing us both, me and Riley, his colleague and his childhood sweetheart. Like many cops, she didn't like reporters. We had first clashed when she was a rape squad sergeant, long before we realized we were also personal adversaries.

She grieved his death too.

Sometime after the funeral, Onnie said she was surprised when K.C. contacted her, asking to see Darryl.

"That doesn't sound like her," I said, finding it difficult to mask my incredulity.

"We talked about it. She said that McDonald gave his life to save my son. That there had to be a reason," Onnie said soberly, "and he would want her to watch out for Darryl."

I blinked several times.

"She picks him up after school once a week. They play softball in the park, see a movie, or visit the police horses at the stable. They have dinner somewhere—sometimes she cooks at her place—and she brings him home around eight."

I still stared at her skeptically.

"You know how he's always loved to draw?"

I nodded. Darryl's crayoned creations had decorated my refrigerator since he was four.

"She takes him to an art class over at the Miami Children's Museum every other Saturday. They've been to the Metro Zoo, the Seaquarium, the Indian village in the Everglades, even a couple of Marlins games. It's a blessing for him, and it gives me a little break. She's a godsend."

It was a side of K. C. Riley I had never seen. I knew she was smart and professional, a fearless stand-up cop who backed her detectives. But she could be as tough as nails to deal with, nearly impossible to pry information from, and a real bitch—at least to me.

"Darryl misses you, Britt."

"He sounds much too busy to remember who I am." Did I sound sarcastic and peevish? I guess I did.

"Kathy's a good woman, Britt. You're not still jealous of her, are you?"

"How can you even suggest that? I have no reason to be jealous. He loved me. I got the guy."

Actually, I realized later, nobody got the guy. And I would give anything to go back to that place in time to the rivalry, the green-eyed jealousy, the envy, and pain. I'd embrace it all in a heartbeat—pain is healthier than the numb emptiness of loss. At least you feel alive.

We carried the storage boxes out to the newsroom and exchanged car keys.

Ryan, at the desk behind me, was hard at work on a feature about the ever-growing abandoned litters, packs, and tangled herds of rusting shopping carts blighting Miami's suburbs, endangering motorists, and costing us all. Shopping-cart theft had become an epidemic.

"Nice story this morning, Britt. Can I see more pictures of that honeymoon couple? She's hot. Shame if they're shark bait," Ryan said. "Specially her. She looked so cute in those shorts. Same thing almost happened to me," he told Onnie.

I rolled my eyes.

Ryan had been lost at sea when an assignment from Gretchen, the editor from hell, went awry. She decided that the *News* should set a reporter adrift for a first-person account of the Cuban rafter experience: what it's like to face strong currents and fifteen-foot waves in shark-infested waters, while escaping Castro's Cuba. She chose Ryan, a gentle, seasick-prone nonswimmer from Ohio for the job. He was to remain adrift for twenty-four hours but accidentally dropped his handheld radio overboard. Swept south, he was picked up by a Cuban fishing boat.

Since the authentic escape raft, borrowed from the Coast Guard, was built on Soviet inner tubes, his rescuers assumed he was fleeing the island. A Cuban patrol boat took him to Mariel. The military suspected he was a drug smuggler or a CIA agent. They set him free after questioning, but the tide kept sweeping him back toward Cuba, where he kept being rescued and returned to the same interrogators. Finally they put him on a plane to Mexico City. Since he had no ID or passport, authorities there were about to put him on a flight to Toronto when he managed to call the paper from the airport.

By then, the Coast Guard had abandoned the search and his obituary had been written.

"Anything can happen out there in the Triangle," Ryan said, describing the ravenous sharks that had circled him. Their numbers multiply at each telling.

If Ryan could survive being lost at sea, so could the missing newlyweds, I thought, and checked the Coast Guard for word. No news. Sea and air search still under way. I reported in to Vanessa's parents in Boston. They hadn't heard anything either.

Coast Guard Lieutenant Skelly O'Rourke, the public information officer, invited Lottie and me for a ride along on one of the search-and-rescue flights. The offer was probably motivated by our help with the photos and the public interest generated by that morning's story.

We skimmed in ever-widening circles aboard a Dolphin helicopter, scanning the turquoise sea and the dark blue Gulf Stream, the world's mightiest river, that flows swiftly through it. Eyes straining, we squinted into blinding sunlight reflected off the water but saw no sign of the missing boaters.

Our veteran pilot pointed out Thunderbolt Cay, the secret sub base used by British and U.S. ships during World War II as they hunted the Nazi U-boats shooting at our ships in the dangerous deep water off Exuma. And Spanish Wells, where, he said, inbreeding among descendants of the Royalists has resulted in "a lot of creepy-looking people, albinos with pink eyes, on Iguana Cay."

We arrived back in Miami with no news, good or bad. I called the Hansens, said the Coast Guard was doing all it could, then dug into my dusty storage boxes and eventually found the notebook I'd scribbled in during that hot, unpleasant day in Texas.

Like most reporters, I take notes in my own style of shorthand and abbreviations. Sometimes they are difficult to decipher immediately upon returning to the office from a crime scene; these were nine years old. And, never one to waste paper, I always use both sides of each page and the inside covers.

Lawyers and cops, often eager to seize reporters' notes, don't realize that unless their specialty is hieroglyphics, it won't do them much good, at least not in my case.

I over-report. Always. Better too much detail than too little. One never knows how much space a story will be allotted. It depends on what sort of news day it is, how productive the staff, and the size of the news hole—the space left for actual stories after all that infernal advertising. The problem with over-reporting is you then face the dilemma of what to leave out. Favorite quotes, juicy tidbits, background, and color that you badgered your sources for—and worked your ass off to get—often don't make it into the newspaper.

Everything a reporter knows is never published.

I squinted at my old notes, as baffled as a pet dog trying to read a newspaper. I had the right pages. The little skull-and-crossbones doodle in the margin was clear evidence that I'd been sitting next to Spencer York at the time I drew it.

That story had been yet another skirmish in my daily war with editors. I remembered urging them to leave in more details about York and his "rescue missions" in other states. But space was tight that day, and my editors weren't especially interested in what he'd done outside our circulation area.

Something had to be cut, and that was it.

But as my notes confirmed, York had described snatching children in Arkansas, New Mexico, and Texas. The details came back to me as I read on. One case involved twin boys. He'd mentioned, without a trace of guilt, that their panicked mother had stumbled and fallen down her front stairs after glancing out a window in response to her children's screams and seeing York, a twin tucked under each arm, running to his old pickup truck. What went through that woman's mind before she discovered his explanatory note and her ex-husband's custody papers taped to her mailbox?

I thought at the time that York was damn lucky no one had ever shot him. Then somebody did. What if the publicity he loved had attracted a well-heeled client? Perhaps he had done another snatch to pay the rent. Maybe it went bad. Or a prior victim may have seized the moment, when news coverage made York a visible target. People from his past were all possible suspects.

The Custody Crusader had worked out of a post office box and operated on a shoestring. Where were the storage boxes with *his* notebooks and records?

I snatched up my phone on the first ring. Andy, the police desk rookie, sounded breathless. He had picked up snatches of Coast Guard radio transmissions. A survivor of the *Calypso Dancer* had been rescued and was being airlifted to a Miami hospital. Good news at last.

"Only one?" I asked. "Are you sure?"

"That's what I heard, Britt. It sounds like they're calling off the search."

"Is the survivor a man or a woman?" I held my breath.

"Don't know. I'll keep listening. They haven't put out anything official yet."

CHAPTER EIGHT

Lieutenant Skelly O'Rourke is not the first man who lied to me and probably won't be the last.

The Coast Guard public information officer had sworn he'd page me at the first hint of news about the *Calypso Dancer.* So much for promises.

He answered his phone. "Hey, Britt, I was just about to call you."

"Oh?"

"You bet. We found a survivor from the *Calypso Dancer.* He's being airlifted to Mount Sinai Hospital in Miami Beach."

"He?"

"Sure thing. Marsh Holt, the missing bridegroom."

I closed my eyes tight for a moment, thinking of the Hansens. "Any sign of her?"

"No."

"You're still searching, right?" I didn't say I'd heard otherwise. Reminding law enforcement types that we monitor their radios encourages them to make it more difficult.

"The mission is no longer rescue but recovery," he said. "And that may be impossible. It's seven hundred fathoms deep out there."

"But if he's alive, she may be too," I protested. "What if she's still out there?"

"Unlikely, Britt. Between you and me? They talked to the husband. Poor guy. The vessel sank. She was belowdeck at the time. He saw it go down."

"Oh, no." *He said he'd take care of her.* Her father's words rang in my ears. "What happened?"

"Sudden squall out of nowhere in the middle of the night."

"But they had a radio. Why no distress call?"

"The boat took on water so rapidly he didn't have a chance. You know how fast shit happens."

"Has her family been notified?"

"The Commander plans to give them a call. The son-in-law wants to talk to them first. Then we'll issue the press release."

"How is he?"

"Suffering from sunburn, exposure, and dehydration. Emotional, as you can imagine. But considering he's been adrift, clinging to a small life raft for three days, he's in pretty good shape."

"How'd he manage to find himself a life raft when he had no time to radio a distress call or rescue his wife?"

"That's pretty cynical, Britt. You having a bad day? It's one of those life rafts in a canister. When a vessel submerges it automatically detaches and inflates. They come equipped with a flashlight, laser, transistor radio, and night-vision goggles. Unfortunately, he lost the equipment in rough seas in the dark. Hell of a honeymoon."

Not as bad as no honeymoon at all, I thought.

Just as Skelly O'Rourke broke his promise to me, I broke mine to the Hansens. I had promised to call them immediately with any news, good or bad. I couldn't. Let the son they never had break the bad news, the hunk who vowed to take care of their only daughter.

Life, I thought, is just one broken promise after another. . . .

Lottie's telephoto lens captured Marsh Holt, wearing borrowed sunglasses, being assisted off the chopper at the hospital, a thin blanket wrapped around his shoulders.

After I was certain the parents had been told the bad news, I called.

"Marsh thinks she's gone. He was there," the weeping father said. "We're praying for a miracle."

"Until you hear otherwise, there's always hope," I said.

The hospital refused to put calls through to the survivor from anyone but immediate family. The patient had been admitted for overnight observation, a spokesman said, adding that he would probably be released the following day.

A hospital source gave me his room number. Checkout time was 11 A.M. I showed up at ten.

I carried a clipboard and a manila envelope and tried to blend into the hospital setting. A Channel 7 camera crew had invaded earlier, trying to interview the Honeymoon Survivor, as he had been dubbed on the eleven o'clock news, but had been nabbed by hospital security and escorted off the premises.

My worry was that Holt might have been moved to another room as a result. The door stood ajar. I knocked and then, heart pounding, stepped inside.

He was alone, staring absently out a window at the deep blue water of sparkling Biscayne Bay.

I had pictures of Holt but was not prepared for his striking physical presence. His muscular body made the hospital bed look small. His curly hair was dark, eyelashes long, his tan bronze. I'd seen his expression of numb disbelief many times before, lately in my own mirror.

His sunburned lips were cracked and peeling and he wore several days' stubble, the only outward signs of his ocean ordeal.

I bustled into his room and smiled.

"I brought you something," I said.

"Are you from administration? I'm being released."

I wasn't sure if the husky rasp in his voice was raw emotion or the effects of salt water on his throat.

"I was on the island about the same time you were," I said. "A friend and I found your camera on the beach, washed up on the reef. Twenty-four frames had been shot. My friend's a photographer. When we got back, she had them developed."

He looked confused.

"We had no way to return them. But when I saw the Coast Guard bulletin I knew they would be important to you and Vanessa's parents. I've already sent them a set."

His dry lips parted but he said nothing, so I babbled on.

"You probably don't want to look at them now, but when you feel up to it—"

He ignored my words, took the proffered envelope, tore it open, and began to shuffle through the pictures, lingering over a laughing photo of the two of them on the beach. Eyes swimming, he swallowed hard.

"You found our camera," he said, voice still raspy. "Nessa was upset when we lost it." He raised wet eyes to mine. "These are the last—" His voice broke.

"I'm a reporter," I confessed, "for the *Miami News.* Here, I brought you a copy of the story in today's paper. A photographer and I flew with the Coast Guard on one of their search missions. When we pinpointed where we'd found your camera, it helped narrow the search. Thank God you're safe."

"Thanks for helping," he said bleakly.

"I'd like to talk about what happened."

He looked puzzled when I opened my notebook. "But why . . . ?"

"Your survival's a miracle. People care. It's news."

"News," he said bitterly, "that I couldn't save my wife?"

"It's not your fault. The sea can be treacherous."

He nodded. "The day was beautiful, exactly what we'd imagined. We joked that we'd never go home, just keep sailing away forever. Together."

He studied the photo of her waving, in her white shorts and crop top, legs tanned, hair caught in a playful ocean breeze.

"What happened?"

He described a moonless night in the Atlantic and sheer terror. As Vanessa fixed dinner in the galley, he went topside to check a fish pot they had in the water for lobsters and a net for stone crabs. The wind velocity picked up. He saw the swells begin to build. Within minutes it was a full-blown squall with earsplitting thunder and lightning.

The *Calypso Dancer* bucked, rocked, and bounced. He secured things on deck, thought he smelled gas, and called down, telling Vanessa to turn on the blowers so the bilge fan could clear out the air.

He started down but there was an almost immediate explosion and fire. He shouted for her to stay calm and raced up the companionway for a fire extinguisher mounted next to the flying bridge near the helm. A gigantic wave swept him overboard as he reached for it. Water poured into the boat and gushed up from the bilges. Vanessa, still trapped below, was swallowed by the dark sea as the *Calypso Dancer* swiftly sank. He found himself alone in steep swells, calling her name, in shark-infested waters hundreds of miles from Miami. He came upon the tiny lifeboat amid the floating debris, then rode that tossing raft for three days beneath a blazing sun.

"I knew she was dead," he said, voice ragged. "But at times I felt her there with me. I talked to her."

The crew of a passing freighter spotted Holt and radioed the Coast Guard.

"You were lucky. You were far north of the usual steamship routes, which limited your chances of rescue."

"Lucky?" The word was a hollow echo.

Uh-oh. Dreaded squishy sounds approached from behind me, the rubber soles of comfortable white nursing shoes on the hospital floor.

She wore an *Aha!* expression, eyeballed my notebook, and demanded my identification. Lip curling with unconcealed contempt, she scrutinized the photo on my press card.

I sighed. I admit it is not flattering. Shot on a rainy, blustery, bad-hair day, I resemble a bedraggled spaniel.

"You'll have to leave, miss. Now."

The patient and I exchanged glances.

She tapped her foot.

"It's all right," he protested. "We were talking."

"Hospital policy—" she began.

Holt was about to be released anyway.

"Where are you going?" I asked him, after she left in a huff. I wondered if she'd be back with security guards.

"I'm not sure," he said. "I don't have a credit card or a red cent. Not even shoes. Vanessa's dad is wiring me some cash."

I said I'd drive him to Western Union and then to a hotel.

I picked him up on the ramp downstairs. Despite his protests, he arrived in a wheelchair pushed by an attendant half his size.

"How can I go home without her?" Exhausted, he leaned back in the passenger seat of my T-Bird. "But I have to," he murmured, answering his own plaintive question. "I'm worried about Nessa's parents. They wanted to catch the next flight, but I told them there's nothing they can do here. She has asthma and he had bypass surgery last year. I don't know how they'll survive this, how any of us will. They're like my own parents, but they probably hate me now."

"They say you're the son they never had."

Holt was to make his official statement to the Coast Guard, he said, and meet with a representative from the charter boat company. Then he would arrange his flight home to Boston.

"Sorry to be so much trouble," he said, as we left the Western Union counter at the big supermarket on the bay, "but you're the only person I know in Miami. I'll take it from here. I can catch a cab outside."

I insisted on delivering him to a downtown hotel, close to the *News* building and the Miami Beach Coast Guard station.

"I still want to talk to you about Vanessa. Can the *Miami News* buy you dinner tonight?"

"I can't let you do that."

"I won't. My expense account will. That's what it's for."

I was touched by his loss. The sad, handsome man moved me. He reminded me of myself. Moreover, the tragic sea saga of the star-crossed lovers was a helluva story. Who better to write it than me?

We stopped at the *News* building, where Lottie snapped a few shots of Marsh Holt, still unshaven, eyes haunted. He used the phone on her desk. American Express would deliver a new card to his hotel by morning. A Boston neighbor agreed to go to Holt's apartment and overnight him some ID so he could board the flight home. The sea had swallowed his driver's license and passport.

"What a hunk." Lottie whistled under her breath while he made calls. "And it looks like he's single now."

"Good grief, Lottie," I said, offended.

"Widowers who were happily married almost always marry again soon," she argued. "That's a fact of life."

I gave Holt the name of a downtown men's store near the hotel, dropped him off, and drove home to freshen up before meeting him at six.

I called Holt's room from the lobby. When he didn't pick up for a long time I began to fear he was out there, lost and vulnerable, wandering Miami's mean streets. But he answered and finally arrived in the lobby minutes later. He'd shaved and changed into a new blue shirt and casual slacks.

He turned the head of a pretty young desk clerk when he walked by.

"I'm not sure this is a good idea," he said, as we pulled off the ramp. "I don't feel up to being around people."

"You'll be okay. I won't keep you long."

We found a back table at Joe Allen's. Unlike many local restaurants, there is no water view, the food is good, and the place is frequented more by residents than tourists.

He ordered Jack Daniel's, I had ginger ale. He had begun to sound better. He had a rich and mellifluous radio voice. "You're missing dinner with your family tonight," he said.

"I don't have a family. Yet."

He gave me an oddly knowing look.

"Tell me more about Vanessa. What's she like?"

I am always careful to refer to the recently deceased in the present tense when talking to survivors. Hearing a loved one referred to in the past tense for the first time often results in an emotional meltdown best avoided—unless, of course, you are a crass television reporter whose goal is to make people cry on camera. Besides, no body had been found. Until you know the worst, you can continue to hope.

He hesitated, brow furrowed.

"How did you meet?" I asked.

He nodded slightly. "I was alone in Boston, didn't know a soul. The city is famous for being musically rich. So I picked up a ticket and went to the symphony. That was the first time I saw her, in that bright beautiful hall. She was seated with her cello, up front, close to the conductor. The lights glinted off her hair. She was wearing a simple long black dress, with sleeves down to the elbow.

"She looked so graceful, making music that was so grandiose and spectacular. I kept watching her, couldn't take my eyes off her, and thought about her later. Kept hearing that lush romantic music and seeing her face as she played. I wished I knew how to meet her. It seemed like a dream when I did."

"How did you manage it?"

"Went back to see a rehearsal two days later. She looked different, more approachable, wearing blue jeans and a ponytail. I overheard the musicians talking. She was part of a chamber music group that was to perform at a museum fund-raiser later in the week.

"There were just four of them at the museum that night, two violins, a viola, and the cello. They played light, cheerful, optimistic music from Beethoven and Haydn, the sort of music that lifts the spirits—and the wallets—of subscribers, donors, and philanthropists.

"I saw her outside afterward, wrestling her instrument into her car. The bumper sticker said 'Music Is Magic.' I offered to help. We were in public, on a crowded street, otherwise I'm sure she wouldn't have talked to me. I said I'd heard her play. She said she'd seen me inside. I was flattered that she'd noticed me. She said it was because I was the only person who appeared to be listening. Everyone else was busy mingling, chatting, drinking, ignoring the music. I said that surprised me, and she laughed again. There's a special warmth in her laugh.

" 'That's our fate at these gigs,' she said. 'We're just there to be background music.'

"I invited her for a drink. She said no, but I did persuade her to give me her number." He pinched the bridge of his nose, his expression pained. "If she'd blown me off, she'd be alive. I was the worst thing that ever happened to her."

"I know how you feel," I murmured sympathetically.

"No," he said sharply, "you don't." His eyes flashed. "You couldn't possibly. You may experience a lot in your line of work, Ms. Montero, but you have no idea what it's like to find your soulmate—and then suddenly she's gone."

My lips felt dry. "You're wrong, Mr. Holt. I know exactly what it's like."

He stared at me, stony eyed.

"My fiancé and I returned home from a trip to the islands, planning our wedding. He was killed in an explosion and fire a few hours later. I couldn't work, couldn't think. That's why I went back to the islands, to feel closer to him and our best times, while trying to figure out how to live in a world without him."

Holt said nothing for a long moment. "I'm sorry. When you said you had no family *yet*, I thought you were one of those career women who choose to become a single mother, to raise a child without a father."

"I couldn't do that." I shook my head. "It's unfair. I lost my father very young, but I have a few vivid memories. Our child won't even have that. . . . I related to what you said because he would still be alive had he not been with me that day. But you can't second-guess life. You can't beat yourself up for events you can't control. I *can* share two things I've learned the hard way: Running away doesn't help but talking about it does."

He exhaled audibly, then shoved his barely sipped drink aside. "I don't think either of us is very hungry," he said. "Let's get out of here."

We walked the pink neon streets of South Beach and talked for hours.

"Vanessa gave me a crash course in the three Bs." He smiled at the memory. "Bach, Beethoven, and Brahms. She believes that making music that's hundreds of years old sound fresh and new is like dipping into eternity. She says playing a Beethoven string quartet is unlike anything else a human being can experience.

"She taught me so much about her world. Some people start each day with calisthenics, speed walking, or a morning jog. But did you know that Pablo Casals began each day by playing one of the six suites for unaccompanied cello? She loves to tell me those stories."

At the tender age of ten, Vanessa attended the pre-college conservatory at the Curtis Institute of Music in Philadelphia. " 'Music calls you,' she always says. 'You don't call it.' She always knew exactly what she wanted to do with her life. You can feel her passion.

"Music was a tough rival. The two of them had a long history. She was only five when she started to play. When we began to see each other, I had to convince her that she wasn't cheating on her art."

"How could she play the instrument so young?" I asked. "Her cello must have been bigger than she was."

"I asked the same question. Who knew there are tiny little cellos for tiny little kids?"

Strolling amid visitors, tourists, and strangers on the street, I learned more than I ever expected to about the musical instrument that he compared to a resonant tenor voice.

Vanessa's cello was made of maple, from Bosnia. Professional cellists pay for two seats when they fly.

"The instrument is cumbersome, but I'd never complain," he said. "We always joke that if she'd played the flute, we never would have met."

Their wedding march was Mendelssohn's from *A Midsummer Night's Dream*. At the reception they waltzed to Strauss.

I told him how I met then–homicide sergeant Kendall McDonald across a bloodstained barroom floor after a shooting. How we'd fallen in love despite the obstacles our conflicting careers created. How we had split up and reunited.

And how it ended. How Onnie and her son, Darryl, six, were stalked by her abusive ex-husband, Edgar, after his premature release from prison. Mother and son hid out in my apartment while McDonald and I vacationed in the islands.

"Couldn't she have gone to the police?" Holt asked.

"She tried. She did everything right. They advised her to take out a restraining order against him. She did. The problem is that a restraining order is just paper, and paper can't stop a bullet or a deranged man. He followed them back from church and burst into my apartment to take Darryl.

"Onnie tried to stop him and they struggled. My dog, Bitsy, a little dog with a big dog's heart, attacked Edgar, who stomped and kicked her, breaking several bones. Edgar left Onnie on the floor, battered and bloody, and took Darryl, who was kicking and screaming.

"McDonald and I arrived home shortly after, totally unaware of what had happened. All I wanted was to show off my engagement ring. We found Onnie hurt and terrified. Edgar had called from his mother's house warning that he'd kill Darryl if she called the police. She knew he was crazy enough to do it. The three of us drove over there. Edgar's distraught mother came running out. She said he'd sloshed gasoline all over her living room and was threatening to ignite it, to kill himself and Darryl. There was no time to wait for SWAT, a hostage negotiator, or the fire department. McDonald went inside.

"Moments later, Darryl flew out the front door screaming for his mother. He leaped into her arms as the house erupted with a gigantic roar. The roof lifted, the windows shattered, and fire shot from each opening as a ball of flame hurtled out the front door with a loud *whoosh*.

"Darryl was safe. No one else escaped."

Neither of us spoke for a long time, as we walked in silence side by side.

"When my time comes, I want to be buried at sea," Marsh Holt said at last, as we lingered in front of a Lincoln Road art gallery.

"Makes sense to me. I've been thinking about cremation," I said. "Bright as fire for a moment, then ashes."

My parting advice to Marsh Holt was not to dwell on his own pain. "You're not alone. Everyone since Adam and Eve has suffered heartache and loss. If they haven't yet, they will. You survive by doing what you do best. And when you're really down, repeat to yourself: *I can do all things through Christ who strengthens me.* Make it your mantra."

The last thing he said to me was a quote from Thoreau: *Listening to music makes one invincible.*

I pecked Marsh Holt on the cheek and left him at the hotel. In the morning he would face the Coast Guard and the charter boat people. I hoped they would be kind.

I watched him walk into the hotel and then drove away, alone.

I had shamelessly passed along Lottie and Onnie's inspirational advice, as though it was my own, advice I had ignored. But when I searched my heart for positive words of comfort it suddenly became valid.

No one else could understand our innermost feelings. Holt was right about that. Fate had thrown us together and I was grateful.

I labored over the story the next morning. The poignant material was a writer's dream of star-crossed love. I knew he would read it, as would Vanessa's parents and friends. I hoped it would become part of their history, a keepsake to fold into the family Bible. I called Marsh once to clarify a date. He sounded weary.

The Hansens had overnighted a professional portrait of Vanessa at the cello, her lovely long hair swept over an ivory shoulder, her profile pristine.

I was about to turn in my copy when everything changed.

CHAPTER NINE

The sea had burped up one of its secrets.

Vanessa Holt was no longer lost.

U.S. Coast Guard Public Information Officer Skelly O'Rourke kept his word this time and called. The body of a woman had washed ashore on a remote out island.

Badly damaged by sea life and decomposition, the corpse had been positively identified by dental charts. She was being brought to Miami.

The changes necessary to my story included updated reaction from her family. Her father sobbed unabashedly, his wife wailed and wheezed in the background.

My own eyes swam when he thanked me "for all you did."

I tried to call Marsh Holt at his hotel, but a frosty front desk clerk said he had asked not to be disturbed. Who could blame him?

He called me a short time later. "You heard the news?"

"Yes. Are you all right?"

"No. I'll never be all right."

I asked if he had anything he wished to add to the story, and he did: "Vanessa's death is a terrible loss—to the world, to music, and to me. She can never be replaced."

To me he said, "Thanks for your help during the worst time of my life, especially our talk last night. It meant a great deal."

Lottie was right, I thought. Think of others, not yourself.

But it didn't help my sleep that night. Instead of fire, the girlish face of the dead bride haunted my dreams. Her long hair streaming in the tide, eyes wide, arms outstretched, her torn wedding veil billowing around her on a windblown seabed. Her lips formed words and frantic phrases. I saw her eyes, heard her voice, and strained to listen, but I could not discern the words.

Awake before dawn, I considered my pep talk to Holt and what a hypocrite I had become. If you talk the talk you should walk the walk. I hadn't attended church since McDonald's funeral, and today was Easter Sunday. Onnie's words had sounded comforting when I repeated them to Holt.

So I went to church. It was early enough to make the sunrise service on the beach. But after my vivid dreams, I had no desire to see water, yearning instead for the rock-solid brick-and-mortar of my church.

Easter, of course, is the holiday above all others to arrive early. Those who forgo church the rest of the year suddenly appear on Easter, herds and hordes of them. They fill the parking lots, the pews, and the collection plates, to a lesser degree, then vanish again until Christmas Eve.

I imagined them the rest of the year, propped on pillows, sipping Bloody Marys, curled up in bed with the Sunday newspapers.

I wore a loose blouse but had to fasten my skirt with an extra-large safety pin because I couldn't close the waistband. Another pressing problem I needed to address. Soon.

I slipped into my favorite pew with a good view of the choir. The delicate scent of lilies filled the church. There were hundreds of them, tall, serene, and graceful, some in pots, others in gigantic bowls mixed with yellow forsythia. They covered the huge cross behind the altar. The shadows of palm fronds outside reflected in the stained-glass windows, and the church was alight with a soft natural glow.

The pews and extra folding chairs set up in the back filled fast with pushy strangers.

"Never in my life did anyone ever shoot at me before," an elegant middle-aged Grace Kelly type pouted to a well-dressed young man in the pew in front of me. My reporter's instincts kicked in. Ears pricked up, I managed to catch the words "Jackson Memorial Hospital" and "courtroom," as the Cameron Diaz look-alike behind me described a recent date to her companion; she liked him, but "He's a gun runner."

Glad I was there, for more than one reason, I didn't know which way to lean. To my regret, trumpets sounded at that moment and a great swell of organ music obliterated their conversations. Beside me, a raven-haired model type with big blue eyes turned, watching for someone. She waved at a tall handsome black man who squeezed into our pew to join her. They were obviously a couple. I smiled. This church, Miami Beach's oldest place of worship, built by pioneers, had changed in so many ways, like everything else in this city. I was so glad to be home. I didn't realize how much I had missed it.

The words of the hymn resonated: Love's redeeming work is done; fought the fight, the battle won. The sermon focused on live dreams, fresh starts, and new beginnings; the prayers dealt with how the lost may be restored. As the pastor primed the universal pump, I wished Marsh Holt had been there to hear it too. Why didn't I invite him?

Later, scores of squealing children scrambled across the grassy lawn, filling their straw baskets during the annual Easter-egg hunt.

I had little chance to exchange more than Easter greetings with my pastor, who did take note of my no-longer-girlish figure. He smiled reassuringly, as though it was a good thing. As happy parents snapped pictures of their excited toddlers, I began to think so myself. Somehow, everything would work out.

Back at my apartment, I brewed myself a cup of herbal tea, then called his hotel to tell Marsh Holt what he had missed, and thank him, too, for our talk. I had nearly forgotten what important threads chance encounters can be in the great tapestry that is life.

Holt had already checked out, the clerk said. Must have left early for the airport, I thought, checking the kitchen clock. I saw him in my mind's eye, a sad and solitary figure amid strangers, waiting to accompany his dead bride home. My eyes misted—not for me, this time, but for him. Too bad we had no chance to say goodbye. I wished him a good life and hoped I had been of help to him. Meeting him surely helped me.

I was still thinking about Holt, whom I would probably never see again, as I walked Bitsy along a path beside the rolling green-velvet golf course, amid warbling birds and the lush scent of flowers. A mounted police officer, helmeted and intimidating, materialized unexpectedly, cantering toward us on the green path. I gasped, startled, with my psyche still so wrapped around the Easter drama that for an instant I mistook him for a Roman soldier.

He waved, then bent low in the saddle to avoid the overhanging branches of a sea grape tree, as I stood transfixed, heart pounding.

CHAPTER TEN

I had no time to think about Marsh Holt in the busy weeks that followed.

Another lost tourist, bewildered by Miami's tangled streetscape, lost his rental car, his wallet, and his life when he stopped to ask the wrong resident for directions. The city's brand-new fleet of high-priced garbage trucks began to spontaneously combust, and pet shops were plagued by shoplifters who stuffed expensive teacup puppies down their pants.

The Human Fly continued to confound and outrage both the cops and the Chamber of Commerce. In his most notorious caper to date, he scaled the face of a pricey South Beach hotel, climbed over a fifth-floor balcony, and crept into an unlocked room. There he encountered the latest hard-partying, super-thin young Hollywood star, who screamed long and loud as the Human Fly buzzed off into the night with her handbag and jewelry.

The star spent days spinning her tale of terror, in increasingly vivid detail, on every Hollywood tabloid show, as well as to Jay Leno, Larry King, Nancy Grace, and Greta Van Susteren. The negative national publicity fueled the ire of local politicians and members of the hotel and tourist industry who pressured police to hunt down and swat the Fly. So did editorial writers and TV commentators. But the Fly flew free.

Motorists awoke and found their cars coated by a thin film of red dust. Daytime skies turned milky white with hazy blood-red sunsets. Along the African coast storms had scooped up red sand and passed it off to the wind currents that stream west. Whipped by Africa's desert winds, the monster cloud of red dust swirled across the Atlantic and settled over Miami, where the full moon hung fat and low, a sinister silver dollar tarnished by Sahara dust in the eastern sky. Patients suffering from asthma, hay fever, emphysema, and other respiratory problems packed local emergency rooms.

And U.S. Coast Guard Public Information Officer Skelly O'Rourke redeemed himself for prior broken promises by tipping me to an in-progress high-speed pursuit of suspected smugglers near the Marquesas, a barren swath of islands forty miles off Key West.

Shortly before dawn, radar aboard a Coast Guard cutter had detected a dangerously overloaded boat moving north from Cuba. A smaller Coast Guard vessel approached and signaled them to stop. Instead, those aboard tried to ram the Coast Guard boat and fled, jeopardizing their endangered cargo.

Nobody outruns the Coast Guard. They have planes, choppers, high-speed boats, radar, manpower, really big guns, and long memories. But the fleeing suspects were desperate people. Ruthless smugglers charge up to $10,000 a head to spirit an estimated two thousand illegal migrants a year to Florida under cover of darkness.

When sighted by the Coast Guard, some resort to murder. They throw the evidence, their passengers, overboard or drop them too far offshore to swim safely to dry land. Scores of migrants pay their money and lose their lives every year.

With the chase under way, Lottie and I scrambled aboard a seaplane at Watson Island and headed south to the scene.

We spotted them from a distance, trailing great rooster tails of wake across the deep blue. Lottie captured aerial shots of the speeding boats and the Coast Guard choppers in pursuit. Several of the thirty-six migrants aboard the smugglers' vessel either tumbled or were deliberately thrown overboard during the maneuvers.

The Coast Guard could not save them all. The thrilling chase concluded with the suspects' capture. When the smugglers ignored warning shots across their bow, special shotgun shells were fired to disable the vessel's engines. Many of the remaining refugees jumped into the sea, flailing, and resisting attempts to rescue them.

The price they were willing to pay to escape the island touched my heart and made me think of my father. All these years later, I thought, the dictator still lives and Cubans still die.

Peering through binoculars, as Lottie snapped pictures, I felt an odd sense of déjà vu and thought for the first time in weeks of Marsh Holt, who had escorted his bride's body on their sad journey home to Boston. End of story, I thought. But now, as I watched another tragic high-seas drama unfold, Holt was on my mind.

Then I realized why.

Later, as we met the Coast Guard boat that towed the seized vessel to the Miami Beach Coast Guard station on the MacArthur Causeway, I was sure.

"Lottie," I whispered, as we watched from behind a security fence, "look at the smugglers' boat."

She lowered her camera, stared, then focused her telephoto lens for a closer look. "It's a Grand Banks forty-footer. It looks just like—" She turned to me. "But it can't be. How could it?"

"It is, Lottie. Look at that custom rail. The transom."

She'd seen this vessel before. So had I, in the honeymoon photos of Marsh and Vanessa Holt. The smugglers' vessel was the *Calypso Dancer.* I was sure. The name and the registration number had been scratched off, another engine added, but there was no mistaking its identity.

My mind raced.

Lottie frowned. "I thought it was sleeping with the fishes at seven hundred fathoms."

"That's what everybody thought. How weird is this?"

Guardsmen were securing the seized vessel. "Shoot as many angles as you can, Lottie."

The whirs and clicks from her camera were all I heard for the next several minutes. The smugglers were marched ashore in handcuffs. Then their passengers were brought ashore, to cheers and applause from spectators already gathered behind the fence.

Migrants interdicted at sea are swiftly returned to Cuba, under the U.S. Government's wet-foot/dry-foot policy. Those who reach American soil can stay, but those who don't go back at once.

To bring them ashore like this was unprecedented, the irony bittersweet. Because some refugees had died, the others were allowed to reach shore to testify against the smugglers in court.

At a press conference, Coast Guard spokesman Skelly O'Rourke said that the accused smugglers, two Cuban Americans from Hialeah, claimed that during a fishing trip weeks earlier they had found the boat adrift with no one aboard. They salvaged it, they said, souped it up, and seized the opportunity, using it to scoop up family members from Cuba and bring them to Miami. They denied being professional smugglers.

How they came into possession of the boat was the least of their troubles. The accused smugglers would be charged with murder in the deaths of a four-year-old boy who tumbled overboard and drowned during the pursuit and an elderly woman who suffered fatal head injuries when being buffeted about on the smugglers' speeding boat in rough seas.

More carloads of Miami's Cuban Americans arrived as word of the tragedy spread. Some were seeking relatives who may have been aboard; others came to protest U.S. immigration policy, Coast Guard tactics, and the Castro regime. Some threatened to block MacArthur Causeway, a major thoroughfare between Miami and Miami Beach.

I gathered quotes from a number of them and then rushed back to the newsroom to call Marsh Holt in Boston. His number was disconnected. Not surprising. It was for the apartment where the couple planned to reside after the honeymoon; it would be too painful for him to stay there.

I called the Hansens.

"Every day it becomes more real that she's gone, and she's not coming back," her father said. Mourners had filled the cathedral for Vanessa's funeral, he told me. They played a Bach cantata.

I said I was trying to reach Marsh.

He reacted angrily. "Don't talk to me about him."

"What's wrong?"

The son they never had had departed shortly after the funeral. "Didn't say a thing. Not even goodbye. Left town—for good, I guess. He's gone. No forwarding address."

His wife breathed heavily on the extension. "It's not Marsh's fault," she argued, sympathetic and congested. "He was too heartbroken to stay in the same city where they met and fell in love. I understand. He couldn't take it. I'm worried about him. His heart is broken." Her words resonated with motherly concern.

They had no idea where he'd gone. But they thought Vanessa's maid of honor and best friend, Sally, might know. The two were like sisters. They gave me her number.

Sally had no idea where Marsh had gone or where he'd come from. He'd blown into town with few ties and little baggage, she said. Vanessa did mention once that Marsh had worked in Chicago with a man named Ron Fullerton. Sally remembered the name because she had an uncle named Fullerton; no relation. Vanessa told her the two men had talked by telephone and had seemed relieved, Sally said, by his contact with an old colleague. Marsh Holt had swept her friend off her feet, but Vanessa was an intelligent and cautious young woman. She had been a bit concerned, as was Sally, about his apparent lack of friends, relatives, and history.

"I thought she should wait until she got the chance to meet people he'd known all his life," Sally said. "I mean, he's clearly no crook or ex-con, but they just didn't know each other long enough. He's hot, and funny, and really sweet, but he was like a man without a past. I used to joke that he must be in the Witness Protection Program. Even if he had no immediate family, there had to be friends, neighbors, fellow workers, ex-girlfriends. But there weren't. It was like he dropped out of a UFO."

"How long *did* they know each other?"

"He proposed four weeks after they met. Really romantic but too quick. The wedding was six weeks later. Too soon, if you ask me. But Nessa was crazy about him. She said, 'When you know it's right, why wait?' "

"I didn't realize they'd known each other such a short time." I tried to remember exactly what Holt had told me about their courtship.

"I thought they took the plunge too soon," Sally said sadly. "But we'll never know now, will we? I miss her every day."

I called Skelly O'Rourke at the Coast Guard to say I suspected that the smugglers' vessel was the *Calypso Dancer.* He'd pass it along, he said, but had a ready explanation if it was true. The Boston bridegroom was no seasoned boater and the tragedy took place on a dark night during a sudden squall. He'd been swept away as he struggled to survive in huge swells. When he turned to look and couldn't see the boat, he probably assumed it had sunk. More likely the *Calypso Dancer* had just drifted out of his line of vision. "You can't see anything out there under those conditions," he said.

The fourth Ron Fullerton I called in Chicago remembered Marsh Holt well. "Used to work for me, but we lost touch," Fullerton said. "Nice guy. What's your interest in him?"

"I wrote the story about his wife's death," I said. "Something's come up and I need to talk to him. His old number's disconnected."

Fullerton didn't seem surprised.

"He's had a tough time. Never got over losing her like that. Happened on their honeymoon, you know. Broke his heart. She was the love of his life."

"Right," I said, recalling the bridegroom's despair. "It was very sad."

"Sure was," he replied. "Suzanne was such a talented girl."

"You mean Vanessa."

"No." The word rang with the certainty of a man who knew what he was talking about. "Her name was Suzanne."

"No. Her name was Vanessa. She was a musician." My voice sounded thin. My mind raced. "She drowned."

"You've got it all wrong," he said irritably. "Her name was Suzanne. She fell. They were taking pictures on their honeymoon in Arizona. She stumbled and fell off a cliff, into a deep ravine. Died instantly."

CHAPTER ELEVEN

"That son of a bitch!" I pounded my fist on my desk so hard it hurt.

"What's wrong, Britt?" Ryan asked softly from the desk behind me. He sounded concerned.

"I'm so stupid!" I blurted, on the verge of angry tears. "What's happened to me?"

"Hormones." He nodded wisely. "It happens. I've been reading up on it."

"On what?"

"You know. Pregnancy."

"Why on earth would you do that?"

"So I can help if anything happens."

"Like what?"

He looked hurt. "Well, in case your water breaks, or anything."

"Oh, for God's sake!" Had the whole world gone insane? His sweet, sensitive face stayed in my mind, as I fled the newsroom.

"I bought it, Lottie, hook, line, and sinker. I swallowed his whole damn story. Every word sounded true to me. How could I be so stupid?"

"Everybody bought it," she said, "not just you."

"But what's happened to me? Why did my instincts fail? Where did my street smarts go? My experience?" Was my personal trajectory straight into the toilet? Was I totally unencumbered by the thought process? "He killed them, Lottie. He did it. He killed both those women. There may be others." I took a tentative sip of the herbal tea she offered and grimaced. "I really hate this."

"Don't worry, the good Lord will nail his ass."

"No, I mean this tea! I want to cut out coffee so the baby isn't jittery, but I need caffeine, I *crave* caffeine; it's the only thing that jump-starts my brain cells. Chamomile sucks!"

"It'll grow on you," she insisted.

I paced the photo office in a cold rage. "He lied, lied, lied, right to my face, won me over with his stories, those sad eyes, and that radio voice. Had me driving his lying ass all over town. Had me offering words of comfort on how to survive and piece his life back together. I really related to that bastard, treated him like a victim, and all the while he was thumbing his nose behind my back. Laughing at her and her parents, those poor people who really believed he'd be the son they never had. They're the real victims. So are Vanessa and Suzanne—and God knows who else."

"But why? Maybe he's just a guy who, if he didn't have bad luck, would have no luck at all. Tragedy stalks some people, some places. We've seen 'em. Like that damn boat, the *Calypso Dancer.* Every time it sails somebody dies."

I rolled my eyes and turned away, trying to think about something—anything—other than coffee.

"Well?" she demanded. "Would you charter that floating death trap for a pleasure cruise?"

"It's not the boat," I snapped. "The boat's no ghost ship. It's him. And I know the motive. That son of a bitch. I called Sally, Vanessa's maid of honor, again. She'd neglected to mention, as did the parents, that Vanessa had already mingled her assets with her new husband's, and named him her life insurance beneficiary before the wedding. She had discussed it with Sally, her best friend. He suggested that since they were about to travel outside the country they should take out policies naming each other as beneficiaries. It didn't seem suspicious at the time, only thoughtful and efficient."

"How much?"

"Half a mil, and I'd wager there's double indemnity for accidental death. And that's not all. Just before the wedding, Vanessa moved her savings into a joint account and everything she owned into their new apartment. He sold it all, Lottie, including the wedding gifts, some still unopened, her jewelry, her clothes, even her damn cello, made of wood from Bosnia. I talked to the apartment house manager and a neighbor. Holt had liquidators in the day after the funeral, bidding on everything but the bathtub. Cleaned the place out the same day.

"Her father probably didn't tell me because he's embarrassed, or maybe her mother isn't aware and he's trying to keep it from her. Neither talks on the phone without the other on an extension.

"I'll wager it was the same with Suzanne. Liz, the best researcher we've got, is running Internet searches right now on all possible variations of his name, honeymoon tragedies anywhere in or out of the country, and the deaths of newlywed women in every state. Onnie's helping."

Lottie took a seat across from me, her brown eyes serious. "If he did kill Vanessa," she said hopefully, "maybe she was the only victim. Maybe Suzanne did die accidentally and it gave him the idea."

"I hope you're right," I said, "but I doubt it. The man's a pro, super dangerous to women. My gut instinct says he's done it before and he'll do it again."

Lottie picked up one of the photos she'd taken of Marsh Holt in the office that day. "Evil shouldn't look this good," she said. "Amazin' how women hear his honky-talkin' bullshit blues and agree to marry him twenty minutes later."

"When her parents suggested they wait and get to know each other better," I said bitterly, "Vanessa reminded them that they met at a USO dance four weeks before her father went to war. They got married the day before he shipped out. She waited. He survived Pork Chop Hill; the rest is history. If only Vanessa had realized that Marsh Holt was not like her father. The signs were there. He blew into town a blank slate, with something evil, a ghost in the machine.

"This is a helluva story, Lottie. We can nail the bastard. Expose him in the paper, and see him in the slammer before he marries another poor girl." I checked my watch. "I'll see if Liz has come up with anything." I paused at the door and frowned. "There's another problem. Ryan's out of control. Did you know he's been reading up on pregnancy?"

She nodded matter-of-factly. "I think he hopes to deliver your baby, Britt. I wouldn't advise it."

Liz was hunched over the computer in her little cubicle as usual, fingers flying, expression intense.

"Anything?"

Her ponytail bounced as she spun her chair around and faced me. "Darn right." She pushed her little computer glasses up higher on her pug nose, the lenses reflecting a greenish glow from the fluorescent lights. "Here's what I've come up with so far." She handed me a printout.

Marsh Holt and a Marshall Weatherholt shared the same Social Security number and the same date and place of birth. Before he shortened it, he was widowed under the name Weatherholt: three times. One bride, Colleen, died in a honeymoon ski accident in Colorado. Rachel suffered a fatal snakebite as they explored Mayan ruins in Guatemala on their honeymoon adventure. Gloria, the third, drowned in a Miami scuba-diving accident. As Marsh Holt, he married Suzanne and Vanessa, who experienced the same bad luck.

The brides' deaths had all been ruled accidental. Tragic accidents, perfect murders.

I felt a chill. "Keep looking," I urged Liz.

I found Fred in his office.

"It's a national story," I said, trying to keep the excitement out of my voice. "The man is a serial killer, and no one even suspects any of the dead were murdered. A helluva story. We have to break it first."

"Need some help?"

"No way. I'm all over it. It may involve some travel."

"That might not be wise." He looked skeptical.

"I might agree in a couple of months. But I'm good to go now. I'm healthy."

He continued to frown. "I thought you were working on the Spencer York homicide."

"York's a cold case. He'll keep. He's dead. This guy's still alive, still out there stalking women."

"How about you stay on your beat, which is what you really wanted, if you recall, and we let another reporter do the legwork. Maybe Nell Hunter could—"

"This is *my* story," I said heatedly. "This one's unique. Holt is more evil than the serial killers who stalk strangers and murder on impulse, driven by passions they can't, or won't, control. What he does is incredibly complex and totally premeditated. Patiently and persistently, he courts innocent young women with the intent to steal it all: their hearts, their money, and, ultimately, their lives. It takes months of planning and playacting. What could be more callous? This is a once-in-a-lifetime story!"

"How much time would you need to nail it down?"

"No way to know exactly. But you know me. I'll work as fast as I can. Time only moves in one direction, and in this case speed is of the essence."

He nodded decisively. "Go for it. Keep me posted. Use caution and your own good judgment. Mary will arrange a corporate credit card and help with travel arrangements. Try to keep the travel to a minimum. You know we've closed some of the bureaus and trimmed as much as possible out of the budget. And Britt, when you're on the road, check in with me or the city desk every day, hear?"

"I hear you. Thanks, boss."

"Oh, and I know you're eating for two, but try to go easy on the per diem. Go get him."

I flew out of his office and back to Liz's desk, high on adrenaline.

"I think he went to Amsterdam and was in Canada for a while," she said, scarcely looking up. "He used his original last name."

I searched *News* files for the case closest to home, Gloria Weatherholt's fatal scuba-diving accident six years earlier. It had scarcely warranted newspaper space, only three brief paragraphs. Gloria and Marshall Weatherholt, a Kentucky couple on their honeymoon, diving from a rented sailboat off Key Biscayne. She failed to surface. He called for help. Search divers pulled her from the water three hours later. The medical examiner ruled it an accidental drowning. Fatal water accidents are common in Miami.

I called Sergeant Craig Burch. He sounded irritated and pulled no punches. "We're swamped, working York full-time. We have enough unsolved murders to keep busy longer than any of us will live, and you want us to reinvestigate an old accidental drowning?" he asked accusingly.

"Exactly," I said, and filled him in.

His interest level rose rapidly as he listened, but he wouldn't make any promises. When they got a break, he said, he'd have Stone review the file. That was the best he could do.

I worked the phones and the Internet to glean as much data as possible from law enforcement agencies who'd investigated the deaths, the local medical examiners' offices, and news stories published both at the accident scenes and in the brides' hometowns.

Suzanne, a native of Baton Rouge, Louisiana, was a promising young writer and poet. She had won a national short-story-writing contest, according to a feature in her hometown newspaper, the *Times Picayune.* A prestigious literary magazine had published her prize-winning story. She'd won a grant from a major arts foundation and was at work on her first novel.

Then she met Marsh Holt.

During their Grand Canyon honeymoon, the couple had stopped to snap pictures at a spot with a spectacular view, a news story said. As the budding poet and novelist posed close to the cliff's edge, loose stones apparently gave way and she slipped. *As her new husband watched in horror, she plunged five hundred feet to her death.* It took nearly a day to recover her body. Police described Marsh Holt as "inconsolable."

I called the sheriff's department investigator, who confided that such accidents are not uncommon. "You never know what a tourist is gonna do," he said. "Had one a couple weeks ago where a family stops their RV to let their dog out. The pooch runs off into a hazardous area with rock-slide warnings posted. The owner chases after him, right past the warning signs, until the ground gives way under his feet. He and a ton of rocks disappear into a deep crevasse."

"Any witnesses to Suzanne's fall?"

"None that I know of, other than the husband—and his camera. We processed the pictures. In the last frame he shot, she was standing right at the edge, smiling and waving at him. The man took it hard."

Oh, sure, I thought.

The medical examiner had found that the slick leather soles and narrow two-inch heels of Suzanne's strappy sandals probably played a role. "When she lost her balance, she had no traction and slid right off the edge," she said. No foul play suspected.

I downloaded Suzanne's prize-winning short story from the literary magazine and folded the printout into a file folder to read later.

Colleen was a native of Connecticut and an equestrian who rode in competitions from Madison Square Garden to London, England. She had walls full of blue ribbons, rooms full of trophies, and had competed in the summer Olympics.

Athletic and competitive, she was also an experienced snow skier. Despite the fact that it was nearly dusk, she and her new husband had remained out on the slopes. It had begun to snow, but she insisted on making one more run. The bereaved bridegroom told police that he had reluctantly agreed. He assumed his bride was right behind him. It had begun to snow harder, with limited visibility. Colleen somehow missed the trail and skied right off the side of the mountain. When Marshall Weatherholt turned, she was gone. He stopped, waited, then went for help.

The ski patrol arrived too late. She had crashed into a grove of large fir trees.

Rachel, a clever young entrepreneur, had launched her own business at age twenty-three. Unable to find a high-fashion handbag with built-in, easy-to-reach compartments for her cell phone, credit cards, cash, and cosmetics, she created her own. Friends adored it. Every female who saw it wanted one for herself.

A slick national fashion magazine featured her creation. Then the *Enquirer* photographed Lindsay Lohan carrying one, and what began as a cottage industry took off, with a small factory, scores of employees, and stores like Saks Fifth Avenue and Bloomingdale's stocking the distinctive bags. About to branch out into shoe, fashion, and jewelry design, Rachel met the love of her life and took time out for romance.

Rachel took a sketch pad on their honeymoon, an exotic trek to Mayan ruins in Guatemala. She hoped for design inspirations.

Poisonous snakes are native to the region. Warnings were posted at their hotel and on the trails. As the newlyweds hiked a jungle path, a small but deadly snake apparently dropped out of a tree and down the front of Rachel's blouse, a sunshine-yellow safari shirt she had designed herself. The bridegroom reacted heroically, local police said. He tore away her shirt and removed and killed the snake. But, bitten several times, she died before help could arrive.

Too bad she didn't design a compartment in her backpack for anti-snakebite venom, I thought.

Local police, reluctant to scare off tourists, declined to discuss the dangers further but did acknowledge that a number of such deaths occur annually, among both visitors and residents. They sympathized with the bridegroom. He had been distraught, they said.

The investigators in each case scoffed at any possibility of foul play. After witnessing his Academy Award–worthy performance as grieving bridegroom, no one ever suspected Holt.

Brilliant, I thought, as I transcribed my notes. The self-made widower knew how to manipulate law enforcement's jurisdictional boundaries. The bride's friends and relatives, who might be suspicious, ask questions, and demand answers, were back home, sometimes thousands of miles away. The investigators most often worked for small unsophisticated police agencies in remote resort destinations where they were better trained in tourism and public relations than in homicide investigation. They were also accustomed to the misadventures of visitors on a holiday. Tourists in unfamiliar settings sometimes stumble into deadly accidents.

I had seen it in Miami, had written the stories. Tourists killed while boating, Jet Skiing, sky-diving, swimming, or snorkeling. People normally cautious at home feel invulnerable on expensive annual vacations. They never see it coming.

Patterns emerged. The victims were already successful or climbing the ladder, mostly from well-to-do families. Each was outgoing, creative, and pursuing a central passion in her life, before being swept off her feet by Marsh Holt. They were busy playing music, writing, designing, or participating in national sports competitions, with little time for romance, until he entered their lives.

How does he select them? I wondered. Did he really wander into a symphony hall in a strange city, see Vanessa, and choose her? Is it really that random?

Vanessa at the cello, the stunning professional portrait her parents had sent me, had been published in full color in the arts section of the *Boston Globe* several weeks before they met.

Suzanne had been featured in her local newspaper and in the literary magazine that published her prize-winning short story. The magazine had used a photograph of her with a short bio on the contributors' page.

The business section of Rachel's local paper had featured the young entrepreneur's booming design business, along with two photos depicting her with some of her creations.

Photos of Colleen had been published in the sports sections of numerous newspapers, including a great shot of her and her favorite horse clearing a high hurdle in competition at Madison Square Garden.

So did the killer discover his victims in newspaper stories? A chilling thought. I have always believed that a news story reporting a success or personal achievement is a gift to the subject and an inspiration to readers. Rare, often once-in-a-lifetime occurrences, they are proudly included in résumés and scrapbooks. They are framed and hung proudly in family homes. Loved ones cherish them.

Eventually, obituary writers will see a feature and include the information in your final story. Or a police reporter like me will find it and include the good with the bad to balance the story of your arrest, conviction, or bad ending.

A famous jewel thief once confided to me that he found the names and smiling faces of his victims on the pages of glossy magazines that report on the social lives of the very rich.

Could reporters like me be helping a killer target his victims?

I was about to leave when I heard from Liz. "He spent a year in Amsterdam."

I caught my breath. "Did he get married there?"

"I'm still checking. But he went there on his honeymoon. A girl he met in Canada."

"Is she alive?"

"No, she fell down a flight of stairs. By accident."

CHAPTER TWELVE

"There's another one," I told Lottie. "Number six. The wedding was in Ontario. Her name was Alice."

"Was?"

"Has anybody ever survived a honeymoon with him?"

Lottie had come to my place. We ordered pizza, and I tossed a big green salad. Daintily, she lifted the lid on the still-warm pizza box and did a double take. "Anchovies?" She wrinkled her nose. "Neither of us likes anchovies."

"I ordered that half for me. Just felt like anchovies for a change."

"Uh-huh." She cut her eyes at me.

"I'm not some crazed mother-to-be suffering from hormonal cravings," I said quickly. "Can't I try something different?"

"I'm not saying a thing."

She opened a light beer and I sipped ginger ale.

"Read this." I handed her Suzanne Chapelle's prize-winning short story.

The protagonist of "A Fish for Benji" was a small boy who lived on the bayou with his dirt-poor parents, a harsh mother, and an abusive father. Poignant and rich in atmosphere, with a frightening undercurrent, the story was clear evidence of the young author's promise. Lottie put down her slice of pizza after the first page and read straight through without a word.

"Wow," she said, as she finished.

"Talk about lost potential," I said, scooping ice cream into a soup bowl. "Suzanne Chapelle wrote that at age nineteen. Who knows what she would have written at twenty-five, thirty, or forty-five? Imagine all the poems, books, and stories no one will ever read."

"It ain't right," she said. "What is that?" She squinted at the bowl in front of me.

"Chocolate-chip mint. Want some?"

She wrinkled her nose. "No. Not with pizza and beer. Marsh Holt should be the poster boy for capital punishment. Nobody deserves it more."

"So many jurisdictions are involved." I paused and licked the spoon. "Remember the cross-country murder sprees of serial killers Ted Bundy and Christopher Wilder and Andrew Cunanan? Their faces were on the network news every night. Wanted posters everywhere. Everybody knew who they were. But nobody knows Marsh Holt is out there. Nobody's even aware of the murders. Somebody has to put it all together first; then a cop somewhere will arrest him and a prosecutor will actually take one of these cases."

"Only one way to do it," she said. "Lay it all out in the newspaper, chapter and verse. Once his name hits the headlines, big-name prosecutors will fight to nail his ass."

I nodded. "That's why I'm going to Arizona first thing tomorrow."

The bell interrupted as I packed the next morning. Expecting Mrs. Goldstein, I threw the door open.

My heart sank. It was my mother, bright and shiny as a new penny, in a little navy bouclé suit with white piping and shiny gold buttons.

"Hi there." I kept my voice cheerful. Chaos and angst were the last things I needed at the moment. I knew if I became crazed, I'd forget something important, and I needed to make every minute of this trip count. I already felt extremely self-conscious in my mother's presence. Though I've never lived up to what she believes is my fashion potential, I've always confidently argued the point. But looking in the mirror now . . .

"You should have called," I said, smiling. "I would have had breakfast ready. Come on in. You're just in time for coffee."

She bustled inside, lugging several bulging shopping bags, put down her packages, and opened her arms. I was up for a hug.

"I apologize for the last time I was here," she murmured in my ear. "You just caught me at a bad moment, totally off guard. This was nothing I ever expected."

"Me either," I said truthfully.

She declined coffee. She wanted to drop something off on her way to work.

"Your last months will be during the hottest, ickiest weather, the dog days of summer," she said, moving her packages to the couch and the coffee table, "so I brought a few things to help see you through. Come on," she coaxed, "have a look."

I tore away tissue paper and began to unwrap bundles. Clothes! Maternity clothes! I dove into the bags with glad cries. Her timing could not have been better. This was Christmas morning and my best birthday all wrapped up in one.

Despite her superb fashion sense, I was never comfortable having my mother choose my clothes. But at the moment I was running out of big safety pins, had nothing to wear, and neither time nor money to shop, and the problem was fast approaching critical mass. It's not easy to be optimistic when your fat pants are too tight.

I wanted to weep at the cool, crisp white eyelet blouse paired with both black slacks and a skirt, each with cleverly designed waistbands designed to expand with your own. Best of all were the blue jeans. I didn't know such garments existed. They were classic jeans in every way, except for the elastic panel across the belly.

This was my surprise introduction to the architecturally engineered world of maternity wear. My mom had unexpectedly come through, big time.

I stripped off my baggy T-shirt and drawstring slacks and went into a try-on frenzy. Four or five different tops, mix-and-match combinations, cool, crushable, and as fashionable as such garments can aspire to be. We ooohhed and ahhhed and shrieked and laughed like schoolgirls, until she was hiccuping and I was absolutely giddy.

She spotted my half-packed suitcase as we transferred my new wardrobe to the bedroom closet. I said I was traveling to report a story and would be back soon. It seemed best not to delve into detail. She asked only whether it was safe and I assured her it would be.

She urged me to call her frequently. "One more thing," she said. "Is my grandchild a boy or girl?"

She had actually managed the word *grandchild* without choking up. Go, Grandma.

"Definitely one of the above," I said. "I didn't look when they did the sonogram. I don't want to know."

"But why?"

"The whole thing has been a surprise." I shrugged. "I just decided to keep it that way. I'll know soon enough."

She pondered that for a long moment. "That means the layette is limited to yellow, mint green, or white." She tapped a manicured fingernail against her chin. "Unless, of course, we shop at the last minute, right after delivery."

I nodded guiltily. I hadn't been entirely truthful. Knowing that the baby was she or he would make this child an individual, a real person with wants, needs, and a future. That seemed too daunting right now. I needed our connection to remain abstract for a little longer. When push came to shove, so to speak, it would be real for the next twenty years. For life, probably. I hear one never ceases being a mom.

My own mother, who now sat across from me, her expression concerned and eager, busily scribbling lists of what we needed in her Daily Planner, was proof of that.

When she began to check off items like receiving blankets and baby monitors, I realized how little I knew.

"I have a lot to learn," I admitted.

"Me too." She touched my cheek. "We'll learn together."

After she left, I unpacked my big T-shirts and baggy pants and happily replaced them with my new duds.

Lottie noted my good spirits when she came to drive me to the airport. "I knew you'd lose the blues once you got back to work and into real life."

She also insisted I call to fill her in on my progress every day. If I keep all my promises, I thought while boarding my flight, I'll have no time to work. I'll spend my days on the phone instead, dutifully checking in with Fred or the city desk, my mother, Mrs. Goldstein, Lottie—even Ryan.

Oddly enough, at the moment I just felt incredibly grateful that they cared.

COLD CASE SQUAD

MIAMI, FLORIDA

Detective Pete Nazario, on the phone at his desk, scowled and tried to tune out Joe Corso's unsolicited personal advice to fellow detectives.

Corso's dubious beneficiary was Sam Stone, whose romance with a young U.S. Justice Department investigator appeared to be growing serious.

"Kid, lemme tell ya one of my unbreakable rules of life. This one's right at the top of the list: Never buy a ring for a woman!" Corso nudged Nazario, still on the phone. "Ain't that right, Pete?"

Emma, the lieutenant's tiny middle-aged secretary, peered disapprovingly over her little spectacles.

"Why not?" Stone asked.

"Simple. When you never buy a ring for a woman, you never buy a ring for the *wrong* woman."

"That explains your popularity with the opposite sex," Burch said, from his desk.

Stone frowned. "What are your other unbreakable rules for life?"

Corso ticked a few off on his thick fingers. "Always lock your car. Never sign or tear a check out of the book until you fill out the stub—"

"See, those two make sense," Stone said, "unlike that first one."

"Take it from me, kid, from a man who learned the hard way. *Never* buy a ring for a woman."

"Found 'im!" Nazario ended his phone conversation with a jubilant grin. "Dyson Junior works at a Sunny Isles tattoo parlor. Just talked to Lou, the manager. The kid's there right now."

"Let's go see what his story is," Corso said. "I'll tell you my other unbreakable rules of life on the way." He pointed his finger like a gun at Stone as they left. "Bro, heed my good advice. Don't wanna have to say 'I told you so.'"

Lou, the manager, a muscular shiny-domed man, was a dead ringer for Mr. Clean except for the tattoos covering his thick arms and burly neck. His body was a walking, talking billboard for his business. He summoned Dyson from a back room.

Colin Dyson Jr. had inherited his father's shifty black eyes and shaggy unibrow. Tall and wiry, he wore distressed blue jeans, a green and brown camouflage T-shirt with HA, YOU CAN'T SEE ME printed on the front, and had wavy dark hair to his shoulders. A multicolored tattooed cobra wound around his right arm from his wrist to his bicep, where its open mouth exposed fangs and a darting red tongue.

Nazario introduced himself and Corso. "Is there a place we can talk for a minute?"

"I don't talk to cops," Dyson said sullenly.

"It'll only take a couple minutes," Nazario said affably.

Dyson arrogantly flipped back his hair and turned away.

"Guess you'd rather talk to us downtown," Corso said.

With that, Dyson spun without warning and shot out the front door of the tattoo parlor as though the starter pistol had just been fired for the fifty-yard dash and he was the favorite to win.

"Hey, get your ass back here!" Corso yelled.

He and Nazario exchanged resigned glances, and Corso took off after him.

"Me cago en su madre," Nazario said, and followed.

Dyson darted out onto busy Collins Avenue, dodging heavy traffic. Corso followed, huffing and puffing by the time he reached the far curb.

Nazario outpaced him, sprinting just a few feet behind Dyson, who cut across a fenced-in construction site and ran down toward the beach. Construction workers began to shout.

As the sand slowed Dyson down, Nazario tackled him and wrestled him to the ground. Dyson cursed, kicked, and flailed as Corso, red-faced and panting, fumbled for his handcuffs and piled on.

"That's the kid from the tattoo parlor across the street!" a construction worker yelled.

"Hey!" another shouted at them. "Whadaya doin'?"

"Let 'im go!" A burly worker in a hard hat charged in their direction.

"Police!" Nazario flashed his badge as Corso cuffed Dyson's hands behind him.

The converging construction workers pulled up short to watch.

"What'd he do?" one asked.

"Nothing! I didn't do anything!" Dyson yelled, as the detectives lifted him to his feet.

Curious beachgoers began to gather.

"Let's get him outa here," Corso muttered, doing a double take at two teenage blondes in bikinis.

They marched Dyson back across Collins Avenue in handcuffs, a chorus of boos trailing behind them.

"You couldn't just answer a coupla questions like a gentleman," Corso complained, still breathing hard. "You're lucky I don't rip the coconuts right off your palm tree for this little stunt. You just made things a helluva lot harder for yourself, kid."

Nazario radioed for a patrolman with a cage car to transport Dyson to the station.

"Sorry 'bout that." The tattooed manager watched Nazario shake beach sand out of his jacket. "I shoulda warned ya, the kid's a little edgy."

Corso put Dyson in the back of their unmarked.

"A marked car is on the way," Nazario said. "Let's sit 'im on the curb till it gets here."

"Nah, he's cuffed. He's okay in here." Corso slammed the door.

Nazario emptied the sand out of his shoes one at a time.

Corso was at the Coke machine, and Lou was asking Nazario when he could expect Dyson to return to work, when their car started and began inching away from the curb.

"Hey! *¡Para, hijo de puta!*" Nazario yelled, and ran toward the unmarked Ford. "Stop! Stop right there!"

"Oh, shit!" said Lou, the tattoo parlor manager.

Corso dropped his Coke can. "Son of a bitch!"

Nazario ran into the street in front of the car, hands up like a traffic cop. "Hold it! Hold it!"

Dyson saw a break in traffic and floored it.

The car knocked Nazario off his feet. He landed on the hood, his face hit the windshield, and he stared for a long moment into the driver's eyes. Neither blinked. Dyson stomped the brakes and Nazario rolled off the hood into the center lane, motorists swerving to avoid his prone body.

"Son of a bitch!" Corso pulled his gun, loped into the street, waved traffic away from Nazario, who wasn't moving, took a shooter's stance, and opened fire. He didn't stop squeezing the trigger until his eighteen-shot Glock automatic was empty.

Brakes squealed. A cabbie driving a family of Chinese tourists to the airport swerved onto the sidewalk and slammed into a power pole. Pedestrians and construction workers dove for cover. Lou, the tattoo parlor manager, hit the sun-baked pavement. Bullets flying, he answered his own question about Dyson's return to work.

"Not soon," he muttered.

"Shots fired! Officer down!" Corso radioed, requesting backup and rescue.

The fading echoes of gunfire were followed by piercing screams from a restaurant and the front porch of a retirement hotel down the block.

His still-smoking gun in his hand, Corso knelt beside Nazario.

"Pete, Pete? You okay?"

"I think so," the detective said. "I didn't want to get up with all the cars and bullets flying by. Tell me all that shooting wasn't you, Joe. It wasn't you, was it? Say it ain't so."

"Damn right it was me. That son of the bitch tried to kill you with our own goddamn car."

"Oh, shit! *Coño, que mierda.*" Nazario struggled to get up.

"Don't move, Pete. Wait for rescue."

"No, I'm okay. Get me the hell out of the street."

Corso helped him to the sidewalk. Nazario hunched his shoulders at the curb and shook him off.

"What the hell happened?" he demanded. "You cuffed him behind his back."

"The son of the bitch has gotta be double-jointed," Corso said, "some kinda contortionist. He musta stepped through the cuffs, got them in front of him, climbed over the front seat, and started the car."

"You left the keys in it? What about your unbreakable rule of life? Goddammit! *Comemierda, le diste un tiro al carro nuestro.* You shot our car?"

"Musta hit it a dozen times," he said.

"I don't think so. I've seen you at the range," Nazario said, disgusted.

"You must be in shock," Corso said. "Musta hit your head."

K. C. Riley burst out of her office. "Shots fired at that tattoo shop! Corso's on the radio. He sounds okay but we have an officer down."

"Pete's the only one with him." Stone reached for his jacket.

"Oh, no!" Emma, the lieutenant's secretary, gasped and covered her mouth with her hands.

They all stared at one another.

"Let's get out there," Riley said.

"I hope Corso didn't do any shooting," Burch said. "I couldn't believe he qualified last time I saw him at the range."

The patrol car Nazario had requested to transport Dyson screeched to the curb. "Let's go!" Corso told the rookie behind the wheel.

He had just heard on his walkie that their missing unmarked Ford Crown Victoria had been sighted from an overpass by a Florida highway patrolman responding to a serious multicar pileup in the opposite direction. Dyson was now reported southbound on Interstate 95, speeding toward the city. He had slapped the detectives' blue flasher onto the dashboard and was weaving through heavy traffic.

"Cross the 163rd Street causeway," Corso yelled. "We can cut him off at the pass!" He dove into the front seat. "Wanna come, Pete? You up to it?"

Nazario paused for a moment, watching Corso reload his weapon. He shook his head. Screams still echoed from half a block away.

"I'll check out the collateral damage here."

"Okay, but get yourself checked out first."

The patrol car tore away from the curb, lights flashing, siren screaming.

More sirens as paramedics arrived. Nazario pointed down the street, waving them on in the direction of the screams. His handheld radio was dead, run over in the street by an SUV that narrowly missed him. He limped painfully down the sidewalk toward the retirement hotel.

"Dios mío." A tiny elderly woman, her dress bloodied, lay pale and dazed, holding a blood-soaked towel to her head as shocked senior citizens and hysterical hotel employees milled about her.

Shit, he thought. *Este hijo de puta mato a una vieja.* My God, the son of a bitch killed an old lady.

Medics scrambled to treat the injured woman as Nazario trudged grimly on down the street to the restaurant. Shots had shattered the front windows, showering an early lunch crowd with flying glass. Bullet holes pocked an inside wall. Nazario ventured inside. Broken glass crunching beneath his feet. Small tables and chairs had been overturned in the chaotic stampede. Broken crystal and fresh flowers from the tables littered the floor.

"Everybody okay in here?" he called hopefully.

"It's dead!" The manager raised his head from behind the counter. He was trembling.

"*¿Qué?*" The detective dreaded the answer.

"The cappuccino machine!" the man burbled emotionally. "They killed it. Shot it dead center in the middle of lunch hour. What happened? Was it terrorists?"

"No, not terrorists. *No, no es un terrorista, es peor, un policia comemierda.*"

Miraculously, no one was dead or seriously hurt, though scores of customers had fled during the confusion without paying their checks. The detective stepped out, scanned the street for other casualties, and returned to the hotel.

The news was better than he dared hope. One of Corso's hollow-point bullets had nicked the elderly woman's right earlobe as she rocked in her chair on the hotel's front porch.

Though the wound bled freely, medics believed that Irma Jolly, eighty-six, would be fine. The outcome would have been far different had the slug struck a mere fraction of an inch to the right. *Gracias, señor.* Nazario fought the urge to drop to the ground and give thanks. His battered knees ached too much.

The medics wanted him checked out at the ER.

"Later," he said. "After we get our car back."

Nazario used the radio of a Miami police sergeant who had just arrived. He saw no life-threatening injuries at the scene, he said, and was proceeding with the sergeant in the direction of the chase.

* * *

Corso and the young patrolman were in hot pursuit, with Dyson in sight, still handcuffed and at the wheel of the Crown Vic. The blue flasher on the dashboard alerted motorists, many of whom yielded or pulled over. An angry Metro-Dade bus driver called 911 and complained about cops chasing each other through traffic.

WTVJ-TV launched its news chopper and broke into regular programming to cover the chase live. Lou, the tattoo artist, watched it on TV from his shop.

"Not for a *very* long time," he murmured aloud, and wondered what a help-wanted ad in the *News* would cost him.

Dyson's unmarked police car sideswiped several motorists, then careened down an exit ramp, with the pursuing patrol unit just five car lengths behind. He had located the siren button and was using that too.

"Go! Go! Go!" Corso bellowed to the rookie behind the wheel.

The rookie radioed that Dyson was blowing red lights and stop signs as the stolen car rocketed through a residential neighborhood at a high rate of speed.

"Takes after his old man," Nazario muttered, as he heard the transmission from three miles away. "They should call off the pursuit," he told the sergeant, "before somebody else gets hurt."

In the pursuing patrol car, Corso urged the rookie driver to stop Dyson with the PIT maneuver. Officers trained in the Pursuit Intervention Technique deliberately tap fleeing vehicles with their own cars to end dangerous pursuits. The officer aligns his car's front end with the fleeing vehicle, maintains speed, and targets a strike area between the tire and the bumper. If done right, the fleeing car spins to a stop.

"They taught us how to do it in the academy," the young patrolman said, wrenching the wheel to avoid a smoking city sanitation truck that seemed about to burst into flames, "but I never tried it in a real chase."

"No time like now," Corso said. "It's fun."

Uncertain, the officer radioed for permission to use the PIT maneuver and received an affirmative. But before they could close the gap between them, Dyson lost control, clipped the side mirror off a pickup truck half a block ahead, and careened off a bright yellow Hummer at a stop sign.

"He's losing it! He's losing it!" Corso shouted.

Dyson skidded sideways across a green velvet lawn, through the sprinklers, and slammed into a house. Roof tiles flew as the big Ford Crown Vic crashed through the northeast wall. The front end of the unmarked penetrated the living room, the blue light on the dash still flashing, the siren still wailing. Dazed, Dyson stumbled out the driver's side and fell over a broken coffee table.

"We got 'im now! We got 'im now!" Corso screamed into the radio.

"Sounds like they have him," Riley said, with a sigh of relief, as she and Burch backtracked from Sunny Isles.

"There he goes!" Corso's voice shouted from the radio. "He's running!"

"Oh, shit," Riley said.

"Badder than his old man," Nazario said, listening as they fought heavy traffic. *"Este hijo de puta es peor que su padre."*

Sam Stone, alone in an unmarked car, was closest, as everyone converged.

Dyson sprinted through the backyard of the house he'd hit as a man ran out the front door screaming, "My big-screen TV! It was brand new!"

"I didn't do the PIT," the young patrolman shouted into his radio. "Be advised. It wasn't me. It wasn't me."

A trucker told 911, "A crazy cop just ran me off the road and hit a house!"

Corso and the patrolman bailed out and took up the foot chase as helicopter blades battered the air above them. They were so focused on their quarry that the rookie forgot to put the car in park.

The WTVJ cameraman caught great footage as the police car as rolled down an incline, picked up speed, and crashed into a huge gumbo limbo tree.

Dogs barked, residents shouted, and mothers rushed to snatch up their small children as the chase pounded through backyards and flower gardens.

Dyson, still in handcuffs, leaped like a gazelle, straight up and over a concrete retaining wall and onto higher ground bordering the expressway. He was about to sprint across six lanes of heavy high-speed traffic.

Back in Sunny Isles, Lou covered his eyes. "Go! Go!" chanted the crowd of beachgoers and construction workers clustered around his TV.

Dyson made a false start, then pulled up as motorists leaned on their horns without slowing down. Deciding against becoming road-kill, he scrambled back down the embankment, jumped to the surface street, and dashed for the cover of dense trees and bushes at the end of the block, with Corso and the young cop fifty yards behind.

"I think there's a canal back there," Corso panted. "We've got 'im trapped."

Crashing and stumbling through wild cherry hedges and thick Florida holly, they unexpectedly came face-to-face with Dyson, who stood twelve feet away on the bank of a wide drainage canal.

"Stop right there!" The panting patrolman brandished his gun.

"Like hell," Dyson gasped, chest heaving. "You can't shoot a handcuffed man."

He turned and dove into the water.

He tried to swim but quickly began to flail and thrash as Corso and the patrolman searched the canal bank for something to throw him. But before they found anything, Dyson slipped beneath the water's surface and disappeared.

"What the hell?" Stone stopped behind a damaged patrol car resting against a gumbo limbo tree and looked around. A siren wailed from inside a nearby house as eerie flashing blue lights pulsated in the windows. He ran toward an agitated civilian out front.

"Everybody inside all right?"

"I was the only one home." The man clutched his heart. "Nobody hurt, but my big-screen TV, and the kids' aquarium—"

"What's that smell?" Stone interrupted. The odor was familiar. He skirted the outside of the house to the crumbled wall, the homeowner following. They heard an ominous hissing.

"Oh, shit!" cried the homeowner.

"Get the next-door neighbors out," Stone told him. "Take them across the street. Now! Keep everybody away!"

He radioed dispatch to send City Gas on a three, an emergency signal. "The stolen unmarked struck a gas meter at this location. We've got a broken line with escaping gas.

"Which way did they go?" he asked the retreating homeowner, who pointed to the far end of the street; other residents directed him along the way.

Stone burst through the foliage. He found Corso, red-faced from the chase, hands on his knees, sucking up deep breaths.

"Hey, bro," Corso said, looking up.

"Where's the suspect?" Stone's eyes darted around.

Corso jerked his head toward the canal. "Son of a bitch jumped in. Thought he could swim in handcuffs. He thought wrong."

"He went down." The young patrolman pointed to the spot where they last saw Dyson.

Corso read Stone's expression.

"Not me, I ain't jumping in there," he said. "It's murky as hell. Probably thirty feet deep. I called for divers."

"What's their ETA?"

"Fifteen minutes."

The young patrolman took a step back from Stone's hard stare. "I can't swim," he said.

Traditionally, Miami police applicants were required to swim one hundred yards underwater while carrying a two-hundred-pound weight. The requirement was eliminated several years ago in order to speed recruitment. Today, police officers protecting a city surrounded by water don't have to know how to swim.

"How long?" Stone shouted, stripping off his shirt.

Corso shrugged. "Coupla minutes."

"Here, take my gun." Stone kicked off his shoes.

"Hey," Corso said. "Hold on. You blacks can't swim for shit. We got divers on the way."

Stone dove into the canal, submerged, surfaced, then dove again. This time he didn't surface.

"Holy shit," Corso said.

Stone broke the mirrored surface, shook his head, gasped for air, took several deep breaths, and dove twice more.

After the third dive, Stone surfaced with one arm around Dyson's neck and swam to the canal bank, where the others dragged the unconscious man up the steep incline.

"Is he breathing?" Stone gasped, as he followed. Dyson's face was blue, lips purple.

"No." The patrolman shook his head.

Corso looked puzzled. "I guess some blacks *can* swim."

Stone started CPR.

Back at the tattoo parlor, Lou got up from his TV and propped a hand-lettered HELP WANTED sign in his front window.

"Where the hell is rescue?" Stone gasped. "Tell them to speed it up."

"I wouldn't do that in a million years," Corso muttered, as Stone performed mouth-to-mouth and then chest compressions.

He was still doing CPR when patrol units, K. C. Riley, and Burch arrived.

"Need me to take over?" Burch asked.

A huge amount of water suddenly gushed from Dyson's mouth. His eyelids fluttered.

"Atta boy," Stone panted. "He's breathing." He turned to Corso. "Where's the damn key? Take his cuffs off."

A Fire Rescue unit arrived moments later. "It was hard as hell to find him," Stone said, still breathing hard. "There's a ton of junk on the bottom. I think I even saw a couple of cars down there."

The paramedics inserted an IV, put a cervical collar on Dyson, placed him on a backboard, and lifted him into their van.

Nazario arrived as it departed for county hospital, lights flashing, siren screaming. "Is he alive?"

"If he makes it, he has Stone to thank," Corso said. "So, bro, where'd you learn how to swim?"

"My grandmother took me to the beach growing up," Stone said, words clipped, his tone chilly. "She taught herself to swim so she could teach me, because so many kids in Overtown didn't learn how and drowned." He still sat on the rocky ground, dripping perspiration and canal water and trying to catch his breath.

"That kid didn't fall far from the tree," Burch said. "No mystery who he takes after."

"Somebody obviously pissed in that gene pool," Riley said.

"He ruined my suit," Nazario complained. "It got torn when the car hit me."

"Stone and his clothes look like shit, too," Burch said.

They all turned to Corso.

"Hey," he said, "this ain't my fault. This coulda happened to anybody."

They returned to their cars, as the homeowner rushed toward the flashing yellow lights of an arriving City Gas truck.

As Stone and Nazario briefed Riley, the various police radios around them simultaneously emitted a high-pitched emergency signal: *Female paramedic pushed from a moving rescue van by a violent patient who escaped.*

On the way to the hospital Dyson had yanked out his IV, ripped off his cervical collar, and struggled with the paramedic treating him. As her male partner looked for a safe place to pull over, Dyson shoved the medic out the back door, jumped from the rescue wagon, and fled.

He didn't go far. The female medic suffered only bruises, abrasions, and acute embarrassment. But Dyson broke his right ankle when he leaped out of the moving vehicle. Police tackled him as he limped along, several blocks away.

"What is with you?" Nazario asked Dyson, now sedated and handcuffed to a bed in the hospital's jail ward. "*¿Qué te pasó, cabrón, por qué corriste?* Why did you run?"

"I din't do it," Dyson mumbled.

"What?"

"What'd you want me for?" Dyson asked, his bloodshot eyes wary.

"We just wanted to ask about something that happened when you were eleven years old."

"I din't do it."

Nazario sighed. "Did you ever meet Spencer York? He called himself the Custody Crusader. Wore army fatigues, was an acquaintance of your dad's."

"That sonbitch."

"York?"

"No, my father."

"I don't get it," Nazario said, perplexed. "All you had was an old open traffic warrant. For that you almost kill a cop, half a dozen other people, and yourself?"

"I din't wanna go to jail."

Stone got a tetanus shot and went home for dry clothes. Nazario was scanned, X-rayed, and tested, and treated for cuts, deep bruises, and road rash but declined to remain overnight for observation.

Back at headquarters, facing daunting paperwork, with every phone lit up, Emma interrupted.

"Colin Dyson on the line."

"Jesus Christ!" Riley groaned. "Don't tell me they gave him one call and it's to us."

"Maybe he wants to apologize." Burch picked up the phone.

"It's the father," he told Riley, moments later. "He says there's something he forgot to tell us."

There was something odd about Spencer York's behavior the night of the Fathers First meeting, Colin Dyson said.

"He was off the wall, super hyper. The guy reacted every time a female walked into the hotel. Not like he was looking for a date, like he had the jitters.

"We leave, and he thinks we're being followed. I'm driving and he's watching the mirrors, looking over his shoulder. Once he tells me to turn at the next corner, and takes us blocks out of the way, to see if the car behind us follows. I asked if the cops were tailing him. 'It's not the cops I'm worried about,' he said.

"Then who? I wanted to know. The Feminazis? A woman? I was joking. That's when he said it."

"What?"

"That females are the deadliest of the species, the cause of all the trouble in the world since Eve. Went on and on about it. Sounded like he was being stalked by a woman."

"What kind of stalking are we talking about here?"

"Well, the guy wasn't exactly known for his youth, good looks, and sex appeal."

Burch thanked him for calling. "I assume you're aware of what happened today, regarding your son."

"Saw some of it live, on TV," Dyson said flatly. "Told you, didn't I? Biggest mistake I ever made."

"That's exactly what he said," Burch told the others, his expression incredulous. "I'm expecting him to ask about his kid's condition. *How's Junior? Is he seriously hurt? When can I see him? Does he need a lawyer?* Nothing. That guy's no father."

"Takes more than sperm to be one," Riley said.

A sergeant from the police shooting team, which investigates whenever a weapon is fired in the line of duty, arrived to interview Corso, who declined unless he was accompanied by his union representative and his lawyer.

"A cop has the right to shoot the sorry ass of anybody who threatens him after being told to stop," he griped defensively, after the sergeant left. "And that includes sorry asses who speak no English. If they don't understand *stop* or *freeze*, they shoulda learned the language before they came here."

He angrily paced the conference room.

"Dyson understood every word we said, so what does he do? Tries to kill my partner right in front of me. What'd you expect me to do? How'd you all be looking at me now if I didn't do shit? Damned if I do and damned if I don't. Jesus, cops can't win around here."

No one looked sympathetic. "A shooting might be justifiable. It's the quality of the shooting that's in question," Riley said coldly.

"After all I went through, all I did today?" He reacted with righteous indignation. "I almost had a goddamn heart attack when I see Pete, here, go car-surfing right in front of me. And then he's laying in the street. Gave me a flashback to a fatal accident I handled once.

"A kid body-surfing on the roof of his buddy's moving car flies off and smashes his head against a guardrail, like a broken egg. His pal, who was driving, said they'd seen car-surfing on some TV show and decided to try it."

He waggled a finger at Nazario, who stared back sullenly.

"It's the law of inertia. Unless you are secured to a moving object, like a car, you will continue moving forward at the same speed the car was going after the driver hits the brakes. That's why we have seat belts."

Assistant State Attorney Jo Salazar popped her head in the door. She needed help assembling the litany of charges which would be filed against Dyson Junior. A city attorney assigned to risk management was also en route.

The young patrolman, Corso's driver in the pursuit, was eager to assist. He'd already written a stack of traffic citations and was becoming creative. "How about driving while handcuffed? Is that illegal?" he asked the prosecutor, as she settled in.

"That's the least of Mr. Dyson's troubles," Salazar said cheerfully.

She huddled later with K. C. Riley in the lieutenant's office. Old friends, they had gone through the police academy together.

"Cops are usually terrible marksmen," Salazar noted, as they discussed Corso. "They're notoriously poor shots."

"I know," Riley replied, "but he didn't hit the unmarked once after emptying his gun at it. And I've heard he's famous for cheating at the firing range. It's probably the only way he can qualify. Rumor has it that when he finishes shooting and walks down to count the hits, he takes along a thirty-eight-caliber pencil to punch holes in the paper target. Nobody's ever written him up, but there's a lot of talk."

"The city may be liable for damages today, but it could've been a helluva lot worse." Salazar said, running well-manicured fingers through her curly brown hair. She shook her head. "It's a miracle nobody's dead."

"Tell me about it," Riley said grimly. "It could've been the stuff of nightmares. Corso always lands on his feet, but not this time. He's used up all nine lives."

"The screw-up fairy has visited us once again, as you all know," Riley said later, at the team meeting. "The city's looking at a myriad of civil lawsuits. Thank God for Stone." She nodded in his direction. "Good job. I don't even want to think about how much worse it might have been." She glared at Corso.

"Excuse me for not grandstanding in front of the camera on that TV chopper." He lurched to his feet as if to storm out of the room.

"Sit down," Riley said coldly. "Nobody else in this room grandstanded out there today. What you saw from your fellow detectives was old-fashioned common sense and good police work.

"The only way we pull this caper out of the crapper is to solve this case. Even that's no guarantee, after today. We need to focus, focus, focus," she said. "Find Spencer York's motel. Re-interview his bondsman. Talk to the radio reporter who interviewed him. See what he remembers."

"I had something working this morning," Stone offered, "before all hell broke loose. There may have been another South Florida child snatch almost a year before Jason was taken from Brenda Cunningham in Miami. It was a Fort Lauderdale case. The mother died."

The room was silent.

"It's not one York would've bragged about. The death was ruled accidental. It's not clear how the case slipped through the cracks. The victim, Sarah Ann Shields, had moved to Lauderdale from Pine Bluff, Arkansas, with her three-year-old son, Patrick. I talked to an old neighbor this morning. He told police he heard the mother's screams around noon. Took him awhile to pull on some clothes and step out. A car he didn't get a good look at took off, burning rubber. Then he saw Shields stumbling, sobbing, hands to her eyes. She staggered to her own car and drove away erratically at a high rate of speed. Hit the curb, he said, and was all over the road.

"Her speeding car slammed into a bridge abutment near Las Olas Boulevard a few minutes later. She was ejected. No seat belt. Massive head trauma. Witnesses said she was screaming, swerving, and weaving through traffic right before the crash. The child seat in her car was empty.

"What's that sound like to you? The medical examiner noted an odor on her body, thought it might have been Mace. It wasn't a robbery. Her purse was found back at her place.

"The same neighbor swore he heard her kid, the three-year-old, playing outside his window earlier that morning. Unfortunately, that neighbor, a junkie, wasn't considered credible, and when the ex-husband was contacted in Arkansas a few days later, he said his son was safe with him. He said Sarah had returned the boy a week or so earlier because he had legal custody.

"They ruled it accidental. She's a traffic statistic. I'm thinking dirty. It's possible that Spencer York paid her a visit. He might have snatched Patrick, and the mother died chasing him, trying to rescue her son."

"Jesus," Riley said. "Any paper trail?"

Stone shook his head. "If it was York, I can't find a record of his usual legal papers faxed to the local cops or the FBI."

"That just may mean he saw the accident and wanted to distance himself," Burch said.

"Or maybe somebody didn't want to complicate their investigation of a simple one-car traffic fatality," Nazario said.

"The victim?" Riley asked.

"Twenty-seven, a registered nurse. Just moved to Lauderdale a few weeks earlier. She'd interviewed at a few local hospitals but hadn't accepted a job offer yet. Didn't know anybody here. Wanted a fresh start. Relatives in Arkansas wrote several letters to the Lauderdale police, alleging foul play and asking for an in-depth investigation. They had no proof and no witnesses but insisted that Patrick had been in Lauderdale with his mother. When the call came that she'd been killed in an accident, the first thing they asked was, 'Where's her boy?'

" 'What boy?' the Lauderdale cops say. They check, and Patrick is safe and sound in Arkansas with his father."

"Sounds like a motive to me." Riley toyed with her grenade-shaped paperweight. "Find out more about her family, especially the letter writers, and her possible love interests." She sighed. "This case has more twists and turns than a snake."

"And enough suspects to fill the Orange Bowl," Burch said.

BRITT

CHAPTER THIRTEEN

The Arizona deputy who initially responded to the scene of Suzanne Holt's fatal fall was not happy to see me.

He wore a bored expression beneath his Stetson. "I told you on the phone the other day, ma'am. That case was an accidental death, relatively routine. We see 'em frequently."

He turned sullen when I insisted on seeing the file.

"The medical examiner, somebody from homicide, and me, we all agreed. I been doing this for twenty-two years. Can't tell you how many cases like this I've seen, too many to count. Even if you installed railings and posted warning signs everywhere, which you can't because it would ruin the scenic wonder of Mother Nature's masterpiece, tourists would still find ways to kill themselves. It's the nature of the beast."

He slapped the thin file folder down in front of me and leaned back in his chair, a bit red in the face, one leather-booted foot up on his desk as though challenging me to find a flaw in their expert opinions.

For a death case, the file seemed pretty thin to me. Ignoring his hostile glare, I examined it slowly.

The photos were the centerpiece, the last moments of a brief marriage about to end badly. Very badly.

They had used a disposable camera, as in Vanessa's case. Marsh

Holt, I thought, clearly belonged to the Dixie-cup throwaway generation. Disposable cameras. Disposable brides. Several pictures had been shot at other spectacular locations, some apparently taken by fellow tourists who had obligingly photographed the happy couple. Suzanne's head barely reached Holt's shoulder.

A petite gamine with huge expressive eyes, pretty hands, and long graceful fingers, she sat alone at a rough-hewn log table in a picnic area surrounded by giant trees, her notebook open before her. Did her notes describe the splendor of her surroundings? Was she entering intimate secrets into the journal of a young bride? Were they fragments of a poem in progress?

Did she ever have trouble deciphering her own notes? I wondered.

Only two pictures had been taken at the site where Suzanne plunged to her death.

In the first, Suzanne, a wisp of a girl one tiny step from eternity, stood smiling, her back to the precipice and to a broad vista of unparalleled beauty: rocky chasms, towering clouds, windy ridges, red limestone walls, plateaus, and a distant valley.

In the final photo she stands closer to the edge, as the deputy succinctly pointed out with his ruler. She smiles, seconds from death, waving shyly to the serial bridegroom, the last man she ever loved.

"You think he told her to step back, closer to the edge?"

"Hell, no!" I got the distinct impression he yearned to rap my knuckles with his ruler. "He warned her not to. She wouldn't listen. Laughed at 'im and did as she pleased." His body language and tone of voice implied that most women, present company in particular, deliberately ignore sound advice when they hear it.

"She kep' telling 'im to try to get all the scenery behind her into the picture. Then she moved closer to the ledge. Right after he pressed the shutter she turned to look at the view, lost her footing, and was gone."

"He didn't happen to capture that moment?"

"No, ma'am. The poor man dropped his camera and didn't even

think to pick it up again. We found it lying out there. I've never seen a man lose it the way he did, the poor bastard. Only married three days. He'll never get over it."

"He got over it enough to remarry only six months later."

"I 'member you saying something to that effect on the phone. Sounds like rebound to me. Happens to a lot of people who experience the sudden shock of losing a loved one."

"And the new wife died on *her* honeymoon too, in an alleged boating accident."

The big man leaned forward, the leather around his waist creaking ominously, a glint as sharp as an ax blade in his steely eyes. "Lady, I have no idea what happened in somebody else's jurisdiction. All I do know for sure is what happened here on my turf. This young woman died in an accidental fall, thoroughly investigated by top-flight professionals. Our conclusion was unanimous. Go talk to the medical examiner if you like." He gestured broadly toward the door, inviting me to do so. "But she ain't gonna tell you nothing different."

I asked for directions to the medical examiner's office.

He followed me out to my rental and tipped his hat as I slammed the door. "Sorry you came all this way for nothing, ma'am."

I saw him at his desk, on the telephone, as I drove out of the parking lot and away from the long barrackslike building.

The medical examiner was expecting me. Dr. Daphne Faircloth was middle-aged and simply dressed with short, curly blond hair.

The honeymoon photos were the centerpiece of her file as well, along with a copy of the magazine that published Suzanne's short story. A brief biography of the young writer appeared on the contributors' page, along with her photo, a head shot, dominated by her big, soulful dark eyes. Wispy tendrils of soft short hair framed her delicate face.

The medical examiner's photos revealed that Suzanne's hands and fingers were torn, her nails all broken, as she must have clawed at the rugged cliff face during her plunge. Cause of death was massive head and chest trauma. There were multiple fractures.

"Typical. Little doubt that it was an accident," Dr. Faircloth said. "No foul play suspected." She folded her hands serenely on her desk in front of her.

They appeared much older than her face. The woman must have had some serious plastic surgery, I thought. At first glance, she appeared to be in her forties but was more likely sixty, unless her hands went out in the sun a lot more than she did.

"All her injuries were typical of such a fall."

"What about the toxicological screen? Did she have drugs or alcohol aboard?"

"A very small amount of alcohol. The husband stated that she drank a glass of wine with lunch at noon. She was small in stature, but I don't believe it played a role. The accident occurred about four P.M., enough time for it to be metabolized."

The doctor apologized, saying she was due in court on another matter and had to excuse herself.

I asked for copies of the two photos taken at the site of Suzanne's fall, and her assistant provided them.

From my motel room, I placed a call to Miami, not to anyone I'd promised to call; I needed to talk to Detective Sam Stone at the Cold Case Squad.

"I'm in Arizona," I told him, "and I need a favor."

"We're busy right now, Britt, really busy." He sounded uncharacteristically harried and impatient.

"I'll keep it brief. What's the name of the forensic photo analyst you used in that case last year?"

"Dr. Clark Wilson at the University of Minnesota."

"Thanks. Have you had a chance to take a look at the scuba-diving death of Gloria Weatherholt yet?"

"The sergeant mentioned it, but like I said, we're swamped." He sounded exasperated and I could hear people calling his name in the background.

"What's going on there?"

"I can't go into it," he said, "but believe me, it's been a helluva day."

"Please don't forget about Gloria Weatherholt." I sighed. "I know nobody wants to reopen a closed case, but I'm sure she was murdered and I really need your help."

"Right."

My timing was bad. He was preoccupied, and I knew I didn't have his attention.

"Do what you can, when you can," I pleaded.

"I'll talk to you later, Britt. Hang in and be careful."

"You're implying that I'm not?"

"I think the answer to that is obvious."

"That's something I'd expect from Corso, not you. But I did walk right into it."

"Sorry, Britt. I'll get to it as soon as I can."

I hung up, concerned about the barely controlled chaos behind him. What was I missing in Miami? Too busy to think about it, I called Dr. Wilson, drove to a FedEx office, and overnighted the photos. Two hours later I boarded a flight to Baton Rouge, Louisiana, Suzanne's hometown.

CHAPTER FOURTEEN

His name was John Lacey. His light brown, slightly shaggy hair framed a boyish face, though he was in his mid-twenties. His was a face that would look boyish even at age seventy.

His words were soft, his manner gentle. He wore blue jeans and a T-shirt that said BELIEVE.

I met him at a coffee shop in Baton Rouge, Louisiana.

His name had surfaced in a newspaper search I did on Suzanne Chapelle. Almost a year before she married Marsh Holt, Suzanne Chapelle and John Lacey had been forever linked in print—their engagement announcement in the *Baton Rouge Advocate.*

Lacey was also a would-be writer, advertising copy by day, moonlighting on the Great American Novel at night.

I said I was a reporter who wanted to talk to him about Suzanne.

He loved the girl, he said, and absentmindedly lit a cigarette. I frowned. Normally I don't object, but now I had good reason.

"Smoking is bad for your health."

"Life is bad for your health," he said, his sad face somber.

Then it suddenly occurred to him why I had objected, and he quickly stubbed out the smoke, amid a flurry of apologies.

His hands trembled slightly when he spoke Suzanne's name. They met as barefoot preschoolers in the same neighborhood. They had loved each other since they were ten years old and in the same English class. The teacher encouraged Suzanne to read her poetry aloud. Soon, he too began to write poetry, despite teasing from the other boys. He and she came from poor families and they ate together in the free lunch program.

"We'd meet at lunch and after school to read each other's stuff, make up stories, and talk," he said, as I nibbled on a slice of coffee cake.

Suzanne's father died when she was twelve. Her mother remarried twice: badly. For most of their teens, Suzanne Chapelle and John Lacey had only each other.

He went off to New York to seek his future but returned in less than a year. They missed each other too much. They became engaged. Then she won the contest and her story was published. A lengthy letter from an admiring reader arrived soon after. The writer was new to Baton Rouge, had read and was moved by her story, and hoped to discuss it further over coffee or a drink.

"Her first fan letter," said Lacey, whose sentences tended to trail off into silence when speaking of Suzanne. She was flattered that a stranger admired her work. Lacey wondered if the man had seen her picture in the newspaper or magazine and whether she was what he really admired.

"I sensed it," he said. "On that first day, before they ever met. It was like hearing the distant thunder of a storm coming your way, leaving you nowhere to run. The literary references he used, and the way he understood her story, impressed her so much that she called to thank him. That's all she intended to do. Call, chat, thank him, and politely decline the invitation. But whatever he said during that call made her want to meet him.

" 'Just a cup of coffee,' she said. Nothing to worry about.

"I knew. I watched what was happening like a slow-motion disaster. I had to trust her. We'd always trusted each other. So I dropped her off that evening. She was wearing her engagement ring, pitiful little pebble such as it was. . . . I drove away, but I had a bad feeling. So I went back, parked, walked up, and looked in the front window, like an orphan with his nose pressed against the glass. I didn't mean to spy on her. I saw him. Saw how she looked at him. And I knew."

The fan's name was Marsh Holt.

"For a while I hoped he was just a BF destroyer."

"Excuse me?"

"A BF destroyer—you know, a pickup artist who likes the challenge of seducing women who have boyfriends. If that's what he was, he'd move on and I could forgive her. I would've forgiven her anything.

"But Suzanne was a keeper. He was older, handsome, more sophisticated, and affluent. I was just an average Joe who loved her." He licked his pale lips. "I had trouble breathing, literally, for months after she confessed she'd fallen in love with him. She wanted us to stay best friends, but there was no way. . . . I wanted her to be happy, to have the world and everything she wanted. But I couldn't watch.

"I have years of golden memories, gifts from the gods who ultimately take away."

"Well put. I take it you still write poetry."

His sad smile turned sheepish. "None that I ever share. Suzanne had all the talent in that department. When I heard she died . . . If he hadn't come into our lives . . ." He trailed off, lost in thought. Then his expression changed from melancholy to curious.

"Why is a reporter from Florida interested in Suzanne Chapelle? She didn't publish enough to have this kind of posthumous attention from the press."

"Actually, it's not her writing that interests me," I said. "It's him. Marshall Weatherholt. Marsh Holt. The serial bridegroom."

"Is he . . . ?" His soft gray eyes stricken, he stared at my new maternity top. "He didn't— You're not . . . ?"

"For God's sake, no. I'm a police reporter. I think Marsh Holt murdered Suzanne, that he's a serial killer. I'm working on a story about him, trying to piece it all together." I told him about the other brides.

He sat in stunned silence, generating grief as though it were radio static, interference that at times prevented him from clearly comprehending my words. He'd blink, furrow his brow, repeat something I said.

"I hated him because he didn't protect her, because he let that terrible accident happen," he said slowly, covering his eyes with his hand. "But at the funeral, when I saw how he suffered, I felt guilty and ashamed. But if you're right"—he raised disbelieving eyes to mine—"he intended to kill her from the start, like the others."

I nodded, afraid that John Lacey might begin to weep aloud in that crowded and noisy coffee shop. So we left, or at least tried to.

I had slipped my shoes off under the table, and now they didn't fit. It was as though a practical joker with a foot fetish had swiped my shoes and replaced them with much smaller look-alikes.

"Sorry." I struggled, trying to cram my foot back into my size-five white Reebok, as Lacey stood waiting. "What new hell is this?" I stared in dismay at my swollen feet and puffy ankles. "Must be the airline flights, or a combination of flying and . . ." I dragged my teeth across my lower lip.

Finally I used brute force to jam my feet back into the shoes and hobbled painfully into the street.

"Sure you're all right?" Lacey looked concerned.

"Absolutely," I said, trying not to wince.

I bought a pair of soft rubber flip-flops at a chain drugstore across the street. They were pink, intended for wear in the shower or on the beach. They'd do fine until the swelling subsided.

"You should elevate your feet," he advised. "I have five half brothers and sisters. My mom always swore that her feet grew with every pregnancy. 'You start as a size six,' she'd say, 'and wind up a ten.' "

"No way," I protested. "I have shoes, high heels, that I love. I'll be damned if I'm gonna outgrow them at this age."

I frowned at my pink flip-flops, wondering what my mother would think.

When I said I needed to make some calls and take notes, Lacey suggested his nearby apartment would be more comfortable than my motel room.

His small second-floor apartment was a typically cluttered bachelor pad, except for the room where he labored on his novel. Scrupulously organized reference books lined the shelves, and the walls were adorned with photos of Suzanne.

I was hungry again, so Lacey fixed me a grilled cheese and tomato sandwich in his tiny galley kitchen while I called the Coast Guard in Miami. Skelly O'Rourke was tied up at a press conference. Twenty-one Cuban refugees had successfully made it to U.S. soil, or so they thought. They had clambered from their small boats onto an old bridge in the Florida Keys, home free, they believed, under U.S. policy. However, the unused deteriorated span was no longer physically attached to land. On that basis, they had been scooped up and sent back to the island they thought they'd escaped, inflaming Miami's Cuban community and setting off a firestorm of controversy.

O'Rourke would be tied up indefinitely afterward, conducting satellite radio and television interviews. No one else in the public information office even remembered Vanessa Holt. The dead bride was old news.

I called Ron Fullerton in Chicago. He had not heard from Marsh Holt and had no theories as to his whereabouts.

A spokesman at the U.S. Consulate in Guatemala City told me that local police had long since closed the investigation into Rachel Weatherholt's snakebite death.

There would have to be sufficient proof, clear evidence of foul play, I was told, before anyone would consider reopening the case. Perhaps, he suggested, such evidence might be found if the body was exhumed.

I wondered. Rachel had been dead for three years, and Holt was so clever that finding injuries inconsistent with his snakebite story seemed unlikely. But it was worth a shot.

I called the New York City mortuary listed in her obit to ask where Rachel had been interred. She hadn't. Perhaps there *had* been evidence of foul play. Marshall Weatherholt had had his bride's body cremated. When her parents objected, he insisted that Rachel had once told him that was what she wanted. An oddly morbid conversation between giddy whirlwind lovers *rocketing* toward wedlock, but nobody questioned it. After all, he *was* the grieving husband.

As I continued to work the phone, John Lacey fixed me some soup, tomato with cheesy croutons.

He was right. His study, with its desktop computer, big leather chair, and comfy overstuffed ottoman on which to prop my swollen feet, was far more comfortable than any motel. And the food was better, hotter, and kept coming.

Lacey confirmed that there had been insurance. How much, he didn't know, but Suzanne had mentioned it during those painful days before the wedding.

He had been invited, in fact she had pleaded with him to attend. But he could not bring himself to watch. "How could I?" he said.

Instead, he sat across the street, alone in his car, and saw the happy couple leave the church in a rain of rice and confetti. That was the last time he saw Suzanne.

I selected some of his photos to borrow for my story and even a few of her short poems.

I called the Colorado ski resort where Colleen was killed.

Few employees remembered the tragedy, but a veteran ski lift operator who did remember told me he'd heard something inconsistent with the newspaper accounts. Nothing disturbing enough to notify authorities or challenge the newspaper, but it had never left his mind.

"The husband said his wife insisted on making one last run despite the poor conditions, according to the paper. He said he reluctantly agreed, against his better judgment, and that's when she was killed. Later, I talked to another couple. They'd wanted to make one last run too. The four of them were waiting for the lift. But weather conditions deteriorated so fast that the other couple changed their minds. When they left, they said, the newlyweds were quarreling because she was afraid and didn't want to go back up the mountain, but he insisted.

"Maybe the guy lied and put the blame on his wife out of guilt. If he hadn't taken her up there, she wouldn't have died. You never know how people will react in a crisis."

"Did the couple you spoke with talk to the sheriff's department?"

"Nah. They were leaving first thing in the morning and didn't want to get involved."

"Do you remember their names?"

"Not off the top of my head, but they're regulars. We see 'em every year."

Not concrete proof, I thought, but if witness accounts showed Holt lied to the police, that might get their attention. Either way, it was a damning detail I'd love to use in my story.

I begged him to try to recall their names and to call me at once if he did.

Lacey sat nearby, on the sofa in his little study, listening to me work, peppering me with questions between calls.

I talked to Vanessa's parents in Boston. Without burdening them with too much information, I asked if the son they never had had filed a change-of-address form at the post office before he blew town. Or if a neighbor or apartment manager might be forwarding his mail.

They promised to find out and get back to me.

I didn't want to brief Fred or the city desk until I had a strong lead to follow. With my progress at a standstill, they'd want me back in Miami and I wasn't ready to go. Not yet. Fred would be unlikely to authorize any more travel once I was home.

This was my only shot and I had to make the most of it.

"We have to find him," Lacey blurted, when I was between calls.

"What do you mean *we*?"

"You can't do it alone, not in your condition. I can help. Suzanne and I knew from her work with abused children that justice is rare. Most often, the system fails. We have to try to make it work for her," he said passionately. "She deserves it."

"What's *your* reason, Britt?" he asked later. "I need to be a part of all this for Suzanne. But you'd be happier and more comfortable at home right now, with your family and the baby's father."

"He's no longer in the picture." My voice suddenly sounded weary.

His eyes widened.

"Not by choice," I said quickly, and then I told him, unloaded everything: about McDonald's death and my escaping Miami to mourn the past, and how, in doing so, Marsh Holt, his doomed bride, and I had passed like ships in the night. About my anger and self-doubt when I learned the truth, and my determination to seek justice by exposing him in print.

He nodded, eyes shiny. "The minute I saw you, I sensed we shared a common denominator. People who've never suffered tragedy don't understand. But we do, don't we?"

We talked half the night. He was haunted.

"Suzanne used to dream of falling. She'd wake up with a gasp. What do you think that was," he asked plaintively, "precognition? Some kind of warning? A sign that evil was singling her out?"

"Dreams of falling are common, but I don't rule out anything," I said, thinking of my Aunt Odalys, who dresses only in white and calls upon the spirits of the dead.

Lacey gave me his bed and made up one for himself on his study couch.

When trying to piece a complicated story together, I love to brainstorm with a good detective, or Lottie, or my landlady, or, believe it or not, a bright and interested editor. Lacey was perfect: quick, imaginative, and totally committed.

"Holt's MO, faked honeymoon accidents, is brilliant." I recapped for him what I'd discovered so far, as he threw a thin beige blanket across the couch.

Lacey listened, eyes sick. "When I saw Marsh at Suzanne's funeral, I thought he was careless with the life of my girl. But I never dreamed—"

"Exactly. He's a hell of an actor. Until now nobody's ever doubted his gut-wrenching performance as the bereaved bridegroom. It's Oscar-worthy. He has the role down pat."

"Because he's had so much practice. What do we do next?" Lacey asked, before we said good night.

"I wish I knew."

He kissed my cheek, a sweet and innocent kiss like that of a kid brother.

CHAPTER FIFTEEN

I know Fred Douglas too well, knew what he'd say, and that I didn't want to hear it. So I called early, more than an hour before he'd be at the office. I planned to leave a sorry-I-missed-you, things-are-fine message, breezy and brief, just enough to buy me some time. I was shocked when he answered his telephone.

What the hell is he doing there at 7 A.M.? I wondered, dumbfounded, indignant, and totally caught off guard. Sure enough, he began to fire questions at me. I didn't lie, but ducked a few.

I could hear the frown in his voice. The man knows me too well. "Sounds like you're not accomplishing anything you couldn't do from here," he correctly concluded.

I denied it. "I still have more leads to run down before I come back."

"Okay, but wrap it up and come on in. Try to catch an afternoon flight, tonight at the latest. See you in the newsroom tomorrow bright and early."

I hung up, disheartened. My cell rang immediately, so quickly I thought Fred had called me back. Instead, it was the lift operator from the Colorado ski resort, with good news, I prayed, just in the nick of time. I didn't want to go back to Miami, not today.

"That couple you wanted to talk to," he said.

"You remembered their names?" I wanted to cheer as I groped for a pen.

"No."

"Oh."

"But I remembered that they're members of a ski club. The Miami Ski Club."

"Miami?" The witnesses I needed belonged to the Miami Ski Club, one of the largest in the country. And I was in Baton Rouge.

Fred's right, I thought regretfully. Time to go home.

Lacey arrived back from the Café du Monde with a sack of beignets—sweet sugary pastries—and containers of rich, steaming café au lait. I broke the bad news as we ate.

He called his boss to say he wouldn't be in, and we used the little time left to collect quotes and local color for my story.

We visited Suzanne's grave at the local cemetery and the places she frequented during her short life, the school she attended, the church where her wedding and funeral were held just days apart.

Lacey introduced me to a few of her friends, all of whom embraced him fondly. Her maid of honor let me borrow a wedding picture. A complete set of wedding photos, Holt with each blushing bride, would provide powerful art for the story.

As I was about to make my flight reservation, Dr. Clark Wilson, the nationally known forensic photo analyst, touched base. "This is extremely interesting," he said. "What time did you say these photos were taken?"

"Four o'clock in the afternoon," I said. "She fell shortly after four P.M., according to the police report. The nine-one-one call was logged at four-oh-eight. The last photo, the one in which she stands closer to the edge, was two or three seconds before she fell."

"Nonsense."

"Excuse me?"

"Those pictures obviously were not shot when the photographer claims. They could not have been. On that date, at that time, the sun and the shadows were not in those positions at that location—not at four P.M., three P.M., or even noon. Those photos were taken at eleven-thirty-five A.M., give or take a minute."

"Can you really be that precise?"

He was certain.

Excited, I called Arizona.

The deputy was not impressed. The medical examiner found Dr. Wilson's findings "curious." Neither considered it sufficient proof of anything other than the fact that the shaken bridegroom may have been mistaken about the time he took the pictures.

They stonewalled, but my story was coming together. This was crucial. Dr. Wilson, foremost in his field, published in prestigious journals, had testified as an expert witness in major cases nationwide. How could his findings be ignored?

I called Liz, the *News* researcher. The night before, Lacey and I had brainstormed, trying to determine where Holt had gone by tracking his past patterns. Our admittedly vague conclusion was that he had probably headed north. But where? I asked Liz to search for a paper trail and suggested that his destination might be a northern city.

"He seems to like to go north in the summer and south in the winter," I said.

"Who doesn't?" she said.

I reluctantly booked a 7 P.M. flight back to Miami.

The Hansens called as I checked out of my motel. Vanessa's father sounded confused, his voice shaky, as though he had aged dramatically in the brief time since we first spoke.

"I have something for you." He went on to describe his trip to the post office in laborious detail. The punch line? Holt had not filed a change of address.

Next, Hansen had visited the apartment house where his daughter had planned to live with her new husband. He spoke to the owner and several neighbors. Holt had confided to each of them, they said, that he could not bear to remain in Boston without Vanessa. His only plan, he told them, was to drive long enough to distance himself from his memories.

His grief so touched the building's owner that, in an uncharacteristically generous gesture, the man returned the couple's security deposit along with half the first month's rent.

Another profitable performance by Marsh Holt, the actor, I thought, with a sigh.

"So then we stopped to have lunch at the Fireside," Hansen was saying, his voice querulous. "Do you know it?"

"No, sir." I checked my watch. "I'm not familiar with Boston."

"An excellent choice. They have a very nice menu."

That reminded me that I was hungry. Again. I peered into the empty bakery bag, seeking crumbs.

"My wife ordered the fish, I had chicken. Right after we ordered, she said, 'Isn't that Bob Feldman sitting over there?' She was right. He waved and came over to offer his condolences. He was at the funeral, but there was such a crowd. We asked him to sit."

My eyes began to cross. I had a plane to catch.

"Vanessa had a little IRA," he rambled on. "You know, an Individual Retirement Account. Bob set it up for her. He's been our financial adviser since she was a little girl. Marsh cashed it in. Bob said it took a little time to get the paperwork done. But he wired Marsh the money, $26,552, on Monday."

I dropped the beignet bag and sat up straight, fingers tightening on the phone. "Where? Did he say where he sent it?"

"To a bank in Minneapolis. Marsh gave him the account number."

"You're absolutely sure?"

"That's what Bob told us."

"See if he can give you the name of the bank and the address of the branch it went to."

I called Liz on our way to Lacey's apartment to pick up my laptop. "Holt may be in Minneapolis. He was there a few days ago to pick up some money."

We were about to head for the airport when Liz called back, twenty minutes later.

"Minneapolis," she said. "You were right."

"Is he still there?"

"Definitely."

"How can you be so sure?"

"He wouldn't miss his own wedding." Marsh Holt, she said, had applied for a marriage license.

I repeated her words aloud. Lacey and I stared at each other. His hands shook.

"Who's the unlucky lady?"

"A Nancy Lee Chastain, age thirty-four. Want me to transfer you to the city desk?"

"No," I said quickly. "Don't tell them you talked to me. Find out everything you can about the bride. I'll call you back in an hour."

"Do we still go to the airport?" Lacey asked. "Are you really leaving?"

I nodded. "Can you call the airline for me?" I said. "Cancel my flight to Miami and find the next one to Minneapolis."

I punched numbers into my cell phone. Onnie wasn't at her desk in the library. I waited while someone went to find her.

"There's a Minneapolis flight leaving in ninety minutes," Lacey said. "It's not direct. You have to change planes twice."

I checked my watch. "Can we make it?"

"It'll be close."

"Book me a seat in coach," I said.

Onnie picked up as I heard Lacey confirm my flight. "Two seats in coach," he said.

"Britt?"

"Right here, Onnie, I was distracted for a second."

I asked her to e-mail me the names and telephone numbers of as many Miami Ski Club members as she could find.

Lacey was tossing underwear and toiletries into a duffel bag.

"Why don't I just leave them on your desk?" Onnie said. "I hear you'll be back in the office tomorrow."

"E-mail them," I said, after an awkward pause.

"Or maybe not," she said. "I'll get right on it."

"Do me a favor. Don't tell anybody in the newsroom that we talked."

She sighed. "Okay. My lips are sealed."

I called Liz from the car on the way to the airport.

"Nancy Lee Chastain started out as an anonymous food critic," she said. "She is now the star of her own local cable TV show on food, catering, and entertaining."

"Has she been featured in a newspaper or magazine in the last six months?"

"How'd you guess? The *Pioneer Press* did a huge profile with color art. It started on the front of the style section, then jumped to an entire page inside. Nice space."

She gave me the name and phone number of the bride's parents.

"One other thing, Britt. Better step on it. The wedding's tomorrow."

I repeated her words. We were already speeding, but Lacey's Chevy convertible leaped forward as he floored it.

COLD CASE SQUAD

MIAMI, FLORIDA

No one who met him seemed to forget the Custody Crusader.

Andy Raddis, a silver-haired veteran newsman at WAVE radio, which broadcasts from a waterfront station on the 79th Street Causeway, remembered the man well. He told Sam Stone that when he walked his guest to the exit after their interview, Spencer York paused to carefully scrutinize the parking lot before stepping out.

"Expecting someone?" Raddis had asked, assuming York was watching for his ride.

"When you do live radio," the Crusader said meaningfully, "you never know who, or what, might be waiting for you outside."

"I thought the guy was just being melodramatic." Raddis shrugged. "He was kind of over-the-top, if you know what I mean."

On the other side of the city, Burch and Nazario, who had refused to go home despite his battered knees and aching hip, found the Sea-something Motel.

In a city where skylines evolve overnight, it seemed miraculous that the Sea Voyager still stood nine years later, was still run down and had the same manager.

"What are the odds?" Burch said. "Maybe we're getting lucky."

"About time," Nazario said, limping.

The manager, a seedy, slightly built man with greasy hair, feigned ignorance.

"You remember," Nazario coaxed. "Spencer York, the Custody

Crusader, the guy who made all the newspapers when everybody and their brother was looking for him. He stayed here."

"Oh, yeah," the manager said reluctantly. "That guy. The Crusader. He was here. He took off on me, still owes on the bill."

"We're thinking he didn't take off voluntarily, like everybody thought at the time," Nazario said. "We're thinking he ran into trouble."

"Any of that trouble happen here?" Burch asked.

"No, no. No trouble here." The manager's lazy left eye wandered.

"That's funny. We heard you do have trouble here," Burch said. "In fact, so much trouble, the city threatened to shut this place down as a public nuisance last year. You almost lost your license to operate. You're on probation. Any more trouble and you're out of business. . . . And failing to cooperate with a homicide investigation? Now, that's trouble. Big-time trouble, right here, right now."

"What do you need?" he whined. "I never refused to cooperate."

"Good," Burch said. "I'm glad we understand each other."

"Being that Mr. York left here unexpectedly," Nazario said, "we assume he left his things behind in his room. What happened to them?"

"That was a long time ago." The manager looked uneasy.

"They were his personal belongings," Burch said. "Selling them or converting them to your own use would be illegal. Help yourself to somebody else's property, and that's trouble."

"He hardly had anything," the man babbled, suddenly talkative. "We don't exactly get the high rollers, the big spenders. The guy had nothing worth taking."

"Where is it?"

The manager's eyes shifted toward a small office just off the lobby. "He had one of those little portable typewriters. When I packed up his room, I put it to use in there."

They trailed him into his cluttered office.

"Whadaya know," Burch said. A battered little Smith-Corona sat on an old desk.

"That's it." The manager shrugged. "Take it. You can hardly find ribbons for it anymore."

"What else?" Nazario said.

The manager shrugged. "Buncha junk—papers, notebooks."

"Sounds like evidence to me," Burch said.

"Right, Sarge. Important evidence," Nazario agreed.

The manager scratched the dark stubble on his chin with a grimy fingernail. "Might be a box back in the storage room," he said. "I thought he might show up sometime, looking for it. I don't remember tossing it. Maybe it's still in there."

The storage room, the size of a walk-in closet, was dirty, full of cobwebs, and smelled musty.

The manager had to stoop and slip in sideways. He began to move old lamps, luggage, and boxes, raising clouds of dust as he worked his way toward the low sloped ceiling at the far end. The detectives stood outside and watched.

"I think I got it," he called, coughing in the dust.

His eyes watered as he stepped squinting into the brilliant sunlight, clutching a cardboard storage box.

"That's it?" Nazario said. "Anything else?"

"Nope. That's all. You can see. Here, I marked the date on the box and wrote 'one of one.' So there'd be no mistake if he came back. See that? My handwriting. 'One of one.' "

They went back to his air-conditioned office and wrote him a receipt for the box, its contents, and the typewriter.

"Let me ask you something, pal," Burch said. "When it was all over the TV and the newspapers that York had jumped bond, and the police, the state attorney's office, and his bondsman were all looking for him, how come you didn't drop a dime and let them know where he'd been staying?"

"They were looking for him," the manager said matter-of-factly. "He wasn't here at the time. He was missing here too. What good would it have done?"

"Let's see his room," Nazario said.

"What good is that gonna do now?"

"Maybe we want to conduct a séance," Burch said, "so we can ask him what the hell happened."

"If the bad thing that happened to Spencer York took place in that room, we have sophisticated forensic techniques that might still provide us with evidence," Nazario explained.

Room 8B was currently unoccupied. The room air conditioner was off and the sickeningly sweet odor of bathroom disinfectant mingled with the faint smell of mildew.

Burch kicked up the corner of a stained throw rug.

"From the quality of the housekeeping, we're sure to find evidence," Burch said. "York's socks are probably still under the bed."

"Gimme a break," the manager whined. "This ain't the Fountainebleau. Who are you, the cleaning police?"

"Lock up the room," Nazario said. "Don't rent it out until we get a crime-scene truck over here."

"You're serious?"

"Absolutely."

"Can you ask them to park around back? It doesn't look good out front. It's bad for business. I mean, I *am* cooperating."

"We'll see," Burch said. "We have a few more questions. Did you have any robberies, violent crimes, here at the motel back around that time? Any other guests go missing?"

"Some people skip, don't want to pay the bill. But nobody that I remember back then ever reported getting robbed. A lotta guys will pick up a girl in a bar, bring her back to his room, and then wake up and find her gone with his watch, his wallet, and sometimes his car. Most don't report it. They're embarrassed or afraid their old lady'll find out. But nothing where anybody gets hurt."

"What about visitors?" Burch said. "You ever see York with anybody?"

"Right around the time he took off, he shows up one night with another guy, a businessman type. They hoist a few drinks in the lounge, do a lot of talking, like they're making a deal." He shrugged. "I don't remember seeing 'im after that. You saw the date on the box. I always wait three days before I consider them gone. So he came back with that guy three nights before the date on the box."

"That would be Dyson," Nazario said. "The night of the meeting."

"What about women?" Burch asked. "York ever have a woman in his room?"

"That same night, when I took out the trash, I heard a voice—a woman's voice—in his room."

"Did you see her?" Nazario asked.

"No, who am I? The sex police? You know what we've got walking round this neighborhood."

"Did you recognize her voice? Was she somebody who frequents this place?"

"Hard to say. I don't think so."

"Did it sound like a friendly encounter? Sex? An argument? Confrontation?"

"I didn't listen."

"That night," Nazario said, "York was flush. We know for a fact that he came back here carrying a lot of money—in cash."

The manager's eyes lit up. "How much?"

"Several thou."

"I never saw any of it."

"Sure he didn't ask you to line him up with some of the local talent?" Burch asked.

"No way! I'm no pimp, if that's what you're asking. The guy had his own connection."

"What makes you say that?" Nazario asked.

"He was only here a few days from outa town, but he had several calls from women—*a* woman. I think it was always the same one."

"She leave a name?" Nazario asked.

"Don't think so. Just asked me to ring his room. When he didn't answer, she'd call back and say, 'Tell him I called,' but she wouldn't leave a name. She said he'd know."

The detectives exchanged glances. "She ever call, looking for him again, after he left?" Nazario asked.

"Nah, not that I remember."

"Aha!" Burch said, as they stashed the cardboard box and York's portable typewriter in the trunk of their unmarked. "The mystery woman did exist."

"The manager was telling the truth," Nazario affirmed. He could always tell.

"Who the hell is she?"

"At least we've got it narrowed down . . . to half the population."

"Yo, you guys been dumpster diving?" Corso greeted Nazario and Burch as they arrived with the old typewriter and the dusty storage box.

"These," Burch said, "are Spencer York's personal effects, everything he left behind at his motel. The manager boxed it up and never told a soul."

"Do tell." Corso meandered over to the desk as Nazario lifted the lid off the cardboard box.

"Christ." Corso quickly stepped back. "That dust and mildew'll set off my allergies. Sorry, I can't give you a hand."

As Burch and Nazario sorted through the items in the box, Stone stepped off the elevator.

"Hey, Sarge. I think there's a woman in the picture."

Burch and Nazario reacted. "What makes you say that?"

"I just reinterviewed the bail bondsman. The front man who posted York's bond had to confer during the transaction with whoever actually put up the money. He made a couple of calls. The bondsman swears he was talking to a woman. Thought he even heard the guy call her *ma'am.* At one point, he said he had to call 'er back again. Maybe she was somebody's secretary. Or she mighta been the one who wanted him back out on the street. The bondsman says the bagman looked young, but his Florida driver's license, which later proved to be fake, gave his age as twenty-two."

"Maybe things are coming together," Burch said. They brought Stone up-to-date as the three pored through the musty contents of the box. Local bus schedules. An old Betty Friedan paperback, with a number of the early feminist's passages highlighted in yellow.

"Look at this!" Burch said. "A receipt from Home Depot for a tarp. Odds are it was the one he was wrapped in. Dated the day he was last seen. What'd I tell you?" He turned to Nazario. "He was killed in that room."

"Credit card?" Stone asked.

"We should be so lucky. Paid for it in cash."

There were local business cards, including Dyson's, the radio newsman's, and some they recognized as members of Fathers First.

At the bottom: a black-and-white composition book.

Nazario whistled as he flipped through the pages.

"Looks like a diary and a list of his expenses. Where did that nurse killed in Lauderdale come from?"

"Pine Bluff, Arkansas," Stone said.

"Bingo! York bought gas there, on a date about a year before Cunningham." Nazario quickly turned to the last few entries.

"Listen to this."

Even Corso rolled his chair closer, forgetting his allergies.

"'*M must be in Miami. Haven't had a sure sighting, but I can sense her. Almost smell her.*'"

"That's the date he bonded out of jail."

Nazario turned the page. "Next day. '*M. Did she follow me here? That crazy bitch. What does she want from me now? Will it ever end? I could cut her heart out.*'"

"That's somebody he had a history with," Burch said.

"Sounds like me and my ex-wife," Corso said.

"That's the last entry," Nazario said.

"Stone, find out the ex-wife's name. See if it's Margaret, Melanie, Maureen, Mary Ann . . . you get the picture," Burch said.

They were still sifting through old receipts and logging legal papers when Stone returned.

"You're not going to like this, Sarge. Looks like York never had a wife, despite what he told Britt Montero. No marriage license ever issued in Texas. His own sister says he was a lifelong bachelor."

"Crap," Burch said. "They weren't close. What the hell does she know? Musta been common law; could be a marriage he never made legal."

Stone shook his head.

"Anybody in the family of that dead nurse in Lauderdale have a name starting with *M*?"

"She had a cousin named Marie Rose," Stone said.

"Cousin?" Nazario shook his head. "I don't see it."

"Neither do I," Stone said. "She was twelve when it happened."

Burch frowned. "York was a guy only a mother could love. He couldn't have been involved with that many women. Let's shake loose some travel money, head for Texas, and beat the bushes. Somebody in his hometown has to know her name."

"Unless the woman we're looking for is a mother he victimized in another out-of-state child snatch," Stone said.

"I doubt he had relationships with any of them," Burch said. "I hope not. It's a process of elimination. We need a lucky break. Just one."

Riley agreed. Burch and Stone would fly to Texas first thing in the morning.

BRITT

CHAPTER SIXTEEN

"Why do we have to change planes twice?" I complained to Lacey. Our route to Minneapolis seemed oddly circuitous. "Why do we have to go all the way to Dallas/Fort Worth and change planes again in Cincinnati?"

"Airline rules," Lacey said. "Even when you die, you have to go through Cincinnati."

I like window seats, horizon, endless skies, and towering cloud banks. I love bird's-eye views of my destination and the surrounding terrain. Lacey prefers the aisle. That made us ideal traveling companions. But there was a flaw in the arrangement, a fly in the ointment: For me, aisle seats were now more practical.

The third time I disturbed Lacey to visit the restroom, I felt I owed him an explanation. "I could swear something's pressing on my bladder."

"Wonder what on earth it could be?" he asked, with a straight face.

"Don't make me laugh," I warned, "and pray that I don't sneeze."

When he wasn't the sad and moody boy, his sense of humor was droll. He perked up and seemed more cheerful after we left Baton Rouge.

By 11 P.M. we were camped out on a row of hard plastic chairs in a chilly concourse at the Dallas/Fort Worth airport, our connecting flight blown off schedule by a line of thunderstorms.

Onnie had e-mailed the names of about two dozen Miami Ski Club members. The president was out of town. I caught the secretary at home on Pine Tree Drive, in Miami Beach. My late call, she said, struck fear into her heart.

"I have teenagers," she said. "Now that they're driving, it terrifies me whenever they're out at night and the phone rings. You know how it is."

No, I thought, but I guess I will.

I asked if she had skied in Colorado on the date Colleen died. She hadn't, she said. There'd been a family wedding she couldn't miss.

I mentioned the accident.

"Oh, I know the one you're talking about. The young bride who skied into the trees. I've heard the story."

She'd heard it from Mitzi and Richard Findlater, the couple who could prove Marsh Holt lied. When I called, they were enjoying their customary nightcap on the balcony of their high-rise Portofino apartment overlooking South Beach and the sea.

"That lovely young girl," Mitzi said, "the bride."

"On her honeymoon," Richard said in the background.

"That's the one," I said.

"We rode up on the lift with them a number of times," Mitzi said. "A rather nice-looking but nasty fellow; too bad the girl didn't live long enough to dump him."

"They didn't seem like a match?"

"Hardly." Ice tinkled in her glass.

In the background, her husband mumbled a few mitigating words in support of the bereaved bridegroom.

"A bad day?" she responded to him. "A bad day, sweetheart? On his honeymoon? Tell me you had a bad day on our honeymoon. I think not."

I liked Mitzi.

"It was our last day," she said. "We had to leave very early in the morning. It was late and starting to snow. We wanted one last run ourselves, so the four of us waited for the lift. She kept begging to go back to their room. She said she was exhausted. He insisted she go up the mountain with him one last time. She didn't want to.

"Skiing conditions deteriorated even more as we waited. By the time the lift arrived, it was snowing harder and the visibility was worse. We decided against it. It was our last night. We'd had a wonderful trip; why push our luck? We turned to leave and she tried to follow.

"He absolutely glowered. Kept saying, 'Don't be a baby, Colleen, get *on* the lift.' He smiled when we stared, but it was a chilling smile. He gripped her arm. She was in tears. He nearly dragged her aboard. She turned to me with a pleading look I'll never forget. I'll always regret not intervening, insisting that she come back to the hotel with us. If he was bent on playing king of the mountain, we should have left him to do it alone, without dragging that poor dear girl along.

"At dinner, we heard there'd been a fatal accident on the mountain. I suspected it might be them. As we left at dawn, we saw a ski patrol medic who confirmed it. He said they knew she was dead the moment they saw her. Her head was lying back on her shoulders, her neck broken. How horrible."

"Wasn't it unusual for him to be skiing ahead of her?" I asked.

She agreed. Richard took the phone to explain.

"In the flat light those conditions bring about," he said, "skiers find it extremely difficult to differentiate between smooth terrain ahead and a drop. Generally, the man doesn't go ahead, but he was wearing those expensive tinted goggles that help in that light and should make it easier for the skier following behind him."

He handed the phone back to Mitzi. When I said that Lottie Dane, a *News* photographer, would call her for an appointment, she was fine with it. But I heard Richard grumbling in the background.

"Nailed it," I told Lacey, after hanging up.

He went off to inquire again about our delayed flight. I wandered down the concourse in my never-ending quest for food and restrooms, my flip-flops slapping the soles of my feet. The restroom I found had a vending machine, but it dispensed only combs, condoms, tampons, and temporary tattoos. Nothing edible.

Lacey returned: no new information on our flight. We watched an electrifying lightning display through the big windows, then opened our laptops. Lacey checked his e-mail and tackled a few job-related tasks.

I polished my interview with the Findlaters and e-mailed it to Lottie along with their telephone number, asking her to schedule a photo assignment and shoot them together.

It was nearly midnight and cold. Lacey put his arms around me to keep me warm as we talked about Suzanne, the other victims, and why it's so difficult to persuade law enforcement to reopen a closed case.

"Does anybody aside from the immediate survivors even care about the misery that murder brings?" he asked plaintively. "How many have to die before people notice? They see it on TV, read about it in their newspaper, sip their coffee, and shrug it off."

"Some murders aren't even reported in the newspaper," I said. "But good reporters and good cops become part of the immediate family. We do notice and we do try to do something about it. Believe me, when this story hits the paper, everyone will care.

"In this world full of bureaucratic clock-watching time-wasters, journalists are among the few people left who can make a difference. Report it right, put it in the newspaper, and stand back. The story takes on a life of its own. It's like magic. That's one of the joys of being a journalist. It's certainly not the size of the paycheck."

"I've learned so much watching you work," he said. "The way you glean information from people and then put it all together. I wish I had taken more journalism courses."

"It's never too late."

He nodded, his boyish face earnest. "Hemingway once said that everyone who writes novels should work for a daily newspaper first."

Our flight was finally called at 3 A.M. Then we sat in line on the runway for another hour and three-quarters before takeoff.

"What if we don't get there in time?" I worried.

"If our connections go smoothly from here, we'll be all right," he said.

"But we can't cut it too close," I persisted. "We need time to sit down and explain to the bride and her family. It'll be traumatic, not something you can do five minutes before she's supposed to walk down the aisle. She'll freak."

"Better freaked than dead," he said. "Better to have loved and lost than to be married to a psycho."

CHAPTER SEVENTEEN

Lights were out, most passengers asleep, when the seat-belt warning flashed on and the captain warned of turbulence ahead. More thunderstorms.

As the plane bucked and bounced and was buffeted about, I wished I didn't need to go to the restroom again.

Queasy, I used my willpower to keep us airborne and our captain on course. I exhausted all that energy for nothing. After twenty roller-coaster minutes, our flight was diverted to Davenport, Iowa.

I panicked.

"We won't make it." I squeezed Lacey's arm until he winced. "We can't let an innocent woman leave on a honeymoon with that man; it's signing her death warrant."

"Don't get upset," Lacey said softly. "We'll figure something out. We'll catch the next flight to Minneapolis."

"He'll kill her!"

An older woman in the seat in front of us turned to stare, then whispered to her companion, who also turned to look. I decided to keep my fears and frustration to myself.

We landed in a driving rain. There was no next flight to Minneapolis. No jets were departing for Minneapolis, and all commuter flights had been grounded due to weather.

I used the *News* corporate card to rent a car, knowing as I pushed the card across the counter that Fred expected me in a few hours. What would he say if he knew how far I'd traveled from Miami since we spoke? Now I was using *News* credit to distance myself even farther.

Saving a woman's life was my objective now. Fred would approve of that, I told myself, though I didn't give him the opportunity.

We waited forever at the car rental counter. Neither of us knew the area, so I asked for a car with OnStar or a GPS system. None was available.

All they had was a tiny compact car. The *News* bean counters would be delighted.

We drove north. I was starved, famished, so hungry I felt as though I hadn't eaten for days. But we had no time to stop. Rain pounded in horizontal sheets, crashing nonstop into the windshield as though hurled by a bucket brigade of madmen.

Despairing of arriving in time, we pulled over and I called the bride's home. Reception was poor. This would be so much better done in person, I thought.

A young woman answered against a backdrop of giggles and girlish chatter. "Is this Nancy Lee Chastain?"

"No, she's sort of busy right now," the woman sang out good-naturedly.

"Can I speak to her? This is an emergency."

Bursts of static on the line made hearing difficult, and I feared losing the connection.

"She's about to leave for the church, hon. Nancy's getting married today."

"No," I said firmly. "She mustn't. That's why I'm calling." I spoke calmly and distinctly. "I have to talk to her. She's in danger. Don't let her do this."

"Say again?" she said skeptically. "Is this a joke? Sue Ellen, is that you?"

"No. Put Nancy on the telephone. Now. Please."

"Does she know you?"

"No. My name is Britt Montero, I'm a reporter for the *Miami News.*"

"She doesn't have time for an interview right now."

"Can I speak to her mother?"

"The bride's mother is busy right now too. Please call back another time."

"This is an emergency."

"I don't know who you are"—the young voice became petulant—"but show a little respect. This is Nancy's wedding day."

She hung up.

"Let's go," I told Lacey hopelessly.

"Which way?" He tried without success to see through the flooded windshield.

I bit back a sob of sheer frustration. Our tinny little rental didn't even have a compass. Where the hell were we? Several times we pulled over to consult a road map, but the rain was so torrential that we couldn't even read street signs without one of us getting out of the car and drenched. This was madness. Lacey and I began to snipe at each other as what should have been a three-hour drive took twice as long.

By the time we arrived in Minneapolis, it was too late to go to the house. We had to find the church. I had the address.

"What if the ceremony's already started?" Lacey asked. "What do we do then?"

"You know the part when the pastor asks that anyone who knows why these two should not be joined in holy matrimony should speak now or forever keep their piece? And everybody holds their breath?"

"Oh, shit," Lacey said. "I'm not doing it."

"You have to," I insisted. "How would it look to a church full of strangers for a woman in my condition to stand up and object? Think about it."

"What do they do when someone speaks up?"

"I don't know. I never saw it happen."

We stopped for directions again and were told that the church was about forty minutes away.

The wedding was scheduled for 2 P.M. It was now 1:35 P.M.

As we passed a police station I shouted for Lacey to pull over.

I trotted inside, cold, drenched, faint from hunger, wet hair plastered against my skull, my flip-flops squishing at every step.

"You have to help me!" I told the sergeant. "You have to send a patrol car to the Church of the Little Flower to stop a wedding. Right now!"

The pudgy middle-aged sergeant looked up from his crossword and regarded me, his gaze puzzled. "Why would I want to do that?"

"Long story," I panted. "But it's a life-and-death matter. The bride's life is in danger if she marries him."

His look was long, sad, and searching. "I'm sorry for your trouble, ma'am. But you can't keep a man from getting married."

"Okay," I impatiently conceded. "Yes, I am pregnant. That is obvious. But it has nothing to do with why the wedding has to be stopped."

We went round and round. I displayed my press card and attempted to explain. "The bride's name is Nancy Lee Chastain, she's a local television celebrity. That's what attracted him to her."

"Nancy Lee? The gal on TV with the food show? I watch her all the time." He began to look interested. "That's right, they said something on TV about her getting married. Lucky man. He'll never go hungry."

"He's a serial killer."

His eyebrows shot skyward. "You have proof that he's wanted?"

"He's not wanted yet, no charges have been filed, but there are homicide cases in five or six different jurisdictions. We don't want her to be his next victim."

"You know the case numbers on the homicides?"

"Well, right now," I said, "they're listed as accidental deaths." I listened to what I was saying and knew that even I wouldn't believe me.

He sighed. "You're a long way from home, honey, and I sympathize. But what you have here is a civil matter. It belongs in domestic court. You need to hire yourself a lawyer."

Lacey came through the door at that moment, streaming rainwater, soaked to the skin after parking the car some distance away.

"He won't listen!" I told him.

I turned angrily back to the officer. "I need to see the watch commander!"

"Don't raise your voice to me." The sergeant suddenly seemed less sympathetic. "The watch commander doesn't need to see you. He's a little bit busy right now."

"He won't listen." Lacey instantly assessed the situation. "We're just wasting time. Let's go."

"Good idea," the sergeant said. "You best stay away from that church," he called after us. "Don't you cause any trouble."

Backing out of the parking lot in the rain, Lacey hit a barricade. We climbed out to assess the damage. The rental car's left rear panel had folded like an accordion.

No damage to the barricade.

As we began to drive away, a young cop emerged from the station to flag us down.

We had to file an accident report, he said. He insisted, despite our arguments that we—actually the *News* corporate credit card—would reimburse the rental company for the damage.

In Miami, police don't even respond to accidents without serious injury or major property damage. Drivers can phone in accident reports later. But this was Minneapolis.

The young officer, rain dripping off his cap, was adamant. The desk sergeant watched from just inside the door. I wondered if this was his idea, to delay us, or document our identities in the event we created a disturbance, or worse, at the church.

I tried to call the church, hoping to reach a priest, a wedding planner, a custodian, anybody, but I had no cell signal. The battery was low. I plugged the adapter into the car's cigarette lighter. At least our crappy car had one of those.

The accident report took more than thirty minutes to complete. Then the officer wrote Lacey two tickets, one for careless driving, the other for damaging police property.

Outright lies. There was no damage to police property, not a scratch, not a smudge. Not fair. But would we be there to defend ourselves and dispute the charges in Minneapolis traffic court? They knew we wouldn't.

"There's still a chance," I said, as we finally drove away. "Some wedding ceremonies take more than an hour. And brides are often late. Really late. Latina brides in Miami sometimes keep their grooms waiting for two–three hours or more."

"Nancy is not Latina," he muttered.

"Maybe they started late because of the weather."

Lacey grunted. I got the impression he had stopped speaking to me.

"Seriously, I went to a Greek Orthodox wedding once. The ceremony took ninety minutes. The bride and groom wore crowns and marched around the church three times, I swear."

"Is Nancy Greek?"

"I doubt it."

At least he spoke, but his sidelong look was snide.

"If you hadn't hit that barricade, this wouldn't have happened."

"If you hadn't ticked off that desk sergeant—" He bit his lip. "Britt, it's just you and me. We're strangers here and at a big disadvantage. Let's not fight. If we don't work together, we've got nothing."

"You're right." I teared up and kissed his cheek. "I'm sorry. I think it's hormones."

* * *

The weather was pristine by the time we careened up to the Church of the Little Flower. Perfect wedding weather. Blue skies, puffy white clouds. The door to the beautiful church was open, the interior yawned empty, silent and sweet smelling. No one was there. Perhaps my message had reached the bride, giving her second thoughts, an epiphany, a gut feeling, cold feet, and the urge to run.

The evidence said otherwise. Rose petals and birdseed were everywhere, scattered about the church entrance, littering the flagstone path. Many brides use them now instead of rice, which can be harmful to wildlife. The trail of seeds and petals led into the parking lot.

It was as empty as the church.

"What's the address of the reception?" I asked Lacey, my voice shrill.

He murmured something I couldn't quite make out as I clambered back into the car.

"What?" I asked irritably.

"I said, I think we're out of gas."

CHAPTER EIGHTEEN

The names of the happy couple, MARSH AND NANCY LEE, blinked in lights on the marquee. The banquet hall resembled a Bavarian castle at the height of Oktoberfest. The parking lot was packed.

The wedding reception had been under way for hours by the time we arrived.

I wasn't exactly dressed for the occasion. Stiff from sitting so long, on planes, in airports, and then in the car, I felt painfully aware of my bloated belly, swollen feet, and crumpled appearance.

"You look nice," Lacey lied, trying to be kind as I attempted to drag a comb through my matted hair. It had finally dried, but the combination of rainwater and a cooler climate had produced a thick blob, resembling a cowlick, in front.

"First impressions are important," I said, still irritable, "especially if you want to appear credible. These people have to believe us."

Lacey hunted for a parking space.

My heart pounded. I was about to confront Marsh Holt, at last.

"Won't he be surprised to see me," I said grimly.

"Think he'll go postal?" Lacey looked worried.

"No way." I shook my head. "Cowards like him might drown a trusting woman or push her off a cliff, but not in front of eyewitnesses. He won't become violent in a crowd. What would he gain? He'd make himself look bad and us more believable. No, he'll stonewall, pretend he doesn't know us. He'll tell security we're wedding crashers and try to have us thrown out before we can ask questions. I wish Lottie was here to shoot his picture with the new bride. I'd like a complete set."

I painfully forced my feet into a pair of pumps and tried to smooth out the wrinkles in my no-longer-crisp maternity top. Both efforts were losing propositions.

Why worry? I thought. I'm not an invited guest, I'm a reporter chasing a story. That story is the light at the end of the tunnel, and I have tunnel vision. But normally I didn't look like this. I sighed. Would I ever look normal again?

"Ready?" Lacey watched me dab on lip gloss in an effort to mitigate the damage.

I nodded. "Here's the plan. He'll spot me right away. I stand out like a sore thumb. But he probably won't recognize you as quickly.

"So as soon as we're inside, I beeline right to him and start lobbing questions. Loudly, if I have to. I need a reaction from him, a few good quotes: denials or attempts to explain.

"Meanwhile, find the bride, unless she's standing right next to him. If she is, find her parents instead. Check the head table. Ask anybody, including the help. Everybody knows the father. He's the one writing the checks.

"Take her or her parents aside, explain in private who we are, why we're here, and why Nancy *cannot* leave with him. Here." I slid a color photo from my folder. "Show them their new son-in-law's wedding picture with Suzanne."

Lacey took the picture, his eyes lingering on Suzanne's face.

"Unless he has me thrown out," I went on, "I'll join you and the parents after the groom runs from my questions."

"What will you ask him?"

I shrugged. "Aren't you concerned about Nancy's safety, since none of your other brides survived the honeymoon?

"Do you remember Suzanne, Vanessa, Colleen, Rachel, Gloria, and Alice?

"Did you kill them?

"How rich has their life insurance made you?

"How is it that the *Calypso Dancer* has reappeared after you swore you saw it sink with Vanessa aboard?

"His answers, if any, should make good reading. And the nature of the questions should ensure Nancy's safety, should she be foolish enough to leave with him. Once he knows we know, he won't dare hurt her."

I slipped my notebook and pen into my pocket.

Lacey held my hand as we walked toward the reception hall. "Ready?"

"Let's do it."

The celebration—the music, singing, laughing, and dancing—swept over us as he pushed open the door.

The huge hall was full. A band played onstage as a man at the microphone crooned "You Are So Beautiful." Members of the wedding party were scattered like flowers among the crowd, their same-style gowns in shades ranging from lavender and amethyst to deep purple. Unlike any other bridesmaid's dresses I'd ever seen, they were stunning. Bevies of small boys in tiny tuxes chased adorable little flower girls in miniature bridesmaid gowns. They and the boys skidded, scrambled, and darted across the floor, shrieking and ducking among the dancers, caught up in that giddy hysteria that immediately precedes bumps, tears, and hurt feelings.

Glittery well-dressed guests partied, drank, and ate. The gigantic wedding cake had been cut. An entire layer of what was probably a six-tiered cake remained on a canopied table with silver servers, stacked dessert plates, and scattered rose petals. The rich dark chocolate-espresso cake was raspberry-filled and covered by thick buttercream frosting: spun sugar roses and tulips. The sight nearly brought tears to my eyes.

It took me a moment to discern what was missing from this picture. The goddamn groom; where was he? Did Marsh Holt see me waddle through the wide front door? Did he snatch up his bride and flee?

I scanned the crowd. The star of this event, the woman of the moment, the only female in a wedding gown, should be easy to spot. No sign of her.

I caught Lacey's eye from across the room. He shrugged. He hadn't seen them either.

I mingled, craned my neck, ignored curious stares. The newlyweds had to be elsewhere on the premises, posing for pictures in front of a phony fountain or flower garden.

"Have you seen the bride and groom?" I asked an older couple strolling hand in hand off the dance floor.

"They're gone. They had a plane to catch." She smiled and checked her watch. "They're off on their honeymoon."

"Are you sure?" My knees nearly buckled.

She saw my stricken expression.

"Did you miss seeing them?" she asked sympathetically.

"We tried to make it in time," I croaked, suddenly cold, hoarse, and on the verge of tears. "Storms diverted our flight so we had to drive. We've been driving all day."

"You poor thing," she said warmly. She took my hand and led me to her table. "Nancy Lee will understand. Sit down. Relax. Eat something. Have some cake. Enjoy what's left of the party."

She didn't need to invite me twice. My feet throbbed. It felt as though I were walking on swollen logs. I should never have forced on my shoes. How would I get them off? I dropped heavily into a chair at her table. Her name was Sophie and she introduced me to her husband.

The lace-covered table was bright with silver flowers and crystal, and littered with bridal favors, instant photos of the bridal couple. I glommed a few of the best. Marsh Holt, aglow and happy in well-tailored black tie, looked even more handsome without the sunburn and the sad, heartbroken eyes.

I had hors d'oeuvres in each hand and my new friend, Sophie, had gone off to procure me a piece of the wedding cake when Lacey appeared.

"You were supposed to back me up." His usually placid gray eyes sparked accusingly.

"You've got to taste this." I moaned in ecstasy.

Crisp apples had been scooped into perfect little globes that arrived on toothpicks, accompanied by three ramekins. One contained a warm golden caramel sauce, the second was shredded coconut, and the third finely chopped peanuts.

"Here's what you do." I demonstrated the technique I had quickly mastered. "First, dip the apple in the caramel, then in the coconut, and last the peanuts. How good is that?"

He chewed thoughtfully, nodding his head.

"Sophie said the entire menu is made up of Nancy Lee's recipes. She's writing a cookbook."

"Sophie?"

I nodded in her direction. She waved back from the cake table as she maneuvered a giant slice with a big spun sugar rose onto a tiny cake plate.

I licked my lips in anticipation and smiled back gratefully.

"What happened?" I asked Lacey.

"Gone," he said, eyes hollow. "The bride and groom left more than an hour ago."

"I knew that."

He watched me swirl another crisp apple globe in the golden caramel sauce.

"This isn't the real me," I said, self-consciously wiping the sweet sauce off my chin. "Believe me, I've never been like this before. I have a license to eat."

"Maybe it should be suspended," he said, lips tight. "I tried to talk to the parents. The father blew me off, said he has too much to do and I'll have to wait my turn. He's settling up with the caterers, the band, the bartenders, the photographers, and the parking valets. His wife is indisposed, he said, in a private room upstairs. She drank champagne all day to celebrate. Now she's on a crying jag, hysterical because her little girl got married."

Lacey looked bewildered.

"Figures." I smiled adoringly at Sophie as she slid the cake plate in front of me.

"I brought a big piece for your husband too," she said. "I saw him join you."

I thanked her and checked my watch. "The honeymooners are already in the air," I told Lacey. "Sophie says they caught a ten o'clock flight."

She nodded and filled us in on their plans. The newlyweds had embarked upon a romantic adventure, alone in a remote cabin where they could hike, sightsee, and experience Mother Nature's most romantic phenomenon. The happy couple was en route to Fairbanks to see the salmon swim upstream to spawn.

Fairbanks, Alaska.

"Nancy's so-o-o creative," Sophie cooed. "Another Martha Stewart. She plans to do an entire show on it when they get back. On the salmon, I mean. Not the honeymoon, of course." She looked toward the dance floor and giggled like a schoolgirl. Her frisky husband, who'd been chatting with friends at another table, was doing a solo samba, headed her way. She opened her arms, he whisked her from her chair, and they were off to the dance floor.

"Aren't they cute?" I said, watching them twitch their hips and hug. "Married thirty-two years. He was Nancy Lee's pediatrician."

"Hope we last that long." He winked. "We already fight like a married couple."

"Sorry I didn't correct her when she called you my husband, but she was so nice that I didn't want her to be disillusioned by the fact that we're not married, to each other or to anybody else."

"Fine by me." He shrugged. "But I'm not paying child support."

It was the first laugh we'd shared all day.

"We have reason, good reason, to believe that your daughter, Nancy Lee, is in danger. We tried to reach her before the wedding, but we were too late."

The father of the bride wagged his finger at me.

"Young lady, you must be the one who called my home today. My niece, Marisa, answered. She told us what you said. It upset my wife, one of the reasons she's upstairs in her current state, something else I have to deal with now. All I can say for sure is that you will not spoil our Nancy's honeymoon. I won't allow it. She deserves this happiness. Whatever happens after, we can take care of.

"My daughter, God bless her, is an achiever, a workaholic. She never stops. We were afraid she would never settle down, never give us the grandchildren we dearly want. Our new son-in-law is a blessing from God. The son we never had."

The familiar words chilled my heart.

"I won't listen to any talk against him, no matter what happened in the past between the two of you. He made his choice."

I insisted I had not come to claim paternity, and that Marsh Holt was not my baby's father. "That's utterly ridiculous," I said.

"Good," he said. "Keep saying that."

We showed him wedding pictures: Marsh Holt with Vanessa, Marsh Holt with Suzanne.

He stared at them uncertainly for a moment, then smiled triumphantly. "Computers!" he announced. "That's what people do with computers today. You see it on the Internet all the time. Pictures of

JFK playing poker with Lee Harvey Oswald, Marilyn Monroe sitting on Joseph Stalin's lap. People with computers can insert anybody into a picture with somebody else. These mean nothing; Nancy Lee's happiness means everything. Leave her alone."

No point in arguing with him or his hysterical wife, who wandered out of hiding long enough to see us deep in conversation with her husband in the now shadowy and nearly empty hall. She stared at me, burst into tears, and ran back upstairs.

Before I left, I wrote the Hansens' Boston telephone number on my card and pressed it into the father's sweaty hands. "Please call these people," I said earnestly. "It's important."

We went to a brightly lit all-night diner for coffee and found a booth.

"They're in denial," I told Lacey. "I think they know something is wrong with the man. They just don't realize how serious it is."

We studied the instant photos of Nancy Lee Holt and her new husband.

Nancy, somewhat older than the others, wasn't at all what I expected. But none of Holt's brides were clones.

Nancy's mouth, her smile, her teeth, were all big and very white, perfect for television. She had the hungry look of a woman focused on food, its origins, its character, how to stalk, prepare—and devour it. She appeared to have never missed a meal. She was solidly built and buxom, with ample hips ideal for childbearing, should she live that long.

Unlike the serial killers who stalk look-alike victims to fulfill dark fantasies, each victim Holt selected was different. What mattered most to him was not that they all had pierced ears and long brown hair worn straight and parted in the middle, but that each was ambitious, successful—and insurable. His were not the usual obsessive sexual fantasies. Marsh Holt was all about greed and ego.

What he did share in common with other serial killers was that he depersonalized his victims. Holt saw them as worthless objects who deserved the fate he meted out to them.

My meat-loaf special arrived, and I shoved the pictures aside.

Lacey sipped his coffee, red-eyed and exhausted. "What do we do now?" he asked, as I dug into my mashed potatoes.

"Find a place to sleep," I said, buttering a roll. "Preferably a single room with twin beds. We have to go easy on travel expenses."

He nodded and yawned. "What then?"

"We buy warm jackets and socks, I guess."

"What is the temperature in Fairbanks this time of year?"

"I don't know," I said, as I poured more gravy, "but we're about to find out."

CHAPTER NINETEEN

Eventually, I reached an FBI agent after calling repeatedly during the night. We did the dance. I pushed, he stayed skeptical. I persuaded, he sounded preoccupied. I cajoled, he remained aloof. I dropped the names of several agents I knew in Miami.

"Please, give one of them a call. Ask about me, my reputation, my credibility. A woman is in mortal danger. Her new bridegroom is a serial killer. I am so sure of it that I'm flying to Fairbanks to warn her. He takes these women across state lines and kills them, each one in a different jurisdiction. Surely this is an FBI case."

He called back midmorning to say that an agent would be available to meet with me in Fairbanks the following day.

Hallelujah! I thought. Progress at last. With the FBI involved, the local police would surely cooperate.

I resisted my initial urge to share the good news with Fred. I was already in trouble. I felt like a fugitive on the lam. I hadn't stayed in touch as promised. I'd ignored his calls and e-mails. I had to; otherwise I'd have to explain where I was and where I was going. The man was my boss; he could say no. The *News* was funding all this. Being denied permission would leave me in an untenable position. Instead, I had to duck, run, do what I had to do, and face the music later. This was a great story. Do it right, I told myself, and you'll still have a job.

Unlike me, Lacey dutifully answered his cell phone; his boss was in a state of high anxiety. The annual meeting with major clients, an account for which Lacey was responsible, was thirty-six hours away. Because of me, Lacey had neither completed his presentation nor briefed colleagues who might save the day in his absence. Big deal, big bucks, big crisis. Crunch time; his job was at stake.

"Look," he said. "I'll fly home today, work like hell on the plane, get it over with, then hop the next flight back up to meet you. I'm sorry, Britt, I don't know how else to handle it. I can't afford to be out of work right now."

"No sweat," I said. "You don't need to come to Alaska. While the FBI and the local cops protect Nancy, I'll get everything I'm looking for, wrap up my reporting, and go back to Miami."

I tousled his hair and hugged him goodbye at the airport. Though I'm not quite a decade older, I felt almost maternal toward him.

"I'm letting you down," he murmured, his gray eyes misty.

"Not. Are you joking? You've gone way above and beyond. I couldn't be more grateful, couldn't have come this far without you. I'll keep you posted on everything."

That sad beautiful boy turned to stride down the secured concourse and then hesitated and looked back, as though changing his mind.

I waved him on. "Go! Go!"

He smiled and went.

The *Pioneer Press* weather page listed the nighttime low in Fairbanks as 45 degrees. Typographical error, I was sure. After all, this was almost summer. Nonetheless, my memory bank began to spit out depressing flashbacks of journalism school. The subject excited and stimulated me. But the school was in Chicago, home of pallid skies, frigid winds, and ice-slick sidewalks. I had been miserably cold, depressed, and homesick for Miami.

My new summery maternity attire and pink flip-flops were all I had with me. So I bought a fuzzy sweater, warm socks, a jacket, big ugly boots, and a flannel nightgown I would never wear in Miami.

I used the *News* credit card, ate a good dinner, went to bed early, then took off for Alaska alone, first thing in the morning.

The flight took eight hours, with a refueling stop in Seattle. For Pete's sake, I thought impatiently, people can fly to Europe in eight hours.

The surrounding skies looked vacant, air traffic sparse. Fellow passengers cheerfully assured me that our late arrival was not unusual; the airline holds the nation's worst record for on-time arrivals.

When we disembarked in Fairbanks, the air was cool and crisp, chilly actually. My sinuses ached.

I left a message for FBI Agent Kyle Goddard, saying I'd arrived. We were to meet at police headquarters in an hour. I stowed my luggage in an airport locker and took only my laptop.

The taxi, an older-model pickup truck, dropped me off at police headquarters, a simple cinder-block and concrete building.

The secretary said the chief expected me, and it would be just a few minutes. I worked on my laptop as the wait stretched into an hour. Finally I was ushered into his office.

The chief sat alone, at his desk.

"Agent Goddard hasn't arrived?" I blurted, stating the obvious.

The chief was apologetic. Agent Goddard, he said, would not be joining us.

"But I was told last night that he'd be here. We had an appointment."

"He was called away on a priority matter," the chief said.

"Are you sure?" Frustrated and furious, I felt betrayed by the feds.

"A matter of national security." The chief looked serious.

"Here? What sort of matter—has something happened?" For a news junkie, I was totally out of the loop. Hadn't even heard a radio news report. For all I knew, North Korea had launched a missile or the Russians had crossed the Bering Strait.

"Off the record?" His dark eyes darted around the room, as though secret spy microphones might eavesdrop. "Terrorism."

Was this small-town police chief pulling a snow job? "I wasn't aware that Fairbanks, Alaska, might be a terrorist target."

"Then you're uninformed," the chief said. "The FBI's top terror suspects are known to be active in this area."

"Al-Qaeda?" What on earth was he talking about? My back ached from sitting so long on the uncomfortable wooden chair in his chilly outer office.

"Domestic terrorism." He peered sternly at me over his spectacles. "The ELF and the ALF are top priority."

"Ecoterrorists, who protest for animal rights and the environment?"

He nodded gravely.

"As far as I know, they've never killed or injured anyone." I felt peevish, uncomfortable, and irritated. "Aren't they more like vandals with a cause?" I shifted uneasily in my chair as the baby practiced logrolling on my internal organs. "Nancy Lee Chastain Holt, the woman whose safety is in question, has no protestors to protect her. And she's in a helluva lot more imminent danger than a herd of caribou. FBI priorities seem a bit askew."

He took exception. "Ecoterrorists have become increasingly dangerous," he said, with solemn gravity. "They recruit young people, encourage violence, teach them bomb building and how to torch buildings. Property damage from their arson alone amounts to tens of millions of dollars annually—"

Whoa, I thought. We'd veered way off track. If the FBI was MIA, this man could be my only ally.

"I had no idea," I said, feigning interest. "Amazing. We haven't experienced much environmental terrorism back in South Florida."

Because developers rule and there's little left to protect, I thought.

Crossing my legs demurely at the ankles, I listened intently and soon learned more than I'd ever wanted to know about the topic. Eventually the chief paused for breath and I seized the moment to gracefully steer our conversation back to Marsh Holt and his endangered bride.

Too late. The damage was done.

"I'm surprised that your newspaper let you travel all this distance alone." His eyes dropped to my round belly.

"My editors believe in woman power," I lied cheerfully.

A patrol car would stop by to check on Mrs. Holt's welfare. That was the most he would agree to do.

Where was the stoic patience I can usually muster when dealing with incompetent bureaucrats and their inflated egos? I wanted to scream and shout epithets, pound his desk with my fists, and indulge in a hot fudge sundae, maybe two. Instead, I politely asked to accompany the patrolmen in order to quell my fears about the bride's safety and, if possible, ask Holt a few questions, so I could wrap up my reporting and go home.

The chief considered this for a moment and then agreed, with a word of warning. "No one can or will force this man to speak to you," he said. "Nobody has to talk to a reporter. These people are on their honeymoon; it would certainly seem more appropriate to approach them at a later date."

"That's my point, Chief. Later may be too late for her. Dead is forever."

I sat alone, like a prisoner, in the backseat of the patrol car. The officers, both young and husky, one short, the other tall, discussed the possibility of snow. There had been flurries two weeks earlier.

"Miami?" one asked, turning earnestly to me. "How can you live down there?"

I laughed. "I was wondering how you can live up here."

"We hear Miami's not part of the USA anymore," the driver said.

"Funny," I said good-naturedly. "Most Miamians are probably unaware that Alaska is part of the USA. Seriously."

"Miami's 'bout as far south as you can go," the driver commented, turning uphill, off the main road and onto a narrow, unpaved, tree-lined dirt road.

"Hell, no," his partner said. "Southern Cal is further south."

"No, it isn't," I chimed in. "North Florida is further south than southern California."

"Say again?"

"It's true. Tallahassee, our state capital in North Florida, is south of Tijuana."

"No way," the second cop said.

"Check it out."

The Holts' rustic cabin hideaway brought Abraham Lincoln to mind. But this was larger than Honest Abe's boyhood home, with horizontal logs on the outside and a corrugated metal roof. No other structure was in sight, only snow-capped mountains in the distance, virgin forests, and rushing streams. Fir, spruce, and oak trees towered beneath a chilly but breathtaking azure sky. Bright yellow dandelions sprouted everywhere, along with a native plant as red as flame. The cops called it fireweed. In the past, when I thought of Alaska, which wasn't often, I had pictured Eskimos and sled dogs. Instead, a shiny black Range Rover, probably rented, stood out front.

We crunched to a stop in the gravel driveway. One of the cops opened the car door for me and I followed them up the front steps. The taller of the two rapped on the rough-hewn front door. No answer.

"Nobody home," the other said, turning as if to go.

The first cop knocked again. "Give 'em a minute. They're on their honeymoon, remember?" He snickered. "Give 'em a chance to climb outa the rack."

He rapped a third time. No sound inside.

My heart felt as cold as my feet. Were we too late? I'd risked my job, tried so hard. Bad news would be a bitter pill to swallow.

The high-pitched bray of a woman's laughter resounded from a wooded path behind the cabin.

We all turned as the newlyweds emerged from the brush hand in hand, faces pink from exertion. They wore handsome hiking boots and matching ski sweaters. Her giggle was a rich deep-throated gurgle that sounded almost theatrical.

Her television-personality laugh? I wondered.

They looked startled at the police car out front and us on the porch and approached, no longer laughing. "Is there a problem, Officers?" Holt asked.

He and I made eye contact. The slick, sick son of a bitch never flinched. He was good, really good. He held the arm of his sturdy-looking bride protectively, as though she were a precious and fragile creature.

"There wasn't a fire?" she cried, melodramatically clutching her heart.

"No, ma'am, there wasn't."

Her ample bosom heaved in an exaggerated sigh of relief. "When I saw you I thought for sure I'd left the stove on," she babbled. "Sometimes when you're happy"—she coyly batted her eyelashes up at her new husband—"you grow careless about the mundane little everyday . . ." She had focused on me, eyes becoming frosty as she gave me the once-over.

"Is that her?" She turned to her husband.

He nodded, sadly. "Hello, Britt," he said, resignation in his voice.

I ignored him and spoke to her. "I'm so glad you're all right." I stepped forward. "I hope I can call you Nancy. My name is Britt—"

"I know who you are." Her cold eyes narrowed.

What has he told her? I wondered.

"This young lady's concerned about your welfare," the tall police officer said. "She's afraid you might have a problem."

She turned to her husband, her look a question. He smiled reassuringly, and in a microsecond she returned his smile. They locked arms in mutual support as she turned earnestly to the officers.

"We just saw a moose, only five minutes from our front door," she said, after a pause. "We've seen deer, a bobcat, and foxes. Yesterday we watched pink salmon spawn. The female releases her eggs, the male fertilizes them, and they both die within two weeks. Did you know that?"

"Yes, ma'am," one of the officers said uncomfortably, as we all stood on the creaky front porch.

"Heaven," she said dramatically. "It's been heaven, more romantic than even I could imagine, and I have quite an imagination." She winked slyly at her husband and then dismissed me with a disdainful smirk. "I'm so happy." She gazed adoringly at Marsh Holt. "We couldn't be happier."

He nodded in agreement.

"But now"—her voice rose, taking on an unpleasantly shrill edge—"an obsessed woman who has stalked my husband for years has followed us here to ruin everything."

She flung herself into a porch chair and began to shed noisy tears, punctuated by snorts, snuffles, and ragged gasps.

"Not true," I said calmly. "The man is lying to you. I only met him once, in Miami."

The two cops shared an *Aha!* moment and exchanged I-told-you-so expressions.

"Look, Nancy, I'm tired. I've traveled nearly four thousand miles to warn you. The least you can do is listen. Can I talk to you alone for a moment?"

"There's only one person I want to be alone with," she said, raising her tearstained face to her husband. He smooched it tenderly.

I wanted to gag. For Pete's sake! I thought, and longed to shake her. "Marshall," I said, "do you remember Vanessa, Suzanne, Rachel, and Colleen? What about Gloria? And Alice?"

He sighed and shook his head, wearing the expression of a weary and beleaguered man.

Nancy was staring speculatively at my belly.

"I told you, sweetheart." He reached confidently for her hand. "I have nothing to do with that. Britt lives in a fantasy world. There's been nothing between us since high school."

He'd been expecting me. That much was clear.

His eyes roved out past the police car, beyond the narrow unpaved road, searching. He had obviously expected two of us. Nancy's parents had blown the whistle. They had interrupted their little girl's romantic idyll to tip off the newlyweds after all.

"Shouldn't you be someplace else?" Nancy asked sharply, with a disgusted little shudder. "Lamaze class, perhaps? In a straitjacket, or a nice jail cell?"

"Nancy, think about it," I urged. "You are not safe alone here with him."

"Officers!" she bleated. "Doesn't the law protect people from stalkers?" Taking an angry step forward, she pointed a manicured index finger at my heart like a gun. "Keep her away from us!"

"In other words, ma'am," the shorter cop said, "you're saying you don't want to be rescued."

"Told ya," the other cop muttered.

"Let's go." The first cop firmly took my arm. My pen dropped from my hand and vanished into the thick grass below as he led me down the front steps.

"Ask him to tell you about Vanessa, Colleen, Rachel, Gloria, Alice, and Suzanne," I called over my shoulder. "They married him too. And they all died on their honeymoons."

Marsh Holt thanked the officers and wrapped his arms around his bride. She hugged him back so hard they nearly toppled off the porch.

* * *

They told me to get out of town and warned me not to go within a mile of the honeymooners. If I contacted Marsh Holt or his bride again, I'd be arrested, the cops said.

"Mess with them again and we put your ass in jail," the tall one said succinctly.

Apparently it was his partner's turn to play good cop. "Look, lady," he said. "We understand that sometimes people become obsessed with another person who doesn't . . . uh, return those feelings. But you have to understand that you can't force a person to want you."

And you can't save someone who refuses to be rescued, I thought mournfully.

"Life doesn't work that way," he went on. "Suck it up, go home, and get yourself some help."

He spoke slowly and distinctly, the way one speaks to an unruly child, a misbehaving dog, or a deranged adult.

Humiliated and furious, I let them put me in a cab to the airport. Once there, I dragged my suitcase from the locker, rented a car, found a room at a small local hotel, and beelined back to the Holts' cabin.

It felt late, but it never grew dark. A strange sun never crossed the sky; the dusky orb slowly circled east to north instead, literally rolling around the horizon of this strange and surreal world. I was Alice down the rabbit hole. Clutching the banister, I dragged myself up the front steps one at a time, banged on the door, and turned the knob. The door swung open.

Nancy puttered at a wood-burning stove, her back to me, a long spoon in her right hand. She wore a frilly apron and little else. An enticing aroma came from a big iron skillet simmering over a low flame. Logs crackled in the fireplace. A champagne bottle sat in an ice bucket next to an intimate table set for two. The scene was warm, inviting, and romantic.

The shortie nightgown under Nancy's frilly apron exposed dimpled thighs. Dimples in the wrong place, I noted mean-spiritedly. Who, I wondered, packs aprons in their trousseau? Domestic divas, that's who.

"Bonjour, sweet face."

She whirled in a giddy impromtu pirouette, lips shiny with raspberry-colored gloss, her expression coy. No sign of the groom. My heart leaped. This, I hoped, was our chance to speak alone.

"Hello, Nancy."

She howled like a banshee, flung herself back against the pine wall, pointed her long spoon at me, and screamed again. The woman had the lungs of a bagpipe player.

"Stop it!" I pleaded. "Don't do that. Listen to me."

Marsh Holt burst through the door like gangbusters. Exactly what I didn't need. The firewood he carried clattered to the floor.

"What the hell are you doing to my wife?" he demanded.

I sighed.

"Marsh! Thank God! She sneaked up behind me! Find a man of your own!" she screamed, still waving the spoon like a weapon. "Leave him alone! He's taken! Taken! Leave us alone!"

Her high-pitched screeches literally hurt my ears.

The patrol car arrived quickly. You would think the police would have better things to do. These two cops were strangers but had obviously been filled in on the obsessive stalker. Me.

"You were warned," one said.

"Don't worry, folks," the other assured the newlyweds. "We'll take it from here."

Marsh Holt comforted his distraught wife, now wearing a terry-cloth robe over her Victoria's Secret ensemble. He stroked her hair tenderly and glared at me.

"She won't bother you again," the cop promised.

"That's what they told us this afternoon." Holt sounded indignant. Mr. John Q. Public, taxpayer and good citizen, rightfully upset by the dubious quality of local law enforcement. He played the role well.

I rolled my eyes.

They assured him that this time I was really in trouble.

Nancy's malevolent mascara-smeared left eye peeped out at me from her husband's manly chest.

"He'll try to kill you," I warned, trying to stay calm. "At least six other women died accidentally when they were with him." I intended to form finger quotes around the word *accidentally* but was thwarted by an officer who seized the moment to cuff my wrist.

"Sure, and he's Jack the Ripper, Son of Sam, and the Zodiac Killer too," the cop said, before advising me of my rights. "He's been a bad, bad boy." He winked at Marsh Holt.

Again, I sat alone in the backseat of the police car, like a prisoner. But this time I *was* a prisoner.

"Nobody likes to put a pregnant woman in jail," the arresting officer informed me, as a female cop patted me down and removed my wristwatch.

She placed her hand on my stomach, and the baby gave it a few swift kicks. "Oh, my," she said, cheerfully assuring them that I was, indeed, pregnant.

"Some people never learn. You were warned," the other cop repeated.

You were warned, I thought. They should write that on my tombstone.

I was desperate enough to eat the bologna sandwich they gave me and drink their watery coffee.

My cell's only positive feature was the layout. The toilet stood only a few convenient feet from my cot. And since it never grew dark, I didn't have to grope about trying to find it during the night. The negative was that it became really, really cold. My fingers and toes and the exposed skin of my face—even my bones—felt painfully cold, in spite of the blanket they gave me.

They hauled me into municipal court first thing in the morning. At least I thought it was the morning. It was difficult to tell whether it was 9 A.M. or 9 P.M. The meal at the jail, another bologna sandwich and more watery coffee, offered no clue. It might have been breakfast, lunch, or dinner. The sky looked no different. The temperature had skidded down to a tooth-chattering 35 degrees. "It's the williwaw," a jailer told me, explaining that was the name of a strong cold wind.

It had to be morning, I finally decided, unless this was night court.

All of us lawbreakers sat in an empty jury box waiting for our cases to be called.

"Heard about chu," whispered the prisoner next to me, a Native American with thick black eye makeup, big hoop earrings, and a leather biker's jacket. "You go, girl. Kick his worthless butt. Squeeze him for child support every day for the resta his no-good life. Good for you. But today," she said, wrinkling her nose sweetly, "play nice. Say whatever they wanna hear and get your ass outa here. Jail is no place to birth a baby."

"You are absolutely right," I said. "Thank you."

The judge, the jailers, even the court clerk, a chubby motherly type, looked troubled to see me. But none were as troubled as I. My back pains were more intense, my legs were stiff, my feet hurt, and I was desperately hungry—hungry for Miami, its warmth, its food, its Cuban coffee, and the people I loved.

My public defender introduced herself five minutes before my case was called. She told me that the police had tried to verify my story, that I was on assignment for the *Miami News*. The editor they had spoken to on the city desk overnight was surprised and dismayed to hear I was in Alaska, much less behind bars. She had disavowed knowledge of any assignment. According to her, I had failed to show up for work days ago, without explanation. I was AWOL. Gretchen, the editor from hell, I thought. It had to be. Who else? She got me.

I saw I was outnumbered and caved.

"Your Honor," I said, "I apologize for my mistakes and deeply regret any trouble I've caused. Hormones may have something to do with it. All I want is to go home to Miami as soon as possible. I'm not feeling well and it would be extremely inconvenient to give birth here, thousands of miles from my obstetrician. I don't wish to be a burden on your state."

I hated myself. Have you no scruples? I wondered, as I used the baby excuse.

The prosecutor scanned the small courtroom. "The complainants, visitors from Minneapolis, here on their honeymoon, don't appear to be present, Your Honor."

The judge, an older fatherly type, gazed down kindly at me from the bench. "I'll make you an offer, young lady. I'll sentence you to time served, without an adjudication of guilt, *if* you promise to board the next flight out. Go home and get yourself some help. It's never too late to turn your life around."

"Yes, sir, I promise," I lied. "Thank you, Your Honor."

The prisoner in the black eye makeup and leather jacket smiled and gave me a thumbs-up.

My rental car had been towed away from the cabin by the police, so I took a taxi back to my hotel. I yearned for a warm nap, hot soup, and a reconnect to reality, but the desk clerk said I had a problem: my credit card.

I asked him to swipe it again. He did. It came up canceled.

"Give me a minute," I said confidently, "and I'll take care of it." I collapsed into a lobby chair and tried to think.

I called Fred at the *News*.

"You canceled the credit card," I said accusingly.

"Thought that might get your attention," he said dryly. "Nothing else did. I take it you have a ticket home."

"Yes," I said. "I bought an open-ended round-trip back."

"Use it," he said grimly. "When you left here for Arizona you were told to check in daily. Yet we had no idea where you were until we heard you were in police custody in Fairbanks, Alaska."

"Fred," I said breathlessly, "listen. I am not the sportswriter you sent to the Super Bowl two years ago, the one who partied all night, passed out, and didn't wake up until after the game. Or Danny Jacobs, the reporter sent to Vegas to cover the world heavyweight championship fight. He wined and dined a showgirl and bought her an engagement ring, all with the *News* credit card, while you, his wife, and three kids all thought he was working. I am not like them. I'm pursuing a once-in-a-lifetime story. Marsh Holt is here now, with a new bride, a Minneapolis TV personality, if you can believe that. I'm working every minute."

"I don't doubt that, Britt, but I'm taking heat from the people upstairs. There is growing concern that you may well become a major liability, that you weren't ready to come back to work, and that I used faulty judgment. Lord knows, I fought for you, balls to the wall. But it's a no-win battle when you take off like a runaway freight train, fail to keep us informed, and still expect our support."

"Two more days, Fred. Just give me two more days." I clutched the phone like a lifeline. "Reactivate the credit card," I pleaded, "so I can wrap it up here."

"I can't do that, Britt. Come back and we'll talk."

"Look. I was afraid if I mentioned coming to Alaska you'd say no," I confessed.

"You were right."

See, I thought. I knew it. I just knew it.

"I wish I *was* in Miami," I blurted. "More than anything. I'm lonely, broke, and cold as hell, but I can't walk away from the story now."

"I hope to God you're taking care of yourself." His voice softened. "You sound terrible. But my ass is on the line too. Mark Seybold has advised the publisher to rein you in. Period. Anybody who pays a lawyer for advice is a fool not to take it, and the publisher's no fool. I don't know what else to tell you. You're like a pit bull, Britt. You hang on. And never let go. That's what makes you such a good reporter. But there comes a time in life when one has to let go. This is that time. I'll see you in my office. Soon, I hope, for your sake. Sorry."

The desk clerk stared, watching me balefully from behind the counter.

I cheerfully signaled that I needed one more minute and punched in another number.

"Holy shit, Britt," John Lacey murmured, when I filled him in.

"I need help, Lacey. I'm not sure what to do. I can't leave because when Holt hits the wind, he's gone. Next time you can bet he won't be so easy to find."

I began to cough. What new hell is this? I wondered. Fred was right, I realized. I sounded terrible and felt worse, achy and congested, probably from my night in that cold cell with only a thin blanket.

"I was wrong about one thing," I croaked. "I came here with three major goals: to keep Nancy alive, expose Marsh Holt, and finish my story. I even pissed off the local police chief by insisting that Nancy's life was more important than a herd of caribou. After meeting her, I owe the caribou an apology."

"Two out of three ain't bad." I heard the smile in Lacey's voice. "At least you still have your sense of humor."

"She and Holt deserve each other," I muttered miserably.

"First," he said, "let me talk to the goddamn desk clerk. I'll give him my credit card number to cover your room, and I'll call you there in twenty minutes."

"I'll pay you back," I swore, my throat raspy.

Twenty-three minutes later, the phone rang in my room.

"I'll see you tomorrow," Lacey said. "I just made a reservation. Sit tight. Order room service. Don't leave your room until I get there. Don't answer the door unless it's me. I talked to a friend of mine who went to law school. He says that if the judge meant what he said, they could arrest you for just being on the street."

"Okay," I said numbly. "I'll wait for you."

I checked my e-mail and the voice messages on my cell phone. Most were those I'd ignored from Fred as he asked, urged, then demanded that I get back to him. Why didn't I listen?

You were warned, I thought.

Feverish and exhausted, I ordered hot soup and crisp toast. I'd drift off but kept waking up, wondering how long I'd slept. Four hours or sixteen? Was this day or night? A.M. or P.M.? Neither my watch nor my travel alarm could tell me.

Was the sun rising or setting? I staggered to the window several times to search the sky. Once I thought I saw the Southern Cross and was grateful, knowing it would guide me safely home. But then I realized I couldn't have seen it in this place. It isn't visible north of Miami. I must have been dreaming or hallucinating.

The sky was blank, no stars at all. It never got dark enough. How did people here ever get their bearings?

An aberrant crescent moon hung ramrod straight in the eerie twilight, or was it dawn? I had never seen the moon in such an odd position before.

I asked Lucy, the pale and quiet dark-haired young woman who brought my soup, what it's like to live here in the winter.

"Dark," she said softly. "I hate waking up in the morning and going to work when it's so dark. The sun rises around noon and sets three hours later."

I imagined police patrolling a midnight shift that lasted twenty-one hours.

"We have something in common with Florida," she told me shyly. "We have our own little Cape Canaveral. They launch rockets into the Northern Lights."

"Why?" I sat up in bed, sipping soup from a mug.

"To learn more about them. For better insight into the relationship between the earth and the sun."

"What do the Northern Lights look like?"

She hesitated. "Imagine translucent fabric curtains whipping back and forth across the sky."

I couldn't.

Lucy, a native of Alaska, had spent her childhood living above a little outpost grocery store owned by her parents. Often, she told me, they'd be awakened at 3 A.M. by would-be customers pounding on their door, tourists who thought it was three o'clock in the afternoon.

Time is slippery when you are feverish, half dreaming, and disoriented. I slept erratically, kept ordering soup. I waited for days, but Lacey never came.

I left message after message for Detective Sam Stone in Miami, hoping he had checked out the scuba-diving death of Gloria Weatherholt. But he was never there, and no one could tell me when he would be.

Lacey had forgotten me, I realized, and I finally resigned myself to confinement in that small room forever.

When my phone finally rang, I couldn't find it. I fumbled about among the blankets and sheets, looking for it, then answered wanly.

"Pack up," Lacey said. "Get ready to check out, I'll pick you up in half an hour."

"Who is this?" I yawned and blinked.

"Lacey. What's wrong, Britt?"

"Where are you? Why didn't you ever come?" I complained drowsily.

"I did. I'm here."

"But it's been four or five days."

"We talked yesterday, Britt. Are you all right? You sound funny."

As though in a dream, I dragged myself out of bed, took a shower, packed my things, and waited until he called from the lobby.

Lacey pulled the car, a rented Ford Explorer, up close to the lobby door, carried out my bag, and hurriedly helped me into the rental.

"I didn't want to risk having a cop spot you from a passing patrol car. You sure you're okay? You don't look so good."

"Thank you," I murmured. "Nice to see you again too."

He felt my forehead. "Shit. You have a fever."

"I'm okay. I just want to finish my story and go home."

"What more do you need?"

"Is Nancy still alive?" I mumbled. Why couldn't I stop yawning?

"We'll know soon." He swerved onto the rutted unpaved road to the honeymoon cabin.

CHAPTER TWENTY

"Wait!" I sat up straight. "We can't go *there*," I said. "They'll call the law."

"We're not visiting them—yet," he said. "We're just driving by. We're their new neighbors."

I stared at him in disbelief.

He smiled. "There was a vacancy, the cabin closest to them, not quite a mile away. It's rented to Mr. and Mrs. John Lacey. I thought it best not to drop your name. Watch it, I think we're passing their place right now."

"That's it." I scrunched down in my seat.

"Nobody around," he reported. "There's a black Range Rover out front."

"That's the car they've been using."

"The next left should take us to our place," he said, consulting a map.

The engine strained, climbing higher and higher up the mountain. There seemed to be only woods and wilderness until another rustic cabin came into view.

"Bingo," Lacey said. "We're home."

He had grocery bags stashed in the back of the Ford. The rental agent had stopped by earlier to prepare the place. Flames crackled and sputtered in the fireplace. The cabin was warm, cozy, and welcoming.

"Thanks, Lacey. Remember, I'm running a tab. Save your receipts. I'll pay you back. How did you afford this?"

"Maxed out my credit cards." He shrugged.

"Sorry."

"It'll be worth it," he said, "to see that bastard's picture in the paper, to see him behind bars for life—or, better yet, in the ground. If not for you, Britt, I wouldn't have known what really happened. There never would have been justice for Suzanne."

Without the cover of darkness, it would be tricky to surveil Holt's cabin.

"I thought we'd stay in touch by cell phone and work in shifts, so if he took Nancy somewhere, we could follow them. If the situation started to look dangerous, we could raise hell, make a lot of noise, and call the cops. But I don't think you're up to it."

"I am," I assured him. "Don't worry, I've caught my second wind."

He nodded, but his eyes remained concerned. "If I can catch Nancy alone, I'll try to get through to her," he said. "I brought some pictures of Suzanne to show her."

"Been there, done that. It didn't work." I shook my head. "She's smitten. And what honeymooner is ever alone long enough to listen to reason?"

"Don't know," he said sadly. "I've never been one."

"Me either," I said.

He cooked hamburgers and vegetables and insisted I eat.

I just picked at the food, no longer the ravenous chowhound I'd been for months. I cleared the dishes and Lacey left on a "recon mission" to check out Holt's cabin. He returned, excited, after forty-five minutes.

"They're home," he said. "I looked in a window. They were eating dinner. Looked romantic, like they're in for the evening, but he could be planning anything."

"You shouldn't have gotten that close. What if he caught you?"

Lacey ignored the question. He looked agitated, full of restless energy and fearful possibilities. "Holt could be planning a fatal walk in the woods for her, or a fire, or even a fake accident with the Range Rover. He might even try to drown her in one of the streams."

"She's looks pretty strong physically," I said. "And even though she didn't believe me, hearing my warnings over and over must have made her start to look at him in a slightly suspicious light, if only subconsciously. She may not be as easy to kill as the others."

Lacey showed me a pair of small binoculars and a small compass he'd used. "Follow it due south, to their cabin," he said. "Due north brings you back here." He paced the room, the firelight casting shadows on his boyish face. He looked so young it scared me.

"This is no game, Lacey. He's older, more experienced, and very dangerous. If he had caught you at that window—"

"Don't worry, I won't get hurt. What I'm worried about is you, Britt. Don't you have enough to just go home and write your story now?"

"Probably," I admitted reluctantly. "But it's better to overreport than under. When you wrap up a big investigative piece and have the bad guy dead to rights, that's when you want to talk to him. Your final interview is always your target. It can make great copy. They tend to protest too much, try too hard to explain, and you can catch them in one damning lie after another. Holt is so slick and smart, that may not happen in this case. But if nothing else, I want to see Nancy safely out of his hands before I leave. Though when you meet her, you'll wonder why."

He sat across from me at the rough kitchen table. "You know, Britt, at first I seriously considered buying a gun and taking care of Holt myself," he confessed. "But thanks to you, I'm thinking straight now. I believe your story will do it for us."

Before returning to stand first watch at the honeymooners' cabin, Lacey took a swig of the blackberry brandy he'd brought to keep warm. This may have been early summer in Alaska, but we were both thin-blooded natives of warmer climes.

He'd be back, he said, when he was sure Marsh and Nancy had retired for the night.

"Be careful," I pleaded. "Stay away from their windows. He'll probably try to hurt her on one of their daily outings. We can follow them in the morning. That's our best chance to catch him in the act."

Lacey set his cell phone on vibrate in case I had an emergency. I hugged him goodbye, then napped in a chair by the flickering fire, cell phone in my lap.

I wasn't sure what time it was when I awoke. It still appeared to be dusk, but it felt cold and the fire had gone out. I checked my watch and saw it was six hours later. Six hours? Where was Lacey?

Too worried to sit and do nothing, I struggled to pull on my boots, listening, hoping to hear his key in the lock. He had the compass. But normally my sense of direction is good. I put on my jacket and began to plod south through the woods, but the uneven light and the clouds that shadowed the landscape made the unfamiliar terrain tricky. Ungainly and clumsy, I stumbled, slid, and skidded several times, unable to get my bearings. I couldn't risk falling down out here alone or becoming hopelessly lost.

Then I remembered another compass, the one in the instrument panel of the Ford Explorer.

With a sense of urgency, I made my way back to our cabin and wasted more time frantically searching for the car keys. Did Lacey take them with him? Then I remembered where he usually put them and, sure enough, found them atop the back tire up under the wheel well.

The clean fresh smell of Lacey's shaving lotion made me feel less alone as I drove the Ford back toward Holt's cabin. I pulled off the road about three quarters of the way there and cautiously continued on foot, watching for him through the trees.

What I saw made me gasp and prickled the hairs on the back of my neck. The Range Rover had been moved. Now it was parked on the far side of the cabin. No lights. The newlyweds had to be in bed.

Increasingly clumsy as my energy drained, I slowly but surely worked my way around the cabin, trying to search in a grid pattern. No sign of Lacey. Then, suddenly, there was. A glint of metal caught my eye, about a hundred and fifty feet from the cabin. It was a compass, the little whistle-shaped compass Lacey had shown me. Did he drop it and become lost?

I eased myself into a sitting position on the forest floor, hoping they didn't have fire ants in Alaska and that I would be able to get up again. I searched, groping through the undergrowth around me. Suddenly a strong smell assailed my senses and something gummy dripped onto my right shoulder. I stared up and saw sap oozing from a deep wound in a pine tree right over my head. The smell was piney, and the fresh gash appeared to have been made by the blade of an ax. I trained my little penlight onto the ground beneath the wound, not far from where I found the compass. It was as I feared. The ground and its carpet of pine needles were disturbed, as though there had been a struggle.

My groping hands connected with something wet and sticky, but the uncertain light of the endless dusk made it impossible to determine whether it was mud, blood, or tree sap.

"Oh, no," I whimpered, fearing the worst.

Panicked, I scrambled away on all fours, gripped a sapling to pull myself to my feet, then used the compass to find my way back to the Ford. Standing behind it for cover, at the fringe of the woods, I took out my cell phone.

We had agreed that I would only call him in an emergency. This was an emergency. I knew his phone was on vibrate.

No answer. I left a pleading message. "Lacey, please call me. I'm panicking. I'm out looking for you now. I need to know you're safe."

Every sound, every leaf that fell, chilled my blood. How could I protect myself out here alone? Suddenly my heart stopped and I braced, frozen with fear at the *whoosh* of an ax swing from behind me. The blow never landed. What I'd heard was only the rush of wings, a startled night bird taking flight. I wondered if the creature felt as helpless, endangered, and disoriented as I did.

Forcing myself to stay calm, I slowly made my way to Holt's Range Rover, pausing every few steps to watch and listen for any movement near the cabin. I touched the hood. The engine felt warm. I ran my fingers around the doors feeling for blood, body fluids, or other evidence of foul play. I whispered Lacey's name, in case he was inside and could hear me. Nothing. I lightly tapped a fender with my fingernail. Not enough force to set off a car alarm, but enough for him to hear in case he might be conscious, tied up inside.

No response. Nothing.

I steeled myself and crept closer to the cabin. Trembling, I inched my way around to what had to be the bedroom. The windows were too high to see inside, and I couldn't find anything to stand on. As I stood beneath it, alert, focused, and straining to hear, there came the sounds of muffled laughter.

The honeymooners were frisky. But where was John Lacey?

I carefully made my way back toward the Explorer, desperately searching the gloom for any sign. Suddenly a car approached up on the road about forty feet to my left. A patrol car. I crouched as it passed, heart pounding, resisting the impulse to run out and flag them down. No one would believe me. How could I help Lacey, or Nancy, from a jail cell? The police would only complicate matters, and I still hadn't e-mailed the latest version of my story to the *News.*

I began to think clearly as I cut through the trees, moving stealthily on the soft pine needles. With my immediate future uncertain, my mission was to dispatch the updated story to the *News,* with a copy to Sam Stone. Then the truth would be alive and out there, in case I wasn't. I prayed the cops wouldn't spot the Explorer and stop to check it out.

Panting, I paused to catch my breath. That's when I heard footsteps behind me. Moving through the trees, gaining on me. I heard his rapid movement and heavy breathing. Too exhausted to run, I turned to confront Holt—and gasped.

I looked up into the soft brown eyes of a moose. Startled, he stopped. We stared at each other. The huge animal could have stomped me into the ground in a heartbeat. But in that breathless moment of eye contact I felt a connection; it was as if the giant wild creature sensed my fear and despair.

We stood motionless for several beats, until the great beast snorted, flared his nostrils, broke eye contact, and walked slowly into the dusk. I watched, breathing hard, until he disappeared.

I prayed to find Lacey, or a note from him, waiting at the Explorer. Nothing. I drove slowly back to our cabin, inching along the roadway, scanning both sides for a clue to his whereabouts. Nothing.

No sign of him at the cabin either. I locked the door behind me and picked up the fireplace poker to use as a weapon against anyone who tried to break in.

The time difference between Fairbanks and Miami is four hours. I worked on the story as I waited, counting the minutes until I knew Sam Stone would be in the office. Then I called, praying to hear his voice. He was my last hope. His voice mail answered. Again. Where the hell *was* he?

"Stone, you've got to help me," I said breathlessly. "Holt may have killed John Lacey, the man I told you about. He went to surveil Holt's cabin last night and never came back. I'm afraid he's either dead or injured. Please call me back."

A mindless computer voice prompted me to press nine to send the message.

I did and was about to hang up when the mechanical voice added: "To speak to someone else, press zero." I did that too.

It rang several times as I continued to pray that God and the machine would connect me to a live human being. My heart leaped when I heard a voice. Not a tape, not a computer, a real person.

"Lieutenant Riley, can I help you?"

My energy level crumpled; I wanted to weep. Why her, why did it have to be her?

"Hello?" She said it again.

Any voice, even hers, from home, four thousand miles away, triggered my emotions.

"Kathy?" My broken whisper echoed through the vast void between us. "Don't hang up."

I had never called her Kathy. Lieutenant Kathleen Constance Riley had threatened to break the kneecaps of any reporter who called her Kathy, or even Kathleen, in print.

McDonald had called her Kathy.

"Who is this?"

"Britt." To my dismay, my voice quaked. "I need your help. I don't know if Sam Stone has kept you apprised of the investigative piece I've been reporting."

"I didn't recognize your voice," she said. "You sound terrible. Are you all right?"

"No," I whispered, and began to cough.

"Is the baby all right?" The concern in her voice caught me totally off guard.

"I think so." Fighting tears, I took a deep, ragged breath to regain control. I had never felt so weak and helpless. "One of the victims of suspected serial killer Marsh Holt was a girl from Baton Rouge. A young man, her former fiancé, was here helping me. His name is John Lacey and he's been playing amateur detective, seeking justice for the girl he loved. He was trying to keep Holt under surveillance. Now he's missing and may be dead. I can't call the local police; they'll arrest me on sight. The *News* cut me off, canceled my credit card, and I'm sick. I'm broke. I don't know where else to turn. I need help."

She didn't speak though she was still on the line. I could hear her breathing.

Dammit, I thought. I pictured her smiling, laughing at my desperation.

"I need help, goddammit! I think he killed Lacey."

"Where are you, Britt?"

"Alone in a cabin on Old Black Hawk Road outside of Fairbanks. Fairbanks, Alaska."

"You're in Alaska? You couldn't get into trouble in South Beach? North Miami? Fort Lauderdale? Even Orlando? You are aware that Alaska is out of our jurisdiction."

"I know you hate me, Kathy."

"Don't call me that," she said wearily. "I don't hate you most of the time. But what the *hell* do you think you're doing?"

I explained at length.

"Your persistence always has annoyed me," she said coolly. "But it's also why I often wished you worked for me. I know you didn't ask for my advice. But don't ever become so discouraged that you stop—or so stubborn that you won't. I always tell my detectives that when you wear yourself out, trouble comes sooner and stays longer."

"Too late," I said. "Trouble is here, and I'm already worn out. Did Stone ever look into Gloria Weatherholt's scuba death?"

"No." She sounded businesslike. "We've been focused on Spencer York, the Custody Crusader. Where did you say you were? The address?"

I told her. "Promise not to let the local police know where I am. I don't want to go to jail again."

"Let me think about this," she said. "I'll get back to you."

COLD CASE SQUAD

MIAMI, FLORIDA

"I need you to make a call to the Fairbanks, Alaska, police department," Riley said.

"Sure." Nazario looked up from his desk. "Any word yet from Stone and the sergeant?"

"Not yet," she said. "Let's hope they get lucky in Texas."

WACO, TEXAS

Three spotted hound dogs dashed from the house to meet the detectives' rental car. They were wagging their tails.

Spencer York's sister, Sheila, a tall and plain strong-jawed woman in her fifties, stood on the front porch wearing a simple cotton housedress and sensible shoes.

"I'm the detective who called you from Miami," Stone said, introducing himself and Sergeant Burch.

"Come on in, git yourselves outa this heat," she said, leading them into her parlor.

"We're working on your brother's case," Stone said. "We have some leads, but we need a few things clarified."

She served hot, strong, delicious coffee and homemade cake topped with chopped pecans and cinnamon, before they talked. She insisted. The detectives got the distinct impression that Sheila Whitaker had few visitors.

Her husband, she said, was away a lot. So was her son.

"Spencer told a Miami newspaper reporter that he had marital and custody problems of his own, which motivated his crusade," Stone said. "I doubt the reporter misunderstood. Unlike most, she's usually accurate and right on target. So it surprised us when you said that Spencer never married and had no children. If that's so, why do you think your brother would tell her that?"

She thought for a moment, hands placidly in her lap. "Most likely because it would make sense. It would give him . . ." She fumbled for a moment. "What's the right word?"

"Credibility?" Burch said.

"That's it." She nodded. "Exactly."

"So what would his real motivation be?"

"Spencer always was a hard man to understand."

She lifted her delicate china coffee cup, dwarfed in her large callused hands, and sipped daintily.

"He just got ideas, couldn't get them out of his head until he followed through."

"We suspect," Burch said, "that a woman might be involved in his murder. We recently found a sort of diary that he kept. He wrote that he thought she had followed him to Miami. That would rule out anyone he may have met in South Florida."

Spencer York's sister put down her cup.

"So our thinking," Stone said, "was that perhaps she might be an ex-wife or former sweetheart, a woman he knew well in some sort of intimate relationship. He referred to her as M."

Something odd flickered in the woman's eyes. She looked away, self-conscious.

She knows, Stone thought.

"He wasn't married, never came close," she said softly, eyes still averted. "Not that I know of. Had two or three dates as a young man, but never with the same girl twice. None of 'em would ever go out with him a second time."

"Did any have the initial *M*?" Burch asked. "You know: Marilyn, Marie, Maureen?"

She sighed and paused again. "Not that I recall."

What is she hiding? Stone wondered.

"Can you help us figure out who this woman might be?" Burch asked.

"He stole children from lots of women. I don't know their names." She got to her feet. "Here," she said. "After that reporter called, I drug out the old family scrapbook." She took the book from a sideboard and opened it on the coffee table between them. "There he is, about seven years old."

Spencer York, his hair dark blond in childhood, sat bare chested on the back of a pinto pony. He was scowling.

She began to leaf through the black cardboard pages. "Wait," Burch said. "Is that the two of you?"

She nodded.

A dark-haired, big-boned woman wearing a severe suit and a perky hat with a small veil sat on a couch against an inside wall with two small children, a boy and a girl. The woman held a Bible in her lap. All three solemnly stared straight into the camera's eye in that moment captured a half century ago.

"That your mother?" Burch asked. "Attractive woman."

She nodded. "A very religious woman, strict Southern Baptist. Had a hard life."

"What about your dad? I don't see any pictures of him in here."

"He left right after my little brother, Emmett, drowned. He went off to work for the railroad and never did come back. Spencer was about eight and I was five."

"Sorry to hear that. It couldn't have been easy," Burch said.

Stone had flipped to a later page in the scrapbook, to a photo of Sheila, her husband, a tall, lean mustachioed man, and their small son.

Back then she looked much like her mother had in the earlier picture, minus the Bible and the perky hat.

Her son was curly-haired, chubby-cheeked, and grinning.

Stone smiled back at the toothy toddler. "Where's your boy now?"

"Over in Killeen, doing right well. Twenty-six years old." She smiled proudly. "Engaged to a schoolteacher, a fine girl. He's a firefighter for the county. They come to dinner every Sunday. It's hard to believe. Child raising," she said, "is never easy."

"Tell me about it," Burch said. "I've got three, two girls and Craig Junior, the middle child. He's thirteen. My oldest is sixteen and starting to date. That keeps me awake nights."

"What it all comes down to," she said, looking Burch straight in the eye, "is influences. When a strong-minded individual exerts a negative influence, things happen. No matter who it might be, you have to keep that negative influence out of their lives."

Burch nodded.

Her eyes dropped meaningfully to the scrapbook as the men rose to leave.

Burch handed her his card at the door and asked her to call him or Stone if she thought of anything that might help.

Something unsaid remained in her eyes. The detectives lingered.

"When did you lose your mother?" Stone said. "When did she pass?"

"Oh, she didn't. She's alive."

"Sorry. I just assumed . . ."

"She's seventy-five years old now, in a nursing home up in Grand Prairie."

"Where is that exactly?" Stone said.

"About a two-hour drive northwest up Highway Thirty-five."

"Think she'd remember anything that might help us?" he asked.

The woman shrugged, eyes blank. "Her memory has not failed."

The dogs followed them out to the car. So did their owner. "Want some more cake? I'll wrap it in plastic and fix you a thermos of coffee, to hold you over during the drive."

GRAND PRAIRIE, TEXAS

The nursing home sweltered in the Central Texas sun. The long white one-story building had a tall front gate, wheelchair ramps, ragged hedges, and a dry fountain.

They rang a bell and an overweight woman in a white uniform emerged from behind swinging doors to meet them at the front desk. Her eyes widened in surprise when they asked for Roberta York.

"She doesn't get many visitors." She opened a register for them to sign. "Poor thing doesn't even have a roommate right now, what with her being so difficult and all."

She summoned a sandy-haired aide, a pleasant-faced young fellow in rumpled scrubs and sneakers, to show them to Mrs. York's room.

"She still reads the Bible every day. Watch out," he warned, "or she'll start quoting from Revelation. Some scary stuff in there. I guess Jesus loves her, but the rest of us think she's an asshole. Good luck." He knocked, then opened the door.

The detectives caught their breath as they stepped into the dimly lit room. It was at least ten degrees hotter inside.

Roberta York sat in her wheelchair as if it were a throne, her back straight, the room nearly dark, drapes blocking the sun. She was frowning at a soap opera that flickered silently in a corner, the sound on mute.

She turned the TV off with the remote and studied her visitors curiously.

The dark hair, the perky hat, and the unsmiling faces of her little children were long gone, but the Bible remained, well worn and well read. Several, in fact, were within her reach, along with spectacles and a large magnifying glass.

Her hair was now steel gray, but the large bones did not appear shrunken.

The detectives explained who they were and why they had come.

"Nine years ago," Stone said, loosening his collar in the oppressive heat, "everybody believed that your son, Spencer, jumped bond to avoid trial in Miami. But that wasn't true. He'd been murdered. His body was recently discovered and positively identified."

She nodded, eyes alert and interested.

"He didn't run away," she said. "I always knew that." Despite the heat, she hugged her arms as though cold. "But I wouldn't blame anyone for fleeing that city. From what I have seen, your South Beach is a modern Sodom and Gomorrah."

"It can be pretty wild," Stone admitted.

She focused on the young black detective. "Do you read your scripture, son?"

"Yes, ma'am. My grandmother, who raised me, wouldn't have it any other way."

Smiling approvingly, she offered advice.

"Take and lead the righteous. Flee that wicked place before the reign of fire, when dead bodies will lie stacked in the streets."

"It *is* getting harder to raise kids there," Burch said mildly. He gazed at the ceiling. "Look at that," he said. "That's why it's so hot in here." The air-conditioning vent was closed.

"I can fix it in a minute," he said, looking for something to stand on.

"No!" she said quickly. "I like it this way."

"Sorry," he said. "I thought it seemed a little uncomfortable for you."

"We know you must find it difficult to discuss your son's death," Stone said, "but we hoped you could help us."

She nodded, picking up a small Bible. "Spencer was my firstborn."

"We need to find a woman with whom he had a relationship. Her name may begin with the letter *M*."

She stared at them.

"Do you know her?" Burch said. "Perhaps a girlfriend, an old flame, a common-law wife?"

She continued to stare and then broke into laughter. She laughed and laughed. "What makes you think any woman would have him?" she finally gasped. "He hated women. He had no romantic relationships and no wife, common-law or otherwise."

"Yes, ma'am," Stone said. "We spoke to your daughter, Sheila, earlier today. She indicated that as well."

The woman's eyes narrowed. "Thou shalt hate the whore." Voice rising, she spit out the words. "Make her desolate and naked, eat her flesh and burn her with fire!"

"I take it you two aren't close," Burch said.

"When I had a stroke, she seized the moment of my weakness and put me here, against my will." Her hands gripped the armrests of her wheelchair.

"This does seem to be some distance from home," Burch said. "Is there a rift in the family?"

"My grandson," she muttered, "was the only one worth saving."

They could barely see her eyes in the shadows. "How about some light?" Burch reached for the drapery cord.

"No!" She flung an arm in front of her eyes and shrank in her chair. "Don't open it. I'm sensitive to bright lights."

Burch dropped the cord and pulled a chair up close to hers.

"Do you recall the last time you saw Spencer?" he asked.

She nodded, smiling.

"When and where was it? Did the two of you enjoy a good relationship?" Stone asked.

She looked nostalgic, as though recalling good times.

"We want to find out who killed him and why," Burch said.

She blinked, as though surprised that they had missed the obvious. "He was the devil," she said, her voice flat and matter-of-fact. "He was Satan, with all his power, his signs, and his lying wonders."

The detectives exchanged glances.

"Somebody had to stop him."

"Who did?"

She raised her chin expectantly, smile chilling, her eyes still in shadow.

"Have you ever been to Miami?" Burch asked softly.

"Once." She smiled demurely. "Somebody had to do the Lord's work."

The silence was electric. He took a deep breath. "Were you alone?"

"We drove. My grandson—Sheila's boy, Roland—had just graduated from high school. My gift to him was a road trip to Florida for the two of us. His mother allowed it. He was happy to come."

"Before we go any further," Burch said, "I'd like to advise you of your rights."

She listened, looking bored.

"Do you understand?"

"I answer to a higher power," she said. "Spencer was evil, the beast with the lion's mouth. I told my grandson that we were posting his uncle's bond as a surprise, so they could get to know each other."

"So Roland went to the bondsman?"

She nodded. "That boy could always be relied upon to do as he was told."

"Who shot Spencer?"

"I did, for the glory of God. My grandson helped me put Spencer into the car and dug the grave. I told him it was the right thing to do, and he was a good and obedient boy. But later, he disobeyed me and told his mother, who turned on me. She'll pay for her sins with her life." She tapped her Bible ominously. "Just like the others."

The detectives stared.

"I brought them into this world," she said loudly, "and I can take them out of it. I can put them in the ground."

"Not in our jurisdiction," Burch said. "It's against the law."

"Not God's law." She leaned forward as if to confide a secret. "I saw the sign of the beast in my youngest son when he was only two. He had the devil in him. God wanted him cast into the bottomless pit, into perdition! So I dropped him in the well. He wailed all the way down, then cried and splashed for a while. Then he was quiet." Her smile was radiant. "God was unpleased and later revealed to me that Spencer was the devil himself!"

"I see." Stone nodded. "When Spencer wrote letters or sent messages, how did he address you?"

"Never Mother. Just M."

Stone slipped out to call local police for a stenographer. Burch stayed in her room, to stoke the fires and keep them burning.

After the stenographer arrived, they talked for hours.

"No wonder the woman doesn't have a roommate," Stone said later, as they walked down the hall, weary, dehydrated, and overwhelmed by the smells of urine, disinfectant, and bad food.

"They'll probably find her incompetent to stand trial," Burch said. "And the juvenile, the grandson, was just the gravedigger and the front who posted Spencer's bond. The statute of limitations lapsed on him a long time ago. Poor kid had a helluva graduation trip."

"Yeah," Stone said. "Most high school grads get to go to Disney World or Aruba."

"Instead, she takes him on a journey to commit murder in the name of God."

"It's the in thing right now, all over the world," Stone said bleakly.

"Wonder when we should expect the reign of fire?"

"Don't joke about that, Sarge. It gives me the creeps."

"I think Corso's the devil, myself," Burch said thoughtfully.

"You want to shoot him? Or bury him?"

"I'll toss you for it," Burch said. "Seriously, he's already buried. No way Corso can beat the jackpot he's in now. He's done, finito. Hopefully, if he's not suspended as we speak, his sorry ass is already back in uniform pounding a beat. How much you wanna bet?"

"You know he always comes out smelling like a rose," Stone said. "The guy's got nine lives."

"He's used 'em all up. He beats it this time, it's proof he's the devil."

"Then we will have to kill him."

They called K. C. Riley at home late that night after interviewing Roland Whitaker. The young firefighter held nothing back. He remembered all the horrifying details he'd wished he could forget.

Sworn to secrecy by his grandmother, he had become withdrawn, unpredictable, and prone to angry outbursts. He had gone from being a typical wholesome teenager to a young man suffering from guilt, bad dreams, and flashbacks of that nightmarish trip. The story eventually unfolded during counseling with his concerned parents. They immediately cut off all ties with Roberta and then considered their heart-wrenching dilemma. If they exposed his grandmother, Roland might face the trauma of a murder trial, public scrutiny, and possible criminal charges.

As they agonized over what to do, the decision was taken out of their hands.

As next of kin, Sheila was notified when Roberta was found unconscious. When it appeared that her mother would survive the stroke, Sheila found the most distant nursing home in the region and placed her there, in a prison of her own.

Slowly, through therapy, Roland had gotten his life back on track.

"With all the possible suspects, who'da thought the mystery woman was York's own mother," Riley said. "But it all fits. Crime scene has confirmed that he was murdered in his motel room. Luminol picked up blood on the floors, the walls, and the furniture: Spencer's blood type. There's no doubt that DNA will confirm it's his. Nice work. Damn. What a case."

"Too bad Britt isn't around to write the story," Stone said, on the extension. "Anybody hear from her?"

"I need to talk to you about that. She's left you some messages."

"We'll be back tomorrow," he said. "We're arranging for Roland, the fireman, to give us a formal statement."

"York's whole family is cooperating," Burch said. "I'll call ADA Salazar tonight, run everything by her. Anything new at home plate?"

Riley paused. "Yeah, there is. I planned to wait till you two got back. I wanted to see your faces, and didn't want to spoil your trip."

"Spit it out."

"Yeah," Stone said. "Don't leave us hanging."

"It's Dyson Junior. Guess who he is? The Human Fly, the burglar who climbs tall buildings; that damn kid is the thief that's been Miami's most wanted for the last six months. Witnesses, including that actress, all came forward after his picture was on TV and in the papers. We got 'im. When they served a warrant, they found all kinds of evidence and stolen property.

"Corso's a hero. The mayor wants to give him the key to the city. There's a picture of him on the front page of this afternoon's paper with Irma Jolly, the senior citizen whose ear he nearly shot off. He has his arm around her and she's gazing up at him like he just rode in on a white horse. The woman hasn't had this much attention in eighty years. She's loving it. She wants to adopt him.

"Nazario wants to put his gun to his own head."

"So do I," Stone said. "Kill me now."

"Told you he was the devil," Burch said.

BRITT

CHAPTER TWENTY-ONE

A heavy rain pounded the roof, rattling the shutters as I worked feverishly on the story, listening, hoping for a footstep at the door yet fearing the sound, hoping that Riley would keep her promise and call me back.

When I finished, I attached the photos with detailed captions, added a cheerful *See you soon!* and, with a great sense of relief, e-mailed the entire package to Fred.

At least I tried to send it.

"Not now," I moaned, as my laptop froze. "Don't crash on me now. Please, not now." When you are desperate and need it the most, modern technology never fails to turn on you. Nothing I tried worked.

I had saved the package on a CD. Little good that did. There was no Sir Speedy, Office Depot, or FedEx box just down the block.

Lacey's laptop! I thought. Brilliant. Where is it? I tossed the entire cabin but didn't find it. Frantic, I closed my eyes to visualize him as he walked out the door, playing the scene over and over in my mind. He wasn't carrying it. But he had it when he arrived. I stumbled out to the Ford through the rain. I found nothing beneath the driver and passenger seats. But when I reached under the backseats, there it was. "Thank God," I murmured, praying I could make it work.

I opened it on the table beside my worthless piece of crap.

The screen blossomed to life, then requested the password. Son of a bitch.

I typed in variations of John Lacey's name and the company that employed him. Access denied. I tried the word *novel*, then *Suzanne.* That one worked.

"Thank you, Lacey," I murmured. "Thank you, Suzanne."

Hearing her name brought flashbacks, terrible images of her fragile body shattered on the canyon floor. "You are not forgotten, Suzanne," I whispered. "I promise, you are not forgotten."

I transferred the contents of the disk into the laptop and then opened his e-mail, using the same password. Thank God Lacey was consistent. I prayed to see him alive again.

I sent everything to Fred.

Your message has been sent.

I sighed with relief. Then sent the same package to Detective Sam Stone. He had never called me back.

Neither had K. C. Riley. I don't know why that surprised me. What should I expect? I regretted begging for her help, giving her that satisfaction.

Except for the baby I carried I was completely alone here, closer to Russia and North Korea than to Miami and Cuba. How surreal is that? I wondered. I began to wish that I'd learned the baby's sex. This isn't fair, I thought. None of it is fair.

Lacey's e-mail had dozens of saved messages, both sent and received. I clicked on one at random and blinked as it opened, startled by the intimate and personal content.

From Suzanne, I thought. I know people who have kept messages from dead loved ones on their answering machines for years. They cling to that final connection.

The e-mail was a love letter. So were most of the others. Their audacious language and lush overripe endearments titillated the voyeur in me. The lovers' wild libidinous energy, their passionate, poetic, and lyrical prose, exposed a relationship fraught with erotic drama, angst, and storm-tossed sperm. My jaw dropped as I read.

Streaks and pricks of light exploded like fireworks in my brain. I felt as though I were drowning.

This must be a feverish dream, I thought. I reread a number of the messages in stunned disbelief. Was I delirious? Delusional? Totally irrational? No. The truth was perfectly clear. The lovers who exchanged these passionate letters were John Lacey and Marsh Holt.

CHAPTER TWENTY-TWO

I stared zombielike at the computer screen, then scrambled into the bathroom to be sick.

I sat gagging on the side of the old-fashioned claw-footed tub, gasping for breath and coming to terms with the fact that in this strange place, surrounded by hostile strangers, I was the only one I could trust.

My last hope was gone. Nobody was coming. No rescue. No knight on a white horse. It was up to me.

I forced myself to eat something. There were sourdough rolls and canned soup in the cupboard. I fixed a sandwich and heated some soup, a strange breakfast. I added a tablespoon of blackberry brandy to the soup, hoping to calm both myself and the baby.

In Miami, I kept a gun in the glove compartment of my T-Bird. Having it now would be a comfort. Why, when I need it most, is it always out of reach? The rain had finally stopped. I slipped an oversized loden-green sweater on over my maternity jeans, replaced Lacey's laptop under the backseat, along with the fireplace poker, then drove back down the mountain toward Holt's cabin. According to the car radio, the temperature was 51.

I parked off-road within walking distance and trudged through the damp woods. I sat on a fallen tree trunk and watched the cabin through the binoculars.

Within twenty minutes, Marsh Holt appeared on the front porch. He bent and stretched for several minutes, scanning the road and surrounding woods as he exercised and limbered up. I held my breath. He didn't see me.

He seemed to be waiting for Nancy, who appeared within minutes. They spoke briefly and went back inside together. Five minutes later they reappeared, wearing backpacks and hiking gear.

They skirted the side of the cabin and struck out to the west. After a few minutes, I followed.

Nancy's bright red sweater helped me keep them in sight, but their pace was brisk and I found it difficult to keep up.

No sign of Lacey. Just thinking of him set my mind and pulse racing. He and Holt obviously shared a long-term relationship; their letters made that clear. How? When did they hook up? What was Lacey's real relationship with Suzanne? Why did he sacrifice her to his lover's murderous scheme?

Greed, I thought. The money. Their exchanges included numerous references to their long range goal, the time when they would be free at last to enjoy each other and their future together, financed by the dead brides' assets and life insurance proceeds.

Up ahead, the newlyweds paused several times, to photograph wildlife, to taste and collect wild berries and native foliage. Even with those welcome breathers, I was panting and relieved when they finally stopped for lunch beside a wide and fast-moving, rocky stream.

I watched, careful not to be seen. They took pictures. Nancy waving, in her red sweater, her short blond hair bright next to the shining water. The hair prickled on the back of my neck as she posed. What if . . . ? What would I do? What *could* I do? This was insane.

They packed up, on the move again. But my heart sank. It looked as though they were about to use slippery rocks as stepping stones to cross the rushing rain-fed stream, a feat I was loath to attempt. The water roared, the current swift and powerful. Who would rescue me if I fell?

Nobody. I couldn't risk it. I had to find a safer place to cross before I lost them. Which way? I ventured downstream. Wrong choice. The sound of rushing water built to a crescendo. Sure enough, cascades, rapids, and sharp drops appeared up ahead. Frustrated, I turned to go back and saw Nancy, about seventy feet away.

She stared, then shrieked and charged me, running full tilt, screaming and waving her arms.

Oh, crap, I thought. I was at a distinct disadvantage and had no desire to grapple with her.

The woman could run. She rapidly closed the gap between us, red-faced and still screaming. No way could I outrun her. I raised my hands in surrender, in supplication, wondering if Holt was right behind her, or me.

"Wait, wait, Nancy. Don't!"

She didn't slow down. I braced for her assault at the last second.

She flung herself at me. Sobbing aloud, she wrapped her arms around me in a crushing bear hug that nearly knocked me down.

"Help! Help me! He tried to kill me," she cried. "You were right! You were right!"

"Thank you." I shook off her hug. "Where is he?" I looked apprehensively around us.

"Back there," she gasped, indicating the picnic area and the stream. "He's after me!"

"Let's get out of here."

"Which way? Which way?" She looked lost and bewildered.

"Come on." I caught her arm and we scrambled into the brush. "Take off that sweater!" I said.

"He tried to kill me, he tried to kill me," she blubbered.

"I won't say I told you so. But take off the damn sweater. It's like a red flag."

"He wants to kill me!"

"So do I," I hissed, "if you don't take that thing off. Get rid of it, or I will. He can't miss you in it."

She looked down, as though hearing me for the first time, and then pulled it off over her head as we ran.

She wore only a little silk camisole underneath.

"Don't bring the sweater with you, for God's sake," I said. "Hide it in those bushes, cover it with leaves."

"Cashmere," she panted tearfully. "Brand new."

"Ditch it!"

She did.

We stayed off the trail. When we paused to listen and catch our breath I asked how she got such a head start on Holt, who still hadn't appeared behind us.

"I knew it, I just knew it," she said, voice trembling, close to hysteria. "You planted the seeds. I began to think. He started to scare me. Last night he went out to chop a few sticks of firewood and didn't come back for hours. I couldn't see him. I don't know where he was, but I thought I heard voices in the woods. He had moved the car and was acting strangely. Just now, at lunch, he kept pouring more wine in my glass. I dumped it in the grass when he wasn't looking. Then he insisted we cross the stream. I was afraid. He knows I'm not a good swimmer. He wants me dead. He told me to butch up, it was the only place to cross. He's never talked to me like that before."

I remembered Colleen, afraid of that last run down the ski slope.

"He said to trust him. But I saw something in his eyes. You were right. I don't know who he is. He was too good to be true. I didn't know him long enough."

"Shush," I said, "he'll hear us. We have to keep moving. Watch for a ranger, other hikers, or anybody. I don't like being out here alone with him."

"Thank God you were here." She began to sob.

"Shut up." I looked around fearfully. "Where is he? What is he doing? Why isn't he right behind you? How did you get away?"

"I hit him hard, really hard, as hard as I could, with the wine bottle." She snuffled. "He fe-fell in the water." She hiccuped.

I stopped to stare at her. "Was he conscious?"

"When he reached out to grab my arm, to drag me onto the rock, I swung as hard as I could. The bottle broke on the side of his head."

I paused and looked over my shoulder. "You think he drowned?"

She wiped the back of her hand across her drippy red nose.

"No. The water just carried him a few feet." She stopped and sniffed. "Then he grabbed hold of a rock and yelled at me to help him. His head was bleeding. I told him you were right and he could get himself out. Then I ran. Thank God I found you."

She tried to hug me again.

"Stop it," I snapped, alarmed. Not only was Marsh Holt homicidal, now he was also soaking wet, bleeding, and mad as hell. As would be Lacey, his lover, who was lurking somewhere, most likely in these very woods.

Even then, as my adrenaline spiked and my fight-or-flight response ratcheted into high gear, I took delight deep down at what a great story this was. Already it needed updating. Again. I could see the new caption under Nancy's photo: THE BRIDE WHO FOUGHT BACK.

She'd be booked on every talk show, a spunky role model for all endangered little girls romanced by the wrong men. Her cookbooks would sell like hotcakes. She'd write a best-selling sequel combining honeymoon recipes with her harrowing tale of heartbreak and survival.

If, of course, we survived.

She was whimpering. "Beautiful wedding . . . expected to be together when we were seventy-five . . ."

"I hate to say this to you too, Nancy, but butch up. I'm not trying to scare you, but another man's involved, an accomplice. He was probably one of the voices you heard last night. He's dangerous too. We have to get to the car and then go to the police. If we walk into headquarters together, they'll believe us and won't arrest me."

At least I hoped they wouldn't. No way, I thought. I had prima facie evidence of the lovers' crimes, plans, and schemes. It was all on Lacey's laptop.

I had my story—but first we had to find our way out of these woods.

I checked the compass to be sure we were headed toward the car.

"Marsh has a gun," she whimpered.

"What?" I hadn't thought to ask. I'd simply assumed that gunplay wasn't his style, since his MO was staging accidents. "How did he get it on the plane?"

"He didn't. He bought it in Fairbanks. Said we needed it for protection from wild animals—and you, because our cabin was so isolated. He said you're dangerous."

I felt a chill, as if someone had walked on my grave. If Holt was armed, Lacey might be too. "Where is the gun?"

"Maybe in the cabin, or in his backpack." She wiped her eyes. "What can I say to my parents, my friends, my television audience? How can I tell them?"

"Come on," I said, weary of her whining. "Hurry." The undergrowth we pushed through had practically shredded her lacy camisole.

"Can you keep up?" Her watery blue eyes focused on me. "You don't look good."

"Just keep going," I panted. "I'll feel a lot better when we get to the car."

My lower back ached. I kept stumbling, clinging to low-lying branches, tree trunks, and bushes for support as I struggled. It took hours. My stomach was cramping. My feet were numb and I couldn't catch my breath. Just when I thought things couldn't be worse, it started to rain. The occasional fat raindrops that splashed onto leaves grew into a heavy downpour that continued to build. Rain pelted my face and my aching shoulders. How could this be any worse? I wondered. I quickly found out. The temperature was dropping. Nancy was shivering.

Then, like a miracle, I spotted a familiar landmark.

"Nancy," I gasped. "We made it! The road is up ahead. The car is beyond those trees to the left, just off the road."

She jogged ahead, hugging her arms for warmth, then turned back to me, an odd look on her face. I drew upon my last ounce of energy, caught up, and staggered into the clearing where I had left the car.

It was gone.

"Are you sure this is the place?" Nancy demanded. "You must be mistaken. The trees all look alike."

"No, this was it," I gasped. "I left it right here." I groped in my pocket for the key, realizing there must have been two. Either Holt or Lacey must have spotted the Explorer and taken it.

"Oh, no," I murmured. The laptop with its incriminating letters, the only evidence to link the two men, was gone with the car.

"This can't be the place," Nancy insisted.

"I can't make it back to our cabin on foot," I said, still trying to catch my breath. "Your place is closer. But it's a risk to go there."

"I could get a sweater." Her teeth chattered.

My feet were cold, wet, and numb. What ever happened to global warming? I wondered bitterly.

I tried to think. "Where are the keys to the Range Rover?" I asked, praying they weren't in Holt's backpack.

Her nose wrinkled as she rubbed her arms, trying to stay warm. "I don't want to be a divorcée." Her eyes welled.

"You don't have to be," I said. "Have it annulled."

"Think I could?" she asked brightly.

"The keys, Nancy, the car keys. Focus. Do you know where they are?"

"You needn't be rude," she pouted. "If life was only candy and nuts, every day would be Christmas."

"Oh, God, Nancy. What the hell does that mean?"

She stared sorrowfully at me through the drenching rain.

"The keys," I said. "The keys."

"Maybe . . . on the hook, just inside the door? Or on the bedroom dresser."

We were tempting fate. Holt, Lacey, or both might be waiting for us. Then I thought of how long it would take me to slog uphill in a downpour through the mud, to the cabin Lacey had rented. And for all we knew, they might be waiting for us there.

"Let's go," I whispered. My heavy boots, full of water, chafed at every step.

Barely able to see through the cold rain, we stared at the newlyweds' cabin from the chilly woods across the road. No lights visible, nothing moving. The Range Rover was still parked where I had seen it last.

If Holt had made it out of the woods before we did, he could be inside.

"Okay, Nancy. Focus. Even if we're lucky and neither one is in there, that could change at any moment. So we go in fast. You run to find the keys, look for the gun, and grab a sweater or jacket, then we're out of there in forty-five seconds or less. If one or both show up, all we can do is run in opposite directions, be brave, fight back, and hope for the best. Got it?"

She began to cry. "This is my honeymoon—"

"It could be your funeral."

"This was supposed to be the happiest week of my life." Rain mingled with tears on her face.

I closed my eyes and wished I felt strong enough to shake her until her big white teeth rattled.

"How long did you know him, Nancy?"

She gasped, shoulders shaking. "Two, almost three months."

"Don't ever do that again. Make it eighteen months minimum before you even consider an engagement."

"He was so handsome, so romantic, so perfect. What gives you the right to be so smug? Look at you."

"This is not the life I chose," I said, itching to smack her hard. "Let's go."

We scuttled across the road one at a time. She climbed the front stairs, fished the spare key out of a flowerpot, and gingerly unlocked the front door.

I watched her step inside and held my breath until she reappeared to wave the all clear.

I dragged myself up the stairs, barking like a drill sergeant. "Okay, okay, okay. Forty-five seconds. The keys, the keys, the keys. The gun. Find the gun. Grab a sweater, a jacket. Let's go, let's go, let's go!"

The car keys were not on the hook by the door. I scanned the room and yelped. Lacey's laptop sat on the rough-hewn wooden table. I snatched it up like a prize.

He had been here, waiting. Neither of them expected Nancy to emerge from those woods alive. Holt had planned to stagger out to safety, feigning grief and shock. The head wound Nancy had inflicted would have served as further proof of how he'd heroically tried to rescue his beloved. He'd spin a tale of how he'd leaped into the rapids to reach her, smashing his head on a rock, risking his own life as the current swept her away.

Nancy emerged from the bedroom wearing a heavy ski sweater and a windbreaker. "Here." She tossed me a man's flannel-lined blue windbreaker. "It's his." Her lips quivered.

I didn't care if it belonged to Beelzebub himself, I gratefully slipped it on.

"And these." She dangled the keys to the Range Rover.

I took them. "Did you find the gun?"

She shook her head.

I sighed and picked up the fireplace poker.

"Where'd that come from?" She stared at the laptop.

"It belongs to John Lacey. He was here. You weren't expected back."

Nancy stopped at the door and turned, eyes roving the room lovingly. She was working herself up again. "I was going to make a soufflé tonight—"

"Don't, Nancy. Let's go. I'll drive."

"I think I should," she said, as we went back out into the rain. "My husband and I are the only names on the car-rental contract. The insurance might not cover anyone else."

"Don't worry about it." Teeth on edge, I heaved myself up into the driver's seat.

The relentless rain made it impossible to see the muddy road, which was slippery as hell.

"We'll go straight to police headquarters," I said. "I just want to get us off this mountain. My plane ticket and clothes are back at my cabin but we can't go there."

"Why?"

"Duh. Think about it, Nancy. If they're not here at your cabin, they're probably looking for us at mine."

Even with four-wheel drive, the Range Rover skidded, and the water made it hard to see the edge of the lane. On a curve it would be easy to drive right off the side. Slowly, we descended to where the rutted dirt road met the pavement.

"Oh, my God!" Nancy said, and began to scream.

"I don't believe it!" I hit the brakes.

There was no paved road, only a raging, dirty brown river.

"Flash flood!" I tried to back up, but the tires spun uselessly in the mud.

CHAPTER TWENTY-THREE

Huge pieces of debris swept by—trees, logs, a roof, and a broken carport—all caught up in the torrent.

"We're gonna drown! We'll drown!" Nancy shrieked.

"No," I said quietly. "We won't. There are three of us here, and that's not going to happen."

I backed up slowly, painstakingly, gaining purchase each time I cautiously fed the Range Rover more gas. I continued backing up the dirt lane as the water followed, rising in front of us. Finally we reached a place wide enough to turn around.

"Where do we go? What do we do?" Nancy babbled.

I found the radio news at 660 KFAR-AM: *State of emergency. Mudslides. Roads closed. River on the rise. Boats rescuing residents.* The water had flowed over bridges and surged through buildings.

I headed back up the mountain through the savage downpour, the windshield so flooded I could barely see. At top speed, the wipers could not move fast enough. The cabin Lacey had rented was the highest shelter I knew. It offered food, warmth, and dry clothes.

My cell phone still had no signal. Nancy had lost hers escaping from her bridegroom.

"We're passing your place," I shouted, over the sounds of the pounding rain and the blaring radio. "Look out that side. See if anyone's there."

If they had returned, Marsh Holt and John Lacey would be furious that the Range Rover and the incriminating laptop were missing. By now they would know that Nancy and I were together.

I turned off the headlights as we approached.

I didn't dare take my eyes off the road, but I saw the Ford Explorer out front. My heart constricted. Nancy had rolled her window down for a better look. Blasts of rain blew into the car.

I heard her gasp.

"What?"

"Somebody on the porch."

"Which one? Did he see us? Are there two of them?"

"I don't know. It was so fast. The rain was hitting my face and I couldn't see."

"I bet he could, watching from a covered porch."

Headlights bloomed in the rearview mirror and my pulse quickened. But just as quickly they disappeared. Perhaps they had turned down the mountain toward the highway, or maybe the driver had simply doused his lights.

"If he headed for the highway," I said, "they'll be back soon."

Nancy burst into tears of relief when we saw the cabin. It looked just the way it did when I left it.

We sat, silent for a moment, the car buffeted by wind and the merciless cloudburst. I dreaded that dash to the door. Dreaded that I might not make it, and fearing what might be waiting inside if I did.

"You're sure you didn't see two men back there?" I asked.

"No, only one. But that doesn't mean the other one wasn't with him."

"Or that he's here, waiting for us." My throat felt dry. "I'll leave the engine running. Move over into the driver's seat. If I don't come out to signal an all-clear in ninety seconds, take off. Hit the gas and get the hell out of here. If you have to, hide in the woods until you're rescued. It won't be too long. The rental agents know how many people are up here. The minute the rain stops, they'll send in choppers, medics, and cops. But whatever happens, don't let go of Lacey's laptop. Keep it with you. Show it to the cops. Insist that they read my story and his saved e-mails. The password is *Suzanne*. Suzanne with a *z*."

Nancy frowned, her eyes narrowed, as though it was all too much to grasp.

Did she hear a thing I said? I was tempted to snap my fingers to test her reflexes, if any, when she blurted, "Absolutely not! I'm not going into those woods by myself."

I sighed.

"No. I'll check the cabin instead." She reached for the fireplace poker and opened the car door. "If he's in there, I can run down those front steps a helluva lot faster than you can."

I paused, then tossed her the front door key. "My condition is temporary," I said. "While you're baking cakes and cookies, and flashing your big teeth for the camera, I'm jogging, swimming, and working out. At least I did. I may be temporarily indisposed but, normally on my worst day, I could outrun you in a heartbeat without breaking a sweat."

"I bet you could," she said, and jumped out of the Range Rover into the rain.

"Be careful," I warned. She didn't hear me. She was already halfway up the front steps, teeth gritted, the fireplace poker gripped solidly in both hands.

My lips moved in a silent prayer as she cautiously stepped inside.

An earsplitting scream sounded almost instantly. The Range Rover leaped forward as my foot stomped the accelerator in a reflex action. More screams. I could hear the sheer panic in her voice above the pounding of the rain. I hit the brakes, switched off the ignition, and groped for something, anything, to use as a weapon.

I remembered the stack of firewood on the porch next to the front door. Head down, I fought my way through the deluge, scrambled up steps strewn with slick wind-blown leaves as quickly as I could, snatched up a heavy piece of wood, and took a deep breath.

Nancy was still alive, still screaming. Water streamed into my eyes as I pushed the front door open and burst inside. The gun, a high-powered automatic, was the first thing I saw.

"You didn't say the other guy was a woman!" Nancy howled. She was crouched against the wall near the fireplace, her hands protecting her face.

"Leave her alone!" I cried, then gasped when I saw the face behind the gun. "What are you doing here? Is it really you?"

"Who is she?" Lieutenant K. C. Riley looked annoyed as she holstered her weapon. "Does she always scream like that?"

"Always," I said, frowning at Nancy, "from the day I met her."

I closed my eyes. When I opened them, K.C. was still there. This was no dream, no hallucination. I dropped the piece of firewood and burst into tears.

"I can't believe you're here."

"I said I'd get back to you. What's *with* this weather?"

I stood there dripping water, barely able to speak. "Thank you for coming," I managed.

"We're investigating the death of Gloria Weatherholt," she said. "It's a cold case, a homicide. She didn't drown. Her scuba tank had been tampered with. She died of carbon monoxide poisoning."

"Thank you," I said. "That is what I've been trying to tell everybody."

She took a step closer. "My God, Britt. You look awful. Get out of those wet clothes and into something warm. Are you all right?"

"It's been a rough week," I said, voice thin.

"Who is this?" She cut her eyes at Nancy.

"Nancy Lee Chastain Holt, survivor bride, the last of an endangered species."

Nancy climbed slowly to her feet, still whimpering.

"Her husband and his lover are probably right behind us. They're armed."

"Lover?" Nancy's eyes welled up.

I explained to Riley where we'd last seen them. She stepped to a front window and peered intently into the storm. "What about John Lacey, the young man who might have been murdered?"

"I was wrong. The son of a bitch isn't dead. He's with her husband. They're a couple. Have been all along."

Riley's eyebrows lifted.

"We have proof," I said. "Did you bring backup?"

"Stone. He's in Fairbanks filling in the local cops. He'll be here soon. I've lost the signal on my cell phone."

"Me too. The roads are impassable, flash flooding."

She nodded. "I barely made it through, had to run a few roadblocks coming up. You two dry off, I'll make some hot tea."

"No," I said, "let Nancy do it. She's a professional."

Riley stood watch while I took a hot shower. I didn't recognize my reflection in the big full-length bathroom mirror. Whose body is that? I wondered. Grotesque. Would I ever be the same again? I sighed and stepped into the shower, luxuriating in the steamy, soapy water. I was rinsing off, still in the shower, when the power went out.

I dressed quickly in the dark and stepped out with a blanket wrapped around me. "Is it the weather?" I whispered. "Or somebody outside?"

"Weather, I think," Riley said. "This must be the worst place I've ever been. It's like Miami, minus the sun."

"Thank Nancy," I said. "She chose it for her honeymoon. How did you get here? I didn't see your car."

"A rental. I hid it on high ground in the woods about a quarter mile north of here. Didn't want Holt to spot it."

I filled her in as I gratefully inhaled the hot tea Nancy brewed. Before the power failed, they had retrieved Lacey's laptop from the Range Rover.

Nancy cried nonstop as she and Riley read the e-mails. I listened, sipped my tea, missed Miami, and experienced a new, highly unusual sensation. I suddenly yearned to scrub my small apartment from floor to ceiling, to reupholster the little chair in my bedroom, rearrange my kitchen cabinets, and organize my closets. None of those things had ever been a priority but now the urge to nest overwhelmed me.

Away from home too long, I began to relate to those who forty years ago believed their exile would be brief, that they would return home to Cuba in a few days or weeks. Most never did and never will.

I stared at dancing flames in the fireplace and wondered. How long before I go home? Will I ever see Miami again?

Nancy whipped up a tasty meal from odds and ends in the pantry and the cans and groceries Lacey had brought. She'd also found some candles. I picked listlessly at my food. Nancy, who'd been hitting the blackberry brandy, soon cried herself to sleep.

The wind-driven rain never stopped.

"Get some rest, Britt," Riley said. "I'll wake you if anything happens."

"I'm too tired to sleep," I murmured. "Maybe, in a while." My body ached. My swollen feet and ankles were blistered, my breasts sore, and my back and belly hurt.

Riley sat at the wooden table, back straight, her Glock in her waistband, the soft firelight glinting off her blond hair. I remembered the sweet-faced girl in McDonald's high school yearbook as I threw a blanket on the couch and tried unsuccessfully to find a comfortable position. We talked softly in the dim light, listening for anything unusual beyond the rain pounding on the corrugated metal roof. It was like waiting for a hurricane's full fury.

"So," she asked quietly. "Is Kenny's baby a boy or a girl?"

I explained why I didn't know, not sure if she believed me.

"I'm glad you're having it. You could have—"

"It crossed my mind for a split second. I never could. Adoption crossed my mind too."

I saw her react even though her features hid in shadow.

"But I couldn't do that either. This is all that's left of him in the world. One reason this story is so important to me is that it's probably my swan song unless the *News* lets me do some sort of work from home. I can't hand this baby off to strangers to raise. No babysitters, no nanny, no day care. Even after he or she starts school, I can't work the police beat, on call twenty-four / seven. That part of my life is over. It's all I've ever done. This won't be easy."

"Nothing good ever is," she said. "You'll find a way to make it work."

I wished I was so sure. Despite my fears and uncertainties I detected envy in her voice.

"You can never predict how life will play out," I said. "When you think you know, you're wrong."

"Everybody has regrets," she murmured. "I drove away the only man I ever loved."

"And I'm to blame for the death of the only man I'll ever love."

"Too bad they were both the same man," she said, her voice a whisper.

"He was the best."

Surprisingly, she disagreed. "He was a great cop, smart as hell, with a good heart and a sense of humor. But he was human, like all cops. He wasn't perfect."

I gave an irritated sigh and frowned in the dark.

"He was a romantic, Britt, attracted women like a magnet. Because he died young, you're convinced you would have lived happily ever after. Maybe not."

"We would have made it," I said quickly. "We were perfect."

"So were we, Britt. Don't place him on a pedestal so high that no other man can ever live up to him."

"I know you two shared a long history."

"Loved him since second grade." She sounded mellow. Somehow the semidarkness made it easier to talk. "We were a couple all through high school. Later, when he fell in love with police work, he wanted to share it. He's the one who recruited me into the academy."

The wind howled outside. Inside, the silence was painful.

"You know it wasn't just you and me, Britt," she finally said. "Women were so attracted to him. The gun is a phallic symbol, and it didn't hurt that he looked good and was great in the sack."

Tearing up in the dark, I knew I shouldn't ask, but I did anyway. "When was the last time you and McDonald . . ."

"Had sex? You don't want to know, Britt."

"He proposed." I propped myself up on one elbow, voice rising. "Bought me a ring. We were about to set the date. . . ."

"You don't know how it would have worked out."

"If McDonald and I had split," I asked, "would you have taken him back?"

"In a heartbeat, God help me. He was the love of my life." She sighed softly in the firelight. "But any woman who married him would have found it a challenge."

"Not me," I said stubbornly.

"Love clouds your judgment," she said. "Don't build him into a larger-than-life lost lover who shadows your future. He had all the usual flaws and foibles, that's all I'm saying. I loved him in spite of it. Always have, always will."

She spoke gently, but her words stung. I sighed in anger and denial. The irony being that, despite it all, I could see what McDonald saw in her.

"Did you hear that?"

"No, what?" I listened, but all I heard was the rain hammering the metal roof, rattling the windows, and crashing like Niagara Falls off the gutter outside the kitchen door.

"A car."

She sprang to her feet and blew out the candles.

CHAPTER TWENTY-FOUR

"Stay where you are, Britt. Don't get up."

Too late. I'd already struggled to my feet, heart pounding, straining to hear, hoping she was wrong.

Riley hunkered down next to one of the two front windows, her back to the wall, gun in hand, peering into the downpour.

I moved to the opposite window, staying out of sight. The visibility on the far side of the glass was nearly zero. I could barely make out the shrouded bulk of the Range Rover parked right out front.

"See anything?" I said softly.

"Not yet," Riley said.

Then I heard the unmistakable thunk of a car door. Or was it? "Hear that?" I whispered.

"Car door?"

"Maybe something fell over in the rain, or a broken tree branch hit the roof," I said hopefully.

I heard it again.

"Two," she said.

"Did Nancy relock the front door when she brought in the laptop?" I asked.

"I double-checked every door, every window," Riley said.

"Should I wake Nancy?" I said.

"Will she keep quiet?"

"Not if she's scared. Is your cell phone still out?"

"Yes."

"Mine too." I suddenly remembered something. "Kathy!"

"What?" she whispered impatiently.

"Lacey has a set of keys to this place."

"There's a one-sided deadbolt, a thumb latch, on the inside," she said.

I had to be sure. I slid down the wall into a sitting position, then crawled beneath the window ledge to the front door and reached up to see if the latch was engaged. It was. I sat, breathing hard for a moment, my back pressed against the door.

"Told you so," she said, in an annoyed whisper.

Just then I sensed, rather than heard, movement on the other side. My spine tingled and the hairs on the back of my neck stood on end. Was it the creak of floorboards? A cautious footfall only inches away? The slight squeak and smell of wet rubber soles?

I waved my arms, gesturing to Riley, as the metal doorknob just above my head slowly began to turn. Then I heard the smooth insertion of a key, followed by a metallic click as it unlocked. He tried to open it, but the deadbolt held. Afraid to breathe, I braced my back against the door in case he tried to kick it open.

Riley had crept up beside me. "He's right outside," she whispered in my ear. "I can't see the other one. Don't know where he is. Take the poker and a sharp knife from the kitchen and go wake up Nancy. Gently, for God's sake. Keep her quiet. Take her into the bedroom closet. Stay there, both of you. Put the wooden chair in front of the closet door and keep low."

"Have you tried your cell?" I whispered.

"Still no signal. If this takes a bad turn, try to get to the Range Rover. If you can't, take to the woods."

I stared at her, startled.

"I don't expect the screw-up fairy, Britt, but it's smart to have a contingency plan."

I groped about, found the poker in the dark, crept into the kitchen, shone my penlight into the drawer, and chose a razor-sharp filet knife.

Careful not to create a silhouette in front of the fireplace's dying glow, I inched into the bedroom where Nancy snored gently beneath a patchwork quilt.

I envied her peaceful sleep and hesitated, hating to wake her. As I reached out to gently nudge her shoulder, an earsplitting crash came from the bathroom, a few feet away. A shower of broken glass tinkled to the floor. A millisecond later, almost simultaneously, something smashed against the front door with the force of a SWAT team's battering ram.

Nancy sat up straight in bed. "What happened?" she murmured. "What was that?"

"Be quiet," I whispered urgently. "They're trying to break in."

She saw the glint of the knife in my hand and howled like a coyote.

I grabbed her arms and pulled her out of bed.

"What don't you understand about 'Be quiet'?" I muttered fiercely in her ear.

I pushed her toward the closet. "Get inside, down on the floor, and stay there!"

Poker in one hand, the filet knife in the other, I cautiously approached the bathroom. The door stood ajar. I stepped closer and was sprayed by icy rainwater gusting through the shattered window.

The floor was wet, and getting wetter, the cheerful red and yellow patterned curtains already soaked.

A huge rock lay amid the glass shards on the floor.

Was he about to climb inside, or had he already done so?

The shock of cold water spray on my face startled and infuriated me. I swung the poker viciously at the closed shower curtain surrounding the tub, knife at the ready. No one there.

Another crash, followed by more breaking glass, in the front room. Again, almost instantaneously, something smashed into the opposite corner of the cabin. Wood splintered and the entire structure seemed to rock on its foundation. They must have rammed it with the Explorer or the Range Rover.

They moved fast, attacking from all directions. If their intent was to frighten and confuse us, it worked on me. I turned to rush toward the front room and collided with Nancy, who was right behind me. She sobbed under her breath.

I nearly wept in frustration. Where the hell were they?

Riley appeared in the doorway.

"Get back in that closet!" she snapped.

"Do you have a backup weapon I can borrow?" I asked urgently.

"No." She shook her head. "Just as well. Too many shooters in these close quarters would be dangerous. You have to worry about cross fire—"

"I may not have police firearms training, but I was trained by a policeman," I snapped. "I know how to use a gun."

Nancy panicked at the word *gun*, screamed, and ran blindly through the kitchen. Riley followed, tipped the wooden table onto its side, and ordered her to take cover behind it.

Nancy's screams drew Marsh Holt to the front room. He hurled a log from the conveniently stacked firewood through a window. He used another to knock out the jagged shards of broken glass around the opening, and stepped through.

From behind the bedroom door I watched the rainwater drip off him onto the cabin floor. Holding a gun and breathing hard, he looked huge and menacing in the flickering light. But, I told myself, he's in for a surprise. He thinks all he's contending with are two unarmed women, one hysterical, the other pregnant.

"Nancy!" he bellowed. "Nancy Lee!" He was so close that I saw the flash of his bitter smile in the shadows. "Where's my goddamn wife?"

Nancy began to whimper in the kitchen.

He heard it too and turned toward her.

"Nice attitude for a man on his honeymoon," I said, hoping to distract him.

"You're to blame for this, you bitch. Where's Nancy?"

She sprang out from behind the table and fled screaming through the kitchen.

I turned to follow and came face-to-face with John Lacey. Drenched, shivering, and holding a gun as though it were a foreign object, he looked as shocked as I felt.

"Lacey," I whispered, "my God. Why?"

"Britt." He stopped and stared.

I heard Holt approach behind me.

"Drop the gun!" Riley said, from somewhere in the dark. "You're under arrest!"

"Who the hell's that?" Lacey's eyes widened.

"What?" Holt spun around and saw Riley.

He fired a shot at her, then turned and fired at me. But I was already sliding to the floor, protecting my belly.

"Oh, no! My God!" Holt rushed at me. I braced and gritted my teeth. But inexplicably, he kept going. As he hurtled past, I summoned up all my strength, lunged, and sliced the back of his right ankle just above the heel as hard and as deep as I could with the filet knife.

He dropped in mid-stride, his outstretched arm unable to reach Lacey, who lay moaning on the floor. I never even heard him fall. In the dying firelight, a dark river snaked toward me across the wooden floor. It wasn't water. Instinctively, I rolled away from the blood, shuddering as I realized that the bullet Holt meant for me had struck Lacey in the side.

"Is he alive?" Blood from the gaping gash in Holt's heel spurted blood that sprayed across the wall and the baseboards. He clutched the wound with both hands and pleaded with Lacey. "J.L.—Johnny. It was an accident, I didn't mean—"

"Sure," I said, "with you it's always an accident."

K. C. Riley snatched up both their guns.

She intended to handcuff Holt to a bathroom pipe but I protested. We were marooned and I had to use the facilities too often to share the space. She cuffed him to a pipe under the kitchen sink instead.

The rain began to let up.

I elevated Lacey's legs and cradled his head. He seemed as bewildered as I felt.

"Why?" I asked again.

"We had enough money. I begged him to stop. But he always said, One more, just one more. He promised we'd never have to work again, I could write my novel . . ."

"How . . . When did you and Holt hook up?"

His smile was a painful grimace. "You guessed it a long time ago, Britt. I had trouble keeping a straight face when you kept saying what a good actor he was. We met in an acting class the year I spent in New York. He knew at first sight. It was all new for me."

"And Suzanne?"

His smile was sad. "We were misfits, best friends, always together. She was clingy, so needy. Once I had a taste of life in New York with Marsh, I could never go back to our old relationship in Baton Rouge. I tried. But she won that writing contest, got so much attention. I couldn't help but be jealous. Marsh was looking for another wife. He suggested her, and I agreed." He winced. "It hurts," he gasped. "Help me, Britt. I don't want to die here, not like this."

"We have to take him down the mountain to a hospital," I told Riley.

"Too dangerous," she said. "In flash floods, the water always wins."

"It's starting to recede, according to the radio," I argued. "We can't wait. His heart rate is way up. He's so pale. His stomach looks distended; he must be bleeding internally. If we just get him down to the paved road, to a roadblock. Medics can stabilize him and get him out."

Marsh Holt joined the argument. "Please," he said, a sob in his voice. "Get us the hell out of here. If you don't, Johnny will die and I'll be crippled for life."

He sat on the kitchen floor, cuffed to the pipe, pressing a blood-soaked towel to his slashed heel with his free hand.

"Don't let him die," he pleaded, tragic and grief stricken, his usual act.

Maybe this time it was real.

By morning the rain had dwindled to a light drizzle. It took the combined strength of all three of us to move Lacey out to the car and make him as comfortable as possible in the back of the Range Rover. Nancy would drive, with K.C. riding shotgun, keeping an eye on the prisoners. I settled in the backseat with Lacey's head on my knees.

Holt sat in the space behind us, clutching the caked towels he used to apply pressure to the still-bleeding wound in his heel. My knife blade had apparently severed tendons and ligaments. He was unable to walk, and the open gash spurted blood at the slightest movement. "I have to keep pressure on it or I'll bleed to death," he protested, when Riley reached to cuff him behind his back.

"Standard procedure," she said flatly. "Prisoners are not transported without cuffs."

"He can't run," I argued impatiently. "He can't even walk. What could he possibly do? He'll bleed out all over the car if you cuff him. All he wants is medical help for Lacey and himself."

Riley grimly removed the cuffs. "You sure you want to do this, Britt? I'd be more comfortable waiting here for medics."

"Stop arguing! Start driving!" Holt cried urgently, pressing another bloody towel to his heel.

"Shut up," Riley told him, her voice cold. "You have no vote. Try anything and I promise to shoot you dead. You make one move, and

I'll dump you by the side of the road in handcuffs. The medics can look for you later. Got that?"

Holt nodded.

"Let's go," I said.

"All right." She chewed her lower lip. "Let's roll."

So we rolled, despite her reluctance, all of us stressed, sleep deprived, and on edge.

We'd gone just a few miles when we spotted a police helicopter, flying low. Nancy and Riley waved. The chopper hovered overhead, as the pilot signaled us to proceed down to the main road.

"They gave us a go," Riley said. "Either the road is open or they have a place to land." The chopper headed south down the mountain and disappeared behind the trees.

"Hear that?" I told Lacey, who'd been drifting in and out of consciousness. "You'll be in a hospital soon. Hang in there."

I wasn't sure if he heard me.

But Holt did and was suddenly talkative. "Nancy? Sweet darlin'? They're lying. You know it. Don't let them poison your mind against me. How can you believe them? They're jealous women. Think about it, Nancy Lee. Baby. Sweetheart. Only you know what we have. You're my wife. Listen to me."

His words resonated with a desperate sincerity. The raw anguish in his voice was heart-wrenching. Marshall Weatherholt, trained actor.

We had warned Nancy, told her not to listen, but she nearly skidded off the road when he spoke her name. When he began the endearments she began to watch him in the rearview mirror. They made eye contact, which made me nervous.

"Okay," I said abruptly. "Pull over, Nancy. It's time I drove."

Riley nodded her approval.

Lacey, holding my hand, opened his eyes, in protest I thought. His lips moved and I leaned over to hear what he was trying to say.

"Suzanne," he murmured, then faded out, his pupils fixed and dilated, his open eyes empty. Gone, just like that.

I sighed, and looked up at Riley, but she was focused on a hairpin turn in the road ahead, watching for a safe place for Nancy to pull over.

From behind me, Holt saw everything. He knew.

With a furious cry, he lunged forward across the seats, caught Nancy by the hair, and jerked her head back. She screamed. Holt cursed. I rolled Lacey's body off the seat and kicked Holt in the side, in the groin, in the ribs, as hard as I could with both feet. He kept his stubborn grip on Nancy's hair as the car fishtailed all over the road.

"Let go." Riley pointed the Glock at his head. "Let go, now!"

Holt didn't. The car careened sideways and began to tip over as though in slow motion.

The explosion hurt my ears as the car rolled, then rolled over again. I felt the shock waves as blood spattered everywhere in a red sheen.

I thought of Miami and home as the car rolled again and again.

I opened my eyes, saw blood and brain tissue, wondered if it was mine, then blacked out.

When I woke up, the car had finally stopped moving. I saw open sky beyond the shattered windshield, a strange sky with a pale orange sun skirting the horizon.

Nancy's screams assured me that I was still alive. So did the fierce pain that made me wince, double over, and cry out.

No, no, I thought. Please. This is too early. Too early for this baby. I remembered Onnie's words, *I can do all things through Christ who strengthens me,* and I repeated them, over and over.

I don't know how long it was before I was lifted from the overturned car on a backboard and felt the whirlwind of chopper blades. I saw Sam Stone's face and heard his words of encouragement and, disoriented, believed I was back in Miami.

Strangers' voices discussed my broken shoulder, possible head injuries, and a fetal monitor. The pains grew surprisingly intense.

"Don't worry, Britt, it's all right," K. C. Riley said. She held my hand.

"I know," I murmured. "Everything will be all right now."

ACKNOWLEDGMENTS

I am grateful to the brilliant star hustler Jack Horkheimer and to the supremely gifted Paul Jacobs, star of the concert stage and the Juilliard School.

New friend J. Jason Wentworth of Fairbanks, Alaska, generously shared his world for this book. So did my old buddies Robert Tralins and Miami Beach super-chef Steve Waldman.

Special thanks go to the world's best pathologists, Dr. Joseph H. Davis, Miami-Dade County Chief Medical Examiner Emeritus, and Dr. Stephen J. Nelson, Chairman of the Florida Medical Examiners Commission and Chief Medical Examiner for the 10th District of Florida. I'm also indebted to the renowned forensic odontologist Dr. Richard Souviron for his help and friendship.

Attorney Joel Hirshhorn, the Reverend Garth Thompson, and my good friend Renee Turolla continue to do their best to keep me out of trouble. It's no easy job.

The usual suspects, Frank and Angela Natoli, Ann Hughes, Mary Finn, Kay Spitzer, Lloyd Hough, Dale Kitchell, Cynnie Cagney, and Arnold Markowitz, came through, as always, when I needed them. So did Patricia Keen and Howard Kleinberg, along with all the other sharp-eyed, quick-witted, Cuban-coffee-drinking Sesquipedalians.

Raul J. Diaz, former homicide major, private eye, and true soldier for justice, was patient and generous with his time and words. Again.

Two razor-sharp young Miami journalists, Andrea Torres and Stephanie Garry, helped me during the writing of this book. As did Glenn Lane, William Dishong, Norry Lynch, Bart Wever, Marie Reilly, Jerelle Farnsworth, Colleen Rudnet, Cristina Concepcion, and Miami Police Public Information Officer Hermina Jacobson.

My heartfelt thanks go to my longtime friend and agent, Michael Congdon, and to the rare and wonderful Mitchell Ivers, an editor who *can* be trusted.

And a special thank-you to that glamorous redhead Marilyn Lane, my chief accomplice, co-conspirator, and getaway driver.

What a sterling cast of characters.

The old saying is true: Friends will bail you out of jail, but good friends are sitting in the cell next to you, saying, "Damn, that was fun!"

ABOUT THE AUTHOR

A Pulitzer Prize–winning *Miami Herald* police reporter and winner of the prestigious George Polk Career Award, Edna Buchanan brings a dynamic and steamy Miami to vivid life in all of her novels. She feels both the heartbeat and the hot breath of this restless, exotic, and mercurial city. Buchanan also won the Paul Hansell Award for Distinguished Journalism from the Florida Society of Newspaper Editors, the Florida Bar Association Media Award, the American Bar Association Gavel Award, the David Brinkley Award from Barry University in 1988, the Miami Police Trailblazer Award, and has been honored by the Association of Police Planning, the Miami Fraternal Order of Police, and the Miami Police Department. The author of sixteen books and numerous short stories, she lives in Miami with two dogs, a herd of cats, and Benjamin, a small brown rabbit.